Rooftop Sonata

BOOKS BY DALE E. LEHMAN

HOWARD COUNTY MYSTERIES

The Fibonacci Murders
True Death
Ice on the Bay
A Day for Bones

BERNARD AND MELODY CAPERS

Weasel Words
Rooftop Sonata

SCIENCE FICTION

Space Operatic
The Belt
Penitence

SHORT STORY COLLECTIONS

The Realm of Tiny Giants
Found by the Road
Manifest Secrets

Rooftop Sonata

A Bernard and Melody Caper

Dale E. Lehman

Chase, Maryland

Rooftop Sonata
Dale E. Lehman

Cover art by Proi
https://99designs.com/profiles/proi

Text set in 11 pt. IvyPresto Text
Chapter headings set in 14 pt. Oxtail OT Bold

Published by Red Tales, 2025
Baltimore, Maryland
United States of America
https://www.DaleELehman.com

ISBN: 978-1-958906-10-1 (trade paperback)
978-1-958906-11-8 (digital)

For Rose, who (I predict) will say
Celeste did exactly the right thing.

No AI tools were used in the crafting of this story. Seriously, where would be the fun in *that*?

Acknowledgements

A few special thanks are in order. First, I owe the existence of Bernard and Melody to author and photographer K. S. Brooks (https://ksbrooks.com), whose photo prompts for the weekly Indies Unlimited (https://indiesunlimited.com) flash fiction competitions brought the duo into existence. Second, my thanks to cover artist Momir Borocki. Momir hasn't just provided me one great cover after another; he provided one that inspired this story! Sounds backwards, I know, but it's true. The *Rooftop Sonata* cover was one of the concepts for *Weasel Words*. Third, a tip of the hat to fellow author J. D. Brayton, who gifted me a copy of Michael Finkel's book *The Art Thief: A True Story of Love, Crime, and a Dangerous Obsession*, which informed a few of the scenes that follow. Fourth, a big thank-you to a trio of fans who took part in a "give Melody a maiden name" contest I ran through my *Story Corner* newsletter:

- Mary Karnes, who provided Melody's maiden name: McGirl.
- Michael Nethery, who suggested Melody's middle name: Jane.
- Pat Mills, who lent Melody's family tree some dignity with Kensington.

And last on this page but always first in my heart, my real-life Melody, my late wife Kathleen, without whose 45-year mentoring and support I would never have written anything publishable.

Chapter 1: Saturday, October 14, 2017

"She's got the body of Venus de Milo, but with more arms."

The words spilled out in a breathless rush, as though the man uttering them had plucked the greatest treasure in the world from the rarified air of the little art gallery. Maybe he had. The exhibit featured no *big* big names, but the works on display were all by up-and-coming artists, young visionaries poised–so the program claimed–to upend our ideas of beauty, culture, relevance, and ourselves.

But no, the man admiring the epitome of feminine beauty wasn't entranced by a sculpture. Not a stone sculpture, at least. His eye was on...

"Don't look now," Bernard Earls whispered to his wife Melody, "but you have yet another admirer."

"Really?" Melody pirouetted like a ballerina, her beautiful auburn hair sailing in a breeze of her own making, her beautiful blue eyes sweeping the gathering until they locked with the wide brown eyes of a dumpy fellow whose jaw must have come unhinged. The guy had a friend, a bit less dumpy but no less unhinged. He, too, was gaping at her.

"I told you not to look," Bernard said. "We don't want attention." Which was a dumb thing to say, because Melody could no more avoid attention than could a sun-sprayed mountainside draped in autumn foliage. With his arm about her, Bernard was the frame to her landscape, a dashing fellow in the mold of Johnny Depp but a few inches taller with a wave of brown hair cresting his crown and a devilish smile–when he felt like smiling–that made women swoon.

Accidentally, though. Bernard had no desire to make any woman but Melody swoon.

But back to the point: they didn't want attention. Probably Mr. and Mrs. Earls were in the wrong business.

"Poor fellow," she whispered. "He looks desperate. Oh, well." Melody finished her turn and ended up where she started, face-to-face with a serene mountain vista, gray ridges behind gray ridges fading into a sepia sky. The painting was small, six by eight, framed in translucent gray plastic. "Where are the trees?" she asked.

"There aren't any." Bernard slipped his cell phone from his left trouser pocket and checked the time. "They should be calling us to the buffet in a few minutes." He put an arm about Melody's shoulders, pulled her close, kissed her hair. "*Please* don't get distracted this time," he whispered.

They didn't have any children, but Melody managed an impressive look of motherly rebuke.

"I only mean—" he started to object.

"I'm not the distracted one, Bernie. Look at this thing." She nodded at the painting. "It's boring."

"It's a Samuel Weston."

"Yeah, who?"

"Samuel Weston. Remember? Destined for greatness?"

"According to whom?"

They'd been through this a hundred times in the past month, but fine, they could manage one more go. "Mr. Jacobi."

"And who is he?"

"Come on, Melody, you know who he is: the guy paying us to nab it."

"Uh-huh. Why?"

"To create notoriety. He already owns a few Westons. He thinks a theft will boost their—"

"What," Melody demanded, "does Mr. Freaking Jacobi know about art?"

"It doesn't matter what Mr. Freaking Jacobi knows about art. He's paying us three grand to—" Bernard glanced around. Why did he always let her get him wound up? Fortunately, nobody had noticed their, uh, conversation. Not yet. He ratcheted down the volume. "To acquire it for him."

Melody snorted, a rarity for her. She was too suave to snort. "For that much, he should want something good. Like that one over there." She pointed three artworks to the left, where a black-and-white photo hung. "See that? A group of naked people arranged to make a flower. Now *that's* art."

Bernard pinched his eyes shut, just for a moment. "It may be art to you, but Mr. Jacobi is looking for an investment. Once this vanishes, his other Westons could be worth a small fortune."

Regarding the Weston, Melody shook her head. "He's no Frank Schlief, that's for sure." She had become enamored of Schlief's bold colors and sensuous lines a year or so back, and now she compared everything to his work. Bernard couldn't fault her taste, but he wished she'd cut it out. "The point is," she continued, "I'm not the distracted one. Both you and Mr. Jacobi are distracted by gold. *Real* art has value beyond money."

Bernard pressed his lips tight and thought, *Fine, fine, whatever, just so long as we get out of here with the painting. And without handcuffs.*

In hindsight, he really shouldn't have thought that. Although he hadn't spoken, he'd inadvertently invoked the "unspeakable law," to wit: *As soon as you mention something, if it's bad, it happens; if it's good, it goes away.*

First, a monkey-suited docent glided into the gallery and announced in ringing tones, "Luncheon is served. Please join us in the adjacent room."

The murmur of conversation waned for a moment, then the guests began a haphazard retreat, rather like liquid sloshing in the bottom of a suddenly tilted glass. Bernard and Melody stepped closer to the Weston, allowing the others to pass by unimpeded. Shortly the room was empty save themselves. In one smooth motion, Bernard gently lifted the painting and secreted it in the largest of the pockets sown into the lining of his suitcoat. He buttoned the coat and tugged the material straight, then turned to escort Melody out the other door, the door not leading to the buffet.

Except she wasn't by his side. She was three artworks down, lifting the naked flower people from the wall.

"No, no, no!" he whispered. "Let's go before…"

"Ma'am?" a new voice intruded. The docent had returned to lock up. Having caught sight of Melody with the photo in her hands, he approached, eyebrows raised, body tense, more than a little disbelief marring his otherwise handsome face.

Melody turned her brilliant smile on the fellow, who halted, simultaneously alarmed and dazzled. The look he gave her was more priceless than all the art in the Louvre. "How much?" she asked. She turned the photo so he could see it better.

The docent hadn't even registered Bernard's presence. Knowing he'd better play to Melody's lead, Bernard removed the Weston from his pocket and waited.

The docent croaked something, cleared his throat, and tried again. "Twenty-eight hundred. But I'm sorry, ma'am, it stays on the wall until you pay for it. We'll package it for you at that time."

"Oh my, I'm so very sorry. I didn't realize." She carefully rehung the naked flower people. The docent eyed the operation. And the operator. "How about that one?" Melody asked, pointing to Bernard. Bernard slowly raised the Weston so the docent could see it.

The man's eyebrows arched again, farther than before. "Twenty-five hundred," he said. "But again..."

"My apologies," Bernard said. He rehung the Weston and brushed off his fingers as though the painting had been caked with dust. Then he came to his wife's side, took her arm, and said, "Come, love. I'm hungry." He escorted her out, knowing without seeing that the docent watched them every step of the way, knowing that by the time they were out of his view, the only thing he'd remember was Melody's swaying hips.

As they left the room, Melody turned a knowing smile on her husband. "See, Bernie?" she said. "I told you the other one was better."

𝄞

Mr. Freaking Jacobi—Bernard thought he might just call him that from now on—had a few choice words for the botched job and its perpetrators, after which Bernard decided he didn't really want Jacobi's three grand anyway. He had just delivered a savage finger punch to the red icon that terminated the call and was about to throw his cell phone through the balcony door when the demonic thing rang again.

Probably Jacobi calling back to continue his tirade. Bernard refused the call.

Half a minute later, the phone rang again.

He refused it again.

It rang again.

Snatching up the phone, he snarled, "Go to hell, Jacobi!"

Laughter, then a wrinkled old voice asked, "Who's Jacobi?"

Bernard squeezed his eyes shut. "You don't want to know. Who's this?"

"Who's *this*? Why, Bernard, love, don't you remember?"

It was a woman's voice, not quite ancient but getting there, somehow familiar. He was pretty sure he'd stolen something from her once upon a time, except his victims didn't usually call him "love."

She waited in silence for him to break his silence. When he didn't, she said. "It's Dolley."

Oh, God, not her.

"Dolley Madison Plaskett. You and Melody attended a couple of my debauches last year."

Melody, who had been in the bedroom, chose that moment to saunter up behind him and shove her cell phone in his face. "Whatcha think of this?" she asked. On the screen, a burnished cedar chest glowed. A thirteen-hundred-dollar price tag glowed beneath it.

He pushed her hand back to get picture and price in focus. "We can't afford that," he said.

"I'm not selling anything," Dolley said. "In fact, I have a proposition for you."

"I only accept propositions from my wife," Bernard grumbled.

"Who are you talking to?" Melody demanded.

"You don't want to know."

"If she's propositioning you, I sure do!"

Dolley laughed again. "God, I've missed you two. Put me on speaker."

Bernard sighed but did as requested. To Melody, he whispered, "It's Dolley."

Melody face-palmed herself.

The Earls had good reason not to want Dolley calling. Several good reasons. First, she was an aging hippie who never outgrew the 1960's. Enough said about that. Second, they'd stolen a weasel from her family—a silver one, not a live one—and while Dolley ultimately found that hysterical, certain of her siblings might still be holding a grudge. And third, although none of the Plasketts ever figured out how the theft had taken place, nor how one weasel had morphed into three in the process, Bernard and Melody didn't care to be associated with any incident that qualified as theft. It wasn't good for their lifestyle.

"The proposition," Dolley said, "isn't anything at all improper."

Bernard wondered why they would want to listen in that case.

She laughed once more—she was good at laughing—and added, "I can't believe I'm saying that."

"So what is it?" he asked.

"I have a friend who's interested in acquiring something of historical value, and she needs a go-between. Naturally, I thought of you."

Bernard looked at Melody who looked at Bernard. She held up her phone and waggled the cedar chest while arching her eyebrows.

"So," Dolley finished, "let's discuss it over dinner. My place, seven o'clock this evening."

"I don't know why you think I'm a negotiator," Bernard said, just to be difficult.

Melody shoved the cedar chest in his face.

"Don't be modest," Dolley said. "You have—what do the young folk say these days? Mad skills?"

That was one way of putting it, although sometimes he wondered if it wasn't a different kind of mad. "All right," he said. "Since you're feeding us, we'll stop by."

"Wonderful. You like crab imperial, I presume?"

Bernard liked anything smacking of emperorship. "Of course," he said.

Melody liked anything yummy. "You bet!" she gushed.

"Then I'll see you at seven." Dolley disconnected without saying goodbye.

Bernard looked at Melody. Melody looked at Bernard.

"Think of the money," they told each other.

"Okay," they both replied.

𝄞

Dolley Madison Plaskett's home, if you could call it that, had walls of gleaming alabaster—or some sparkling white material, anyway—that undulated about the grounds in graceful curves. Standing before it, you'd think it more abstract sculpture than home, but an aerial view revealed something astonishing: the form of a nude woman lying on her side, her arm tucked beneath her head. Bernard had seen that girl once before, courtesy of online satellite imagery. Inside, the place was less astonishing. Enormous, yes. Sinfully well-appointed, yes. Undraped figures prancing and sprawling over the walls, yes, but well-known classical paintings all, one or two possibly originals.

Last time they were here, they were greeted by a short guy with blonde face fuzz, cutoff jeans, and a faded red t-shirt. That had been high summer. Now it was autumn, and the same guy greeted them in blue jeans and a faded green t-shirt. In a fit of embarrassment, he previously refused to identify himself. Bernard didn't bother asking his name now. His paranoid examination of the drive and the grounds and the scattering of clouds floating overhead suggested he remained terrified someone would discover him working here. Before, Bernard thought Dolley's excesses were the cause, but he'd since learned it was the opposite: she and her hangers-on had, in the main, grown too old to perpetuate a shocking lifestyle. The young man found that even more embarrassing than the alternative.

Embarrassed or not, he hustled them in, pushed the door shut, and scurried to the dining room. The Earls had to trot to keep up.

"They're here," the servant announced.

Seated at the head of the table, Dolley waved them in. To her right, her octogenarian partner Bob Wetzlinger had probably dozed off, although his eyes remained open a crack.

"Bernard, dear!" Dolley said. "Melody, dear! Sit, sit, we're about to serve."

Another servant scurried in from a side door with a tray of salads and set them around. In short order, wine and the main course were brought in. Bob woke up enough to gum his meal and occasionally blink at Melody as though he recognized her, possibly as someone he'd slept with six decades ago. Although if she was, she hadn't aged a day, making life way more unfair than he'd ever realized. Meanwhile, Melody effused praise for the flavors, while Bernard enjoyed them in silence and awaited the inevitable.

Eventually, Dolley obliged him. "Do you know the art collector Gerhard Nachtnebel, Jr.?"

Bernard wasn't sure he wanted to know anyone with a name like that. "I don't think so," he said.

"He's famous."

"I can't track every famous guy."

Dolley grinned. "Especially since the advent of social media influencers."

"What about this collector?"

"He has a place upriver in Swampside, a big house, half again as big as mine. Half of it is given over to art events and instruction. Artists, art historians, students, and God knows who else flock there like vultures for classes and to study his collections. It's rumored he has a secret collection, a stash he doesn't let anyone see."

Bernard thought that too strange to credit. Unless...

Melody perked up. "Why? Did he steal them?"

Yeah, unless that.

Dolley's smirk suggested it was exactly that. "I mentioned a friend of mine needs help negotiating acquisition of an item of historical value. That item is said to be in Gerhard's secret collection."

"She wants us to steal a stolen relic." Normally, Bernard wouldn't have used the "s" word, but this was Dolley. She had supplied weed—and God knew what else—to her friends long before it was legal in Maryland.

"Twice stolen, in fact. It's right up your alley. Don't think I've forgotten about those weasels. I still don't know how you pulled that off."

And she never would. "What do you mean?" Bernard asked.

"How you turned one weasel into three."

"About this relic being twice-stolen, I mean."

"Oh. It goes like this. Adolf Hitler assembled a collection of original manuscripts by the composer Richard Wagner." She pronounced it REE-kard VAHG-nur. "They were kept in his bunker. That much is known for certain. At the end of the war, when the bunker burned, they were presumed lost. But the scuttlebutt is that a highly-placed SS officer stole one of those manuscripts before the fire. In fact, he's believed to have swept up a considerable stash of stolen art as the Nazi war effort collapsed. Then, while sneaking it out of Germany, he was allegedly shot by his driver, who stole the stolen loot and escaped. That driver was Gerhard's father."

Bernard figured a story like that couldn't possibly be true.

"A story like that," Melody said, "has got to be true. Right, Bernie?"

"To be honest, love—" Bernard began. He didn't get to finish.

"So what does your friend want?" Melody asked Dolley. "And most important, what's the payout?"

Dolley grinned. "Twenty grand. The target is the original autographed manuscript of the opera *Rienzi*, which someone gave to Hitler as a fiftieth birthday present. That opera, it's been said, was a big inspiration for his career. Can you imagine what that must be worth?"

Not really. The name Richard Wagner meant nothing to Bernard, and as far as he was concerned, anything that had inspired Adolf Hitler should be exorcised and incinerated and its ashes buried in hallowed ground to keep it safe from warlocks and satanists. But the fee was another matter. Twenty grand. Damn.

"Why does your friend want this old parchment?" "Why?" wasn't a question Bernard generally asked, but once again, this was Dolley, and more to the point, the whole thing sounded like some-body's drug-induced hallucination. Which made sense, because this was Dolley.

Bob Wetzlinger looked up from his meal and blinked. "Wouldn't you?"

"Can't think why I would," Bernard told him.

He shrugged, said, "Suit yourself," and resumed eating.

Dolley shook her head at him. "The whole world believes *Rienzi* to be lost forever. Whoever finds it will be famous."

"People like us don't want to be famous," Bernard said.

"I do," Melody insisted.

"Not for stealing a stolen relic, love."

"Oh. Right."

"Nobody will know it was you," Dolley promised. "And you'll have twenty grand, tax free."

"Plus expenses," Bernard said.

Dolley winked. "She can afford it."

"Who?"

"My friend."

Who wished to remain anonymous while becoming famous. Weird. "Will she meet with us?" Bernard asked. "You have her address?"

"She will, and I do," Dolley replied. She slid a slip of paper to him. "We won't speak of this again. The rest is up to you."

Yeah. It always was.

Chapter 2: Saturday night, October 14, 2017

Dolley's palatial palace occupied a generous swath of acreage in the snooty D.C. suburb of Beartrap Falls. The art mecca of Gerhard Nachtnebel, Jr. reposed upstream on the Potomac in the even snootier village of Swampside. Bernard and Melody, though, lived a bit north of the nation's capital in the decidedly unsnooty town of Aschimos, where they rented an apartment in the heart of a blocky building. Bernard found the economic imbalance implied by these facts outrageous, although the prospect of a twenty grand payout tempered his sense of injustice.

The Earls apartment wasn't horrible. It just didn't approach mansionhood. They had a plush tan sofa, plenty of books stuffed into Swedish assemble-it-yourself bookcases, and a very nice flatscreen TV that had fallen off a truck during a delivery to a well-to-do family Bernard had fortuitously been visiting at the time. (And was *that* ever a story, especially the way Melody recalled it.) To round out the illusion of elegance, Bernard owned a roll-top desk that didn't quite look like the particleboard it was. Most important of all, their apartment was a safe unit, tucked into the center of the second of three floors. Four doors separated it from the staircases at either end of the dim hall, the position thieves were least likely to target. Bernard would know.

Then again, being surrounded by tenants had its downside. Namely, noise. The soundscape was in constant motion as neighbors came and went, which they did with some frequency. Indeed, in recent years there had been but two constants. One—unfortunately for Bernard and Melody's hearing—was the apartment to the left, occupied by Dimetrice Cornwell and his quiet (in a wild sort of way) girlfriend Osheena Amadeo. Dimetrice's parties, featuring ear-splitting thunder that allegedly qualified as music, had disrupted Bernard and Melody's blissful existence more times than anyone including God could count.

Demitrice and Osheena were friendly enough, sure. A bit too friendly, judging by the nature of their parties. Yet there were days when Bernard wished they'd vacate the premises—or Aschimos, or Maryland itself—to reduce the noise to background level. But being more broke than even Bernard and Melody, Dimetrice and Osheena weren't going anywhere anytime soon.

The other neighbor not going anywhere anytime soon lived directly across the hall. Mrs. Victoria Clarke, a widow perfectly aged to eighty-two years, was quieter than a starfish. She also loved to bake, and more importantly, loved to share her spice cake with Bernard and Melody. The combination more than made up for Dimetrice.

Except something was off today.

Returning from their encounter with Dolley that evening, Bernard and Melody stopped dead outside their apartment door when a shriek erupted from Mrs. Clarke's abode. "What was that?" Melody gasped.

Bernard frowned at Mrs. Clarke's door. "Sounded like an elephant."

"Why would Mrs. Clarke have an elephant?"

"I don't know."

"She didn't adopt one, did she?"

Bernard fished in his pocket for his keys. "I seriously doubt it."

Scrunching up her face in concentration, Melody asked the next logical question: "How did she get it *in* there?"

"Maybe she's watching a nature program." Bernard held up the key to their apartment and nodded toward their door.

"Oh, yes," Melody agreed. "That must be it."

The elephant trumpeted again, although this time it sounded more like a howler monkey howling. "Definitely a nature program," Bernard said. He took Melody's hand and tugged her homeward.

Melody tugged back. "What if it's Mrs. Clarke?"

Bernard tugged back back. "Mrs. Clarke couldn't sound like that if she tried. It's the TV, love. Come on."

Melody tugged back back back. "But maybe she's hurt, Bernie!"

There it was again, only this time it went on and on and on, either a sound of pain or of giddy delight. It was hard to imagine Mrs. Clarke being *that* happy, so maybe Melody was right. Bernard dropped his wife's hand and knocked on the door. "Mrs. Clarke!" he called. "Is everything all right?"

More elephants or monkeys or whatever racketed through the apartment, and then the deadbolt clicked and the door opened partway, and Mrs. Clarke's gray head popped out. She beamed at her neighbors. "Oh, Mr. and Mrs. Earls! How kind of you to ask. Yes, everything is fine. My great-grandson is visiting me. Isn't he adorable?" She pulled the door open all the way and motioned toward the interior. Something flashed by behind her, shrieking, but whatever it was winked in and out of view so fast that Bernard couldn't have said whether it was human, monkey, cat, or rabbit. Probably not a rabbit. Bunnies didn't sound like that.

"I see," Bernard said, although he hadn't quite.

"How cute!" Melody purred, as though she'd been able to tell. "You must be so proud."

"Oh yes," Mrs. Clarke said, beaming. "I can't quite keep up with him, of course, but that's the wonderful thing about being a great-grandma. You can send them home when it gets to be too much."

The streak streaked by in the other direction, screeching like a screech owl.

"Is he staying long?" Bernard couldn't keep the dread from his voice. Melody elbowed him.

"Just while his mother is at work," Mrs. Clarke said. "For the next two weeks, until she gets him enrolled in a new daycare program. His previous one wasn't..." she glanced back as the elephant trumpeted by. "...suitable. I may not survive it, but it's fun right now." She smiled. "I need to get back to the kitchen. Baking buttermilk brownies. I'd offer you some, but I don't expect there will be any left after Chris-Chris gets done with them."

Melody laughed. "He eats them all?"

"He eats half of one and pulverizes the rest."

They said their goodbyes and two steps later arrived home. They snapped on some lights. Melody dropped her purse on the table and led the way down the hall. They were both exhausted. Who wouldn't be after failing to steal a painting, being bawled out by Mr. Freaking Jacobi, receiving a referral from Dolley Madison Plaskett as the ideal couple to steal a twice-stolen relic held by the son of a Nazi murderer, and not quite meeting Chris-Chris?

"The more I think about this," Bernard said, "the less I like it."

Melody took his hand and led him into the bedroom. "You always liked it before," she pouted.

"Not this. I love this. I don't like that."

"Which that is that?"

"Wagner. *Rienzi.* Gerhard Nachtnebel, Jr."

Melody kissed him gently on the lips. "Twenty thousand dollars," she purred. "Cedar chests."

"Getting shot in the head," Bernard countered.

She pushed him away and pulled a skimpy white nightgown from the dresser. "Why are you always so negative? You've never been shot in the head before, and let's face it, you've had opportunities."

He had to give her that. "Only because you were there. Your luck is eerie."

"You need some luck?" She tossed the nightie on the bed and turned her back on him. "Unzip this thing."

That did the trick.

Chapter 3: Sunday, October 15, 2017

Bernard hadn't looked at the address Dolley gave him, not really, until halfway through breakfast Sunday morning. Melody pulled out the stops and made banana pancakes, bacon, and scrambled eggs. While cooking, she asked him to squeeze some orange juice, which he did. He squeezed it out of the carton and into their plastic glasses while pondering what an oxymoron that was. Plastic glasses. Glasses were called glasses because they were made of glass, right? Whether you drank out of glasses or wore them, the very word signified the material from which they were made. So why weren't these vessels called plastics? Why didn't you say, "I'd like a plastic of wine?"

On second thought, never mind.

Equally obvious was why one might turn down an offer of twenty thousand dollars for stealing from a Nazi, or the son of a Nazi, anyway, who'd held on to his father's ill-gotten gains. Quite aside from the fact that *Rienzi*, which may or may not exist, was hidden in a secret stash which may or may not exist, a mansion filled with art likely had over-the-top security. Just getting in the door would pose a problem. And if they got that far, Bernard still had to locate the alleged hidden treasure room and rummage through it to find the manuscript—assuming he'd know it when he saw it—and escape undetected. And unmurdered. That was a problem far more vexing than why you didn't ask for a plastic of wine.

Bernard toyed with the slip of paper containing the address of Dolley's friend, their employer. No name, no phone number, just an address, suggesting said employer was expecting a visit from them. He tilted his head as he read the town's name: Ford's Ford.

Presumably named for a stream crossing, not a car. Leaving his half-eaten breakfast, he retrieved his laptop from his rolltop and returned to the table while Melody followed him with her eyes.

"What's up?" she asked.

"This address," he said. "It's weird."

"Maryland addresses are like that."

"This one's weirder." He mapped it on MapMania and studied the results. Just beyond the west edge of D.C., Ford's Ford was a cramped cluster of pricey homes bordering an exclusive country club. If ever there had been a stream to ford, it had long since been buried beneath basements or asphalt or the golf course. Maybe it had morphed into a water hazard. The whole place was a hazard of another sort. "Look at this," he said, turning the screen so Melody could see.

She wrinkled her nose. "Eww, traffic trap. I'll bet their chauffeurs can't even get out of their driveways." She retreated to her pancakes, took a bite, assumed a thoughtful look. "Then again, you could save money that way."

Bernard looked up. "Huh?"

"Well, if your chauffeur can't get out of the driveway, there's no sense in having one."

"Which? A chauffer or a driveway?"

"Hmm. Good point. Both."

Best not to pursue the thought. They'd never get back on track. "Unfortunately," he said, "that's where Dolley's mysterious friend lives, so that's where we're going."

Melody clearly didn't like that, but she had a solution. "You be the chauffeur. I'll close my eyes."

He wouldn't dream of letting Melody drive that area. When she got behind the wheel of her red Corvette, anyone daring to navigate the same road was taking their life in their hands. Anyway, Bernard's car was far more elegant, a powder blue Lincoln Zephyr, a vehicle which, despite its fourteen years of service, looked nearly mint. It drew envious sighs in the environs of Aschimos without attracting police attention. Between her driving and her car, Melody was a cop magnet, although she could charm the sunglasses off any police officer. She never received a ticket. Bernard didn't often get pulled over, but when he did, they threw the book at him. Life was so unfair.

Anyway. Bernard turned his attention to another question mark: who the hell was Richard Wagner, and why had Dolley pronounced it so strangely? REE-kard VAHG-nur. The Internet provided the solution. As to the latter, he was German, and of course Germans pronounced everything strangely. As did the French, the Italians, the Spanish, and even the English. Why could nobody but Americans speak right? And even then. Southerners. Westerners. Midwesterners. Bostonians. And all the various racial and ethnic linguistic divergences.

Whatever. REE-kard VAHG-nur it was. As to who he was, Bernard learned Wagner was a brilliant nineteenth-century composer famous for his operas, especially his *Ring* cycle, the second of which was *Die Walküre*, which later inspired some operatic caricatures, including screaming women in horned hats. Okay, main point: the guy was famous. An original, autographed manuscript of his work would be valuable, far more valuable than all the Samuel Weston paintings in Mr. Freaking Jacobi's collection.

After breakfast, Bernard and Melody made themselves ready. Bernard donned a conservative navy suit he'd lifted from a rack at The Suit Emporium. It wasn't exactly expensive. It wouldn't have been even if he'd paid for it. But then, no suit was cheap anymore, and it fit well even without tailoring. As with all his suit coats, Melody had modified it by sewing several large pockets into the lining, for business purposes. He paired the suit with a white shirt and a maroon tie. "How do I look?" he asked his wife.

She waggled a hand.

That usually signaled more disapproval than one would think. "What's wrong?"

"It's too ordinary for a guy like you."

"I'm glad you think so, but I don't want to overdo it. We don't know who this friend of Dolley's is."

"Good point," Melody said. "If she's like Dolley, you might get another proposition. How do I look?"

"Ravishing, as always." She had pulled on a dark red dress that was a finger's width from skin-tight. She'd encircled her neck with a string of faux pearls.

"Oh, good. Then I'll make up for you."

Bernard offered her his arm. Out they went, boarded the Zephyr, and undertook the grueling journey through D.C. traffic to the stately home of their unknown contact, a three-story brick Georgian surrounded by a wrought iron fence. While the house was large, the property was on the small side, shaded by ancient sycamores and tulip poplars that pushed at the boundaries. A huge gate barred the drive up to the garage. A speaker box was posted beside it. Bernard pulled up to the box, lowered his window, and punched the only button in evidence.

The box crackled with static.

"Hello?" Bernard called.

More static.

"I'm here to see..." Well, this was awkward. He didn't know her name.

This time, a voice tried to break through the static. It failed.

He tried a different approach, more for his own sake than for whoever was spluttering behind the electronic interference. "Dolley Madison Plaskett sent me."

An enthusiastic, "Oh!" punched through the white noise this time. "Bernard? Melody?"

"That's us," Bernard affirmed, and the gate rolled open to let them pass.

He cruised up the drive to a shuttered four-car garage, then he and Melody walked hand-in-hand to the front door, which opened before he could ring the bell. The woman admitting them towered over them, easily six foot three, tanned and toned, platinum blonde. Bernard felt overdressed. Their hostess wore jeans and a smock splattered with more colors than Mother Nature herself owned, pushed out by a bust of impressive proportions. The sleeves of a plain white t-shirt wrapped her upper arms. Wielding an artist's paintbrush coated in electric blue, the woman flashed them a dazzling smile. "Bernard! Melody! I'm so pleased to meet you. Please, come in, come in, over here, let's go into the studio and we can talk while I work. This way, this way!"

Bernard braced himself for an exhausting conversation.

She led them through a foyer lined in marble statuary, a sitting room flooded with foliage, and an enormous sunroom cluttered with easels, canvases, paints, pencils, papers of various grades, and sketches and drawings and oils, oh my. Bernard and Melody simultaneously blinked at a charcoal sketch of a nude couple dancing to unheard music. They were anatomically correct except for one small detail. Their heads were missing.

Their hostess noticed their astonishment and laughed. "Everyone has theories as to my intent," she said. "All very deep and symbolic and spiritual and..." She winked at them. "...wrong. Truth is, I never figured out their faces, so I just stopped there."

"You figured out the rest," Bernard said. "That counts for something, I suppose."

Pulling a couple of stools from a workbench, she motioned Bernard and Melody to sit, then snagged one for herself and settled before an easel with a blue, blue sky beneath which blank canvas spread. She dabbed her brush into a pool of blue paint on a palette and extended the sky downward. "My professional name," she said, "is Celeste. You won't need my real name, I'm sure."

Nope. Besides, how hard could it be to discover? She wasn't exactly hiding, not in a house like this.

"Hi, Celeste!" Melody said as though she'd just met a new best friend. "I'm Melody and this is Bernard. I call him Bernie. Best if you don't."

Bernard smiled weakly, but it was the truth. He hated that hypocorism, except when Melody uttered it. Then he loved it.

Celeste winked at Melody. "Gotcha," she said. "How much did Dolley tell you?"

Bernard shifted on the stool. "She claims Gerhard Nachtnebel, Jr. may be in possession of the original manuscript for the Wagner opera *Rienzi* and says you're seeking a go-between to assist in acquiring it. She gave us some details of the item's history and indicated you would be willing to pay handsomely for our assistance." How respectable the proposition sounded when put that way. He gazed respectfully into Celeste's eyes.

"You got it." She turned back to the painting and continued to apply the blue. "Get me *Rienzi*, and you'll earn twenty thousand dollars."

"Plus expenses," Bernard said.

"Expenses? What sort of expenses?"

"I won't know that until I know the effort required."

"Hmm. Now we come to the delicate part, don't we?"

Inasmuch as breaking and entering, burglary, and not getting shot could be called delicate, yes. But Bernard said nothing, and Melody seemed to be holding her breath, which somehow made her look even more beautiful. Bernard told himself to focus. On the job. Not on Melody.

Celeste regarded her sky, then put the brush down and turned to give her guests her full attention. "Access to the Nachtnebel mansion is no problem. It's a mecca for art students. Half the place is given over to instruction, practice, and rubbing everyone's noses in Gerhardt's collections. But–"

Melody's eyes widened. "Why would he want to rub everyone's noses in his collections? Wouldn't that ruin the art and spread germs?"

Celeste blinked at Melody, then laughed. "Yes," she said, "it probably would. But he makes a fortune on registration fees and tickets, so I'm sure he doesn't care."

Melody made an *eww!* face but refrained from further comment.

"There's also his private collection," Celeste continued. "Nobody ever sees that."

"Then how do you know it exists?" Bernard asked.

"Because," Melody said, "his father was a horrid Nazi thief."

Celeste winked at Melody. Clearly, the women were forming a rapport. "That's one thing," she said. "Another is, I've seen it."

At first, Bernard thought that fortuitous, but then logic seized his brain's reins. "Hold on. You said nobody ever sees it. We may never have met before, but I can tell you're not nobody."

"I'm glad you think so. You may have noticed I'm an artist."

"Well, duh," Melody said. She waved her hand to indicate the whole studio. "You draw headless dancers, after all, and paint skies over nothing."

"Don't worry, something will be under that sky eventually."

"Thank goodness," Bernard said. "What about this private collection?"

"I've communed with Gerhard's treasures," Celeste said, "same as a million other unknown artists. And taken a few classes. One day during lunch break, I went to the restroom. I pushed on the door, but it wouldn't open. Locked tight. A guard appeared from nowhere and led me away, more forcibly than required. He told me nobody was allowed in. Not that it was out of order. That nobody was allowed in."

Bernard was almost intrigued. Suspicious behavior, yes, but it could have meant anything.

"What I propose," Celeste continued, "is that you pose as art students and slip into that so-called women's room unnoticed. I'm sure the secret collection is back there. Find *Rienzi* and bring it to me. In and out. Simple."

Oh sure, simple. The woman was practicing burglary without a license. Bernard really wanted to arrest her for that, but, well, twenty thousand dollars. And anyway, her theory was worth testing. Even if what she wanted wasn't locked in that so-called restroom, something of value might be.

Celeste turned her dazzling smile on Bernard. "So, what expenses could you possibly have?"

That one was easy. "Tuition," he said. "And art supplies."

$\oint$

Celeste gave them things. For one, her cell phone number, which Bernard entered in his contacts list. He didn't reciprocate and she didn't ask. She also provided a hand-drawn map of the Nachtnebel mansion, sketched from memory. It looked good enough to frame, lettered like a medieval manuscript, embellished with curlicues and doodles along the edges. Melody thought it elegant. Bernard thought it over-the-top. Artists.

For another, Celeste saved Bernard a web search by pointing him to the website of the Nachtnebel Arts Foundation, where upcoming events at the mansion were listed. And for her encore, she handed over a gem of intel: the name of the Nachtnebel security system, a name guaranteed to strike terror into the hearts of burglars everywhere: Fitzroy

Fortresses, motto: "Don't even think it." That wasn't bravado, either. It was a well-founded warning. A Fitzroy sign outside a home convinced most burglars to pick another target.

But Bernard and Melody were in a class of their own. At the mere sound of *Fitz*, they both thought it. They couldn't help it. Melody even nudged Bernard a few times. Because, you see, they had an inside man, if one could call the geeky Shawn Ueltschi a man. He was more a twenty-one-year-old teenager who hadn't yet crossed the finish line. Bernard suspected that between pulling double duty as a college senior and a junior Fitzroy engineer, Shawn hadn't had time to suss out the full implications of his fiancée Felicity Barnswald's femaleness. Regardless, as of that moment Shawn was on call, whether he knew it or not.

Bernard and Melody took leave of Celeste (real name unknown) and fought through D.C. traffic back to the less congested environs of Aschimos. Dinnertime approached, and they were exhausted. "I'm not cooking tonight," Melody said. "Let's order a pizza."

"Tell you what, love," Berhard graciously suggested. "Let's dine out."

Melody smiled a sappy smile. "You're too good to me."

"Nothing's too good for you."

Soon they were ensconced in a corner booth at their local Burger Bazzar, dining on double Swiss burgers and seasoned fries. They splurged and got chocolate milkshakes. Large ones. Melody was close to swooning.

Bernard let her revel in the luxury while he studied Celeste's map. Although in outline it portrayed the whole of the mansion, only the west wing—the wing devoted to classes and other public events—was drawn in detail. The private east wing was blank. For each of the three floors on the west, Celeste had sketched in a central corridor of ridiculous proportions flanked by classrooms and lecture halls. On the back side of the mansion, a grand staircase connected the floors dead center, with a less grand one—probably for emergency use only—at the west end beside the public entrance. Public restrooms nestled against the grand stairs to the west. Three doors east was a room marked "Bistro" in excessively elaborate script. Bernard figured lunch there had to be paid for in gold.

All three floors were the same, save one detail. On the back side of the third floor, a second pair of restrooms huddled by a door connecting the public wing to the private residence. Celeste had marked those as suspicious. The first and second floors had connecting doors, too, but with classrooms flanking them instead of restrooms. Suspicious indeed. Plumbing dictated the locations of the facilities. Every floor ought to have them in the same place.

"We should get some lemon pies, too," Melody said. She delicately licked fry seasoning from her fingers.

"Uh-huh," Bernard said without registering the suggestion. No way was either of those restrooms big enough to hide a secret art stash. Not much of one, anyway. But Celeste might still be right. Maybe one large room—not a pair of restrooms at all—hid behind those two doors. But why keep a secret stash in a room with public accessibility? Why not bury it in the private wing?

"There's something fishy here," Bernard said.

Melody peered at Bernard's burger. "Doesn't look like fish," she said.

"Huh?"

"You said it was fishy."

"Not that. This." He pushed the map her way and explained his conclusions.

"Maybe it was the only place he had available," Melody suggested.

"In a palace that size?"

"Come on, Bernie, when you're filthy rich, you've got to have grand pianos and fountains and aviaries and all that. They take up a lot of room."

Bernard doubted he'd want an aviary if he became filthy rich. Maybe a fountain. Maybe a piano or two. He didn't play piano and had no interest in learning, but for ostentation, sure. Why not?

"Get us some lemon pies," Melody added.

Leaving the map to his wife, he went. When he returned, he found her puzzling over it. "Find something?" he asked.

"Found something missing."

"What's that?"

"Celeste said a guard came out of nowhere. I don't see nowhere on here."

Melody's peculiar phraseology notwithstanding, it was a fair point. None of the rooms were marked as security offices. Either Celeste had been caught on camera trying to access the forbidden room—except how could a guard have gotten there so quickly?—or he was patrolling and she didn't notice his approach.

"We should take a good look at the third floor," Bernard said. "I'll find us a class and sign us up."

Melody popped her lemon pie out of its box and wafted it under her nose. Her eyes rolled in ecstasy. "Tomorrow," she said. "Tonight, let's just enjoy ourselves."

Bernard tucked the map away and unboxed his dessert. They raised their pies and clinked them, although pies don't clink. In fact, they hardly made a sound. But Bernard and Melody both felt the elegance.

Chapter 4: Monday, October 16, 2017

Over breakfast, Bernard reflected that Monday mornings are always better when you're starting a new project. Like stealing a priceless artifact from a woman's restroom in the heavily guarded mansion of some Nazi offspring.

Okay, not always. How did he get himself into this?

Still...twenty thousand dollars. Focus, Bernard, focus.

He'd made a start. He had a map and some questions. Access to the mansion would be simple. Just find an event, register, and show up. Then case the joint. Easy peasy.

Except for two things. One, he needed a foolproof plan because, well, bullets in the head. Two, he couldn't devise a foolproof plan in just one sitting. He'd need time to study the lay of the land. Or, well, the mansion. Fortunately, they could attend a multiday class. Unfortunately, they had to be invisible during that time. Unmemorable.

The main obstacle to that was Melody. God hadn't meant her to be invisible. He'd made her, for some inscrutable reason, to be as memorable as ripe strawberries dipped in sugar and eaten in the warmth of a late spring sun. Just look at her. She was sitting across from him, wrapped in a light blue bathrobe, sipping coffee from an "I ♥ Sheboygan" mug that she'd pilfered from some rich target's house, not because she knew anything about Sheboygan but because the name tickled her fancy. Her laptop was open in front of her, and she was gazing lovingly at the screen, no doubt at something expensive that would go well with that luxury model cedar chest. When she realized Bernard was looking at her, she looked up and smiled, and his entire being melted.

"I'm going to Chrissy's this afternoon," she said, naming her favorite beauty parlor, though she had no need of greater beauty.

Bernard didn't want her to go. He wanted her right there in her bathrobe, sipping coffee.

"For information," she added. "For the job."

Oh, right. The job. "Information?"

"Some of the ladies are very artistic. Maybe one of them can get us into that Nazi guy's classes."

"That's no problem," Bernard said, "I'll just register online."

Her whole face drooped in disappointment. "Bernie. The personal touch is always better."

"Not where Nazis are concerned."

"But we don't want just any class. We want a good one."

Squaring his laptop before him, Bernard typed in the URL Celeste had supplied. "The quality of the class doesn't matter, love. It's just a cover."

She narrowed her eyes. Even without looking at her, he could feel it. "What about the registration fee?" she asked.

"What about it?"

"We don't want to waste Celeste's money on a second-rate class."

"It won't be wasted. We'll use the time to—"

"I'm sorry, Bernie, but I insist. If we're going, it's gotta be worth it, artistically as well as professionally."

When Melody went to that kind of place, there was no arguing. "All right," he said. "You find us a class, and I'll sign us up."

"In that order," she said. "Don't register before I find out."

"I wouldn't dream of it." Which was true. Bernard had no desire to be an outcast from his own bedroom. Not that Melody would go that far. She never slept well without him wrapped around her. But that didn't mean she wouldn't contrive some other punishment, and could she ever be devious.

Assured by his assurance, she returned to her laptop, punctuating her online window shopping with sips of coffee and occasional gasps of pleasure. Bernard didn't want to know what she'd found, not yet, not before payday.

He browsed the website of the Nachtnebel Arts Foundation, headquartered at the sickeningly elegant Nachtnebel mansion. A full schedule of upcoming courses, seminars, lectures, master classes, and exhibitions populated the coming six months, along with a scattering of private viewings. Drawing classes, watercolor classes, oil painting classes, ceramics classes, even a writing class. None of it came cheap, and (he couldn't help but notice), there were no vacancies for the next five weeks. Maybe it was for the best that Melody had put herself in charge of scheduling. She could worm her way into the most crowded of venues.

Only one offering was free: the Nachtnebel Virtual Gallery, an internet video channel featuring not only images of art housed in the mansion, but drone footage of the grounds and the building itself.

Intrigued, Bernard went for a fly-around.

&

Chrissy Christopher, tall and black and as elegant as a panther, happened to be the aunt of a friend of a cousin of Melody Earls, a happy association that made Melody one of Chrissy's favorite customers and the recipient of a sizeable discount whenever she stopped by. Money was no object to Chrissy. As she catered to women of wealth in her Bethesda shop, she had become one herself, within reason. She wasn't a one percenter, but she made enough to keep her in radiant dresses and Caribbean cruises.

When Melody pranced into the establishment, everyone—customers and stylists alike—lit up like LED streetlights.

"Wow! Melody!"

"Hey there, girl!"

"What an amazing dress! Where'd you get it?"

"Our supermodel returns!"

The greetings tripped over each other in their rush to reach Melody's ears. She cast her smile liberally over the gathering and took them all into an air hug with widespread arms. "Hi, everyone!"

Chrissy all but fell in her rush to gather Melody into a physical hug. "You look better every time I see you, girl!" She had the cutest Virginia accent. Melody couldn't get enough of it. Stepping back, Chrissy examined every inch of her friend. "Nope, you don't need nothin' done to you today. But name your pleasure and I'll try not to mess you up too much."

Melody play-slapped Chrissy's shoulder. "Oh, come on. You're an artist. You couldn't mess up anyone if you tried."

Chrissy smiled, embarrassed. "I didn't say it." Then she leaned close and whispered. "But I know that's right."

The women giggled. Melody took a seat by the window where customers waited for service. She daintily crossed her legs at the ankles and sighed. That was her signal that she had a story for them. Of course she did. She always had a story, usually of glowing success in the world of glamor modeling. Not one of them had ever seen Melody in a magazine, print or online, but they were all sure they had, a testimony to the confidence she exuded.

Besides, they needed her to be a star. It lent excitement to their otherwise dreary lives. Aside from Chrissy herself, the staff seldom got out of their own neighborhoods, while the wealthy matrons they served largely served the whims of their husbands, a shocking truth given it was the twenty-first century. It shocked Melody, anyway, but there it was. They didn't visit Paris or Rome or Kathmandu when *they* wanted to. They went when their men went. Melody knew, because she'd heard their complaints time and again.

She administered a remedy, an injection of a life where women had power and control and the nerve to shape their own destinies. It might not be quite the truth, but it wasn't a lie. It was a public service.

She delivered today's public service announcement in awe-struck tones. "I sold my first painting last week. It went for eight thousand dollars!"

Everyone erupted in cheers and applause and astonished cries of, "I didn't know you were an artist!"

"Oh, yes," she said. "I've been painting since I was in kindergarten." True enough. Then, it had been fingerpainting. "My teachers always said I had talent." Also true, although not generally for painting. Melody's talents tended towards, well, acquiring sparklies and afterward telling scintillating tales to evade punishment. "It's always been just a hobby. But I finally got up the nerve to present something in an art show." True again, after a fashion. She had, indeed, presented the naked flower people to that meddling docent.

At that point, she let her audience take over. Claire, one of the stylists, squealed, "And you got eight thousand for it?"

Everyone joined the noise, which as near as Melody could make out involved proclaiming her the new Georgia O'Keeffe.

She waved off the praise in mock embarrassment. "Oh, you guys. It's not that big a deal."

A customer named Deirdra, a redhead with eyes as fiery as her locks, leaned forward in her chair. "But Melody! Eight thousand!"

"Oh, that's nothing. Some artists get millions for their paintings. I gotta up my game, don't you think?"

That caused more babbling as the women talked over each other in dazed astonishment until Chrissy herself cut through the commotion with a sensible question: "Up your game? What do you mean, girl?"

"You know, study with real artists. Improve my technique. Make as big a name for myself in the art world as I have in modeling." Strictly speaking, she already had about equal fame in both worlds, but the Chrissy's gang didn't know that.

"Well then," Deirdra said, straightening with pride, "I can tell you how to do *that*."

"Really?" Melody said, mock ecstatic. "Do tell!"

"I have a nephew named Thunder who has a wife named Whisper who's a pretty hot painter herself. She's taking a master class that just started. She could probably get you in."

Following that announcement, the beauty parlor grew strangely quiet save the humming of a hair dryer, and even that felt muted.

"Thunder?" Melody asked. "And Whisper?"

"Oh yes, they're quite a cute couple."

"But," Chrissy said. "Thunder? And Whisper?"

Dierdra laughed. "Come on, everyone has a weird name these days."

"I don't," Melody said.

"Half of everyone, then."

Melody didn't see how half of someone could have any name at all. A name belonged to a whole person, didn't it? But it wasn't important. "What about this master class?" she asked. "Is it through an art school?"

"It's in Swampside, at Gerhard Nachtnebel's place. Have you heard of him?"

Bingo. Melody's luck came through again. "Oh, yes! I hear he has a wonderful collection."

"Perfect!" Deirdra tugged her purse up from its resting place at her side and rummaged until she found her cell phone. "I'll call Whisper and see if we can't get you in." A moment later, she was leaving a voice mail.

Melody settled in to wait. The conversation drifted from master classes to art and artists everyone liked, to mild arguments over the relative importance of line and color, to the color of furnishings and draperies and fall foliage and how much it cost to have someone come out and mulch the dead leaves.

Deirdra's phone emitted a curious ring tone that sounded like a hurricane blowing shingles off a roof. "Ah," she said, "that's Whisper." She set the phone to her ear. "How are you honey? Having fun? Oh, that's great. Hey, could you get someone a spot in the class? Melody. Melody. You've heard me talk about Melody, I'm sure. No, not music, she's a supermodel. I met her in Chrissy's like three years ago. Well, she's a painter, too, and she'd like to get in on the class."

Melody waived frantically to get Deirdra's attention. "Oh! See if Bernie can get a spot, too!"

Surprised, Deirdra gaped at her. "He's a painter?"

"Oh, sure. He's a wonderful painter." Which was true. Bernard did a nice job helping Melody's father paint his living room once.

Deirdra gave her a thumbs up. "Whisper, honey, make it two spots. Melody wants to bring her husband. Yes, yes, he is. That would be great. Thank you!" She tucked her phone away and told Melody, "They're taking a short break right now. She'll find out and get back to me. It shouldn't be long."

Conversation resumed, this time taking in winter trips to Acapulco and Rio and—for reasons Melody couldn't fathom—Antarctica. Escaping the mild Maryland winter for someplace frozen solid didn't make much sense to her, but then as her mother always said, it takes all kinds.

Before long, that hurricane noise filtered out of Deirdra's purse again, and she received the wonderful news that Melody and Bernard were most welcome to attend the remaining four days of the five-day master class at the Nachtnebel mansion starting Tuesday morning at nine A.M. sharp, provided they paid the full thousand dollar per person tuition upon arrival. No pro-rating.

Melody clapped with joy, although inwardly she cringed. Bernard would choke on his dinner when he heard the cost. But hey, it wasn't their problem. Celeste was covering expenses.

𝄞

Bernard almost choked on a forkful of mac and cheese. "A thousand a person!" he bellowed once his throat was sufficiently clear. "Did you *have* to tell me that while I was swallowing?"

Melody smiled sweetly. Or sarcastically. With her, it was hard to tell. "At least you weren't drinking," she said. "I don't need a Chardonnay shower tonight."

Not that it would have been. They couldn't afford such elevated wines. This one, a cheap white Melody had picked up at a sale, was barely even a white. More of a gray, Bernard suspected. But it would do. During their eleven-year marriage, they'd gotten so good at pretending to elegance that they even fooled themselves sometimes.

"It's a quality class," Melody added.

"For a thousand a head, it better be."

"A master class." She puzzled over that for a moment. "Does that mean you get a master's degree after attending?"

Since the price bombshell had already been dropped and nothing more outrageous could possibly follow, Bernard hazarded a sip of wine before answering. "It's taught by a master of the art, who usually gives students individual critiques on their work and makes suggestions for improvement."

"Oh, a master! Like Rembrandt?"

"Yes, but with luck it won't be him."

"Why not?"

"He's dead, love."

There was that smile again. "I know *that*, Bernie. But maybe his ghost could teach the class."

"Ghost?"

"Sure. Nachtnebel wouldn't have to pay a ghost, so he could keep the entire thousand for himself." Melody put a finger to her lips and wrinkled her brow in thought. "You know, that might be a good business for us to get into. Ghost master classes."

Bernard forked up some more mac and cheese. In the olden days, he would have wondered why their conversations always bent this way, but no more. There was no explaining it. Melody's mind meandered through surreal worlds with alarming frequency. And yet she could muster deep insights, too, not to mention clever escapes from any dark pool they fell into. Bernard suspected some relation between all those facts, but he'd never figured out how it worked.

"I doubt anyone would pay for that," he said.

She sipped her wine and rolled her eyes in ecstasy. "Of course they would. I could sell anything to anyone."

There was that. "Be that as it may, we won't be taking classes from a ghost this time. Or even from a live instructor if Celeste won't agree to the expense."

"She already agreed to expenses," Melody reminded him. "She made what's called a 'rash promise.' It's a silly thing to do. You end up paying the full week's price for only four days."

Bernard almost choked on another forkful of mac and cheese. "They didn't prorate it?"

She gave him a dull look. "You expect a Nazi would?"

Point. "I'd better get this over with," he said. He retrieved his cell phone from beside his plate and tapped Celeste's name in his contacts list. Setting the device to his ear, he waited for her to pick up.

"Hello, Bernard," she said, which was odd because although she had given him his number, he hadn't given her his. His silence must have broadcast the question. She laughed. "You're the only one who would call this phone," she said. "It's a burner."

Ah. That would do it, although it seemed awfully good trade-craft for a lowly artist. "Hello, Celeste. Not to be blunt, but I need expense funds. Fast."

"If you were going for genteel, you missed it by a mile."

"We can get into a master class tomorrow, but..." Bernard figured she could figure out the rest.

"You didn't have to aim *that* high."

"It was available."

Celeste didn't reply. Bernard wasn't sure she was even breathing, although once she heard the exact number, she might start breathing fire.

"A thousand a head."

"And you have two heads." She chuckled. "Maybe that's how I should have finished that painting. Given each figure two heads." The chuckle became a guffaw, which was better than breathing fire. Once she got her mirth under control, she said, "All right, but if you run off with my money, you'll be as headless as those dancers."

"Ma'am, I'm a professional," Bernard said, doing his best to sound utterly insulted. He did it so well, Melody put a hand to her mouth in astonishment. He waved it off to let her know it was all right.

"I'm relieved to hear it," Celeste said. "How do I send it?"

"MoneyMonkey," Bernard told her, naming his favorite financial app. The app itself wasn't any better than any other, but Melody couldn't help giggling at the name, which made it totally worth it. She had an endearing giggle. She was doing it right now, behind that hand that was still at her mouth.

Bernard gave Celeste the email address he used for the purpose and waited while she sent the money. A ding or two later, his bank account had been enriched. He thanked her, she graciously wished them a fun class, and that was that. Setting the phone down, he said, "That went surprisingly well." He took a sip of gray wine.

"MoneyMonkey," Melody snickered.

Unable to suppress a laugh, Bernard spewed fake Chardonnay all over the table.

Chapter 5: Tuesday Morning, October 17, 2017

The screech of someone being stabbed without mercy jarred Bernard awake. He bolted from bed, shaking as the screech screeched on and on and on and...

"Oof," Melody mumbled. She pulled the sheet over her head.

The sound stopped as suddenly as it had started. Bernard couldn't wrap his brain around it. Did water pipes make that noise? Certainly not someone's ring tone. Anyone creating a ringtone like that should be hanged, drawn, and quartered. So should anyone choosing to use it. Nothing in the apartment complex's lawn service arsenal would make that racket, not unless it was seriously malfunctioning. No, it had to be someone's voice, and voices didn't do *that* unless something horrific was happening.

It sounded again, high-pitched, loud, terrifying. It went on and on for twenty, thirty seconds before falling silent.

Melody pulled the sheet over her head, then stuffed her head under her pillow and mumbled something unintelligible that might have been, "Stop it," or "Mop up," or "Hop on," the latter of which was more like what they'd done last night before falling asleep.

"I better see what that is," Bernard said. "Someone might be hurt."

Melody pushed the pillow and the sheet from her head. Eyes still closed, she said, "Get dressed first."

Good point. Bernard pulled on a pair of jeans and a plain blue t-shirt, stuffed his feet into his slippers, and rushed from the apartment. Then he stood in the silent hall, looking left, looking right, looking at the ceiling–which was pointless, because ceilings never sounded like *that*. Nor did floors, not without seriously injured bodies cluttering the hall, none of which were in evidence. Hmm.

He was about to make for the stairwell at the front of the building when the screech screeched again, now clearly issuing from Mrs. Clarke's, apartment. Bernard pounded on the door, rattled the doorknob, and called, "Mrs. Clarke! Are you all right? Mrs. Clarke!"

The screech stopped.

The door cracked open. Mrs. Clarke peeked out. "Oh, Mr. Earls! Yes, I'm fine. It's just Chris-Chris."

"Chris-Chris?"

"My great-grandson. Don't you remember? He's staying with me."

Bernard might have remembered, just as he might have remembered his clothes without being reminded, had his brain not been shocked into a stupor. "Does he do this every morning?" he asked.

"I guess we'll see." Mrs. Clarke looked over her shoulder. Chris-Chris was in the living room, staring wide-eyed at Bernard while hugging a stuffed T-rex to his chest. "He's quite a bundle of energy. I hope he didn't disturb you."

Bernard liked Mrs. Clarke too much to tell her the whole truth. "I thought someone was hurt."

"You're a saint, Mr. Earls. Thank you for checking up on me."

"Not at all," St. Bernard mumbled. "Have a good day."

Back in the bedroom, Bernard flopped on top of the sheets next to Melody and stared at the ceiling.

"Anyone dead?" Melody asked, still half-asleep but not with her head buried.

"No. It was just Chris-Chris."

"Hmm?"

"Mrs. Clarke's great-grandson."

"Mmm." She tugged at the sheet, but with Bernard on top of it, it didn't move. "Time," she said.

Bernard fumbled for his cell phone. "Six eighteen," he informed her. How the hell early did Chris-Chris's mother go to work? Maybe she had to commute to D.C., in which case she probably left at four A.M.

It was shaping up to be a miserable two weeks.

"Alarm's set for seven," Melody mumbled. She rolled onto her side and managed to open her eyes three-quarters of the way. She gave Bernard a sleepy once-over. "Get off my sheet."

Bernard pinched the bridge of his nose and shook his head to clear it.

"And get undressed."

𝄞

Having done the online fly-around the previous day, Bernard knew what they were getting into. Or at least, he knew the outside of what they were getting into. The drone footage provided by the Nachtnebel Virtual Gallery showcased the sprawling, gated estate replete with stands of silver maple, sycamore, and green ash. Ponds surrounded by formal gardens dotted the grounds. Roses were everywhere, interspersed with native flowers and a few exotics. A bonsai garden was tucked into a stone enclosure behind the mansion.

The mansion itself was an imposing structure, rather like those English estates one saw in BBC mysteries where rich people were always killing each other off: all stone and columns and turrets and everywhere great windows just begging to admit burglars. Not that burglars would get too far. Fitzroy Fortresses was nothing if not thorough. The windows would all be alarmed, even those on the third floor, which couldn't be reached without help from the fire department.

The drive leading onto the estate meandered for a good quarter mile before ending in a parking lot at the west end of the mansion, the public end. Prior to that, a gated road split off toward the six-car garage on the private east end, where the Nachtnebels lived.

The rear of the mansion had a different character, still elegant but not so imposing, bristling with as many balconies as an apartment building. Whatever room you were in above the ground floor, you had access to at least one balcony with wrought iron railings decked with black curlicues and flower blossoms, most furnished with Adirondack chairs and little tables and potted roses and hydrangeas. These all overlooked the bonsai garden, the manicured lawn, and the woods beyond.

The drone had reached sufficient altitude to permit a study of the roof, too, which consisted of a dizzying array of pitched angles, some quite steep, and cones atop turrets. Bernard wondered where the Nachtnebels would find a roofer insane enough to risk his life merely to refasten a loose shingle.

It wasn't all Himalayan slopes up there, though. Bernard always found it interesting how the parts of buildings not meant to be seen degraded into sheer ugliness. In this case, a flat section of roof stretched about a quarter of the way across the mansion dead center, bristling with vents and AC units and two small structures with access doors, one east and one west. Those would be used by HVAC contactors and kamikaze roofers, so no ornamentation had been afforded them or the surrounding area. It could have been a factory roof grafted onto the mansion.

But since the area was well hidden, the Nachtnebel abode overall remained an inspiring place. It particularly inspired envy, an emotion Bernard tried with only limited success to suppress. And now that they were driving up that quarter-mile drive and passing before the façade, he couldn't help himself.

"Let's steal it," he told Melody.

"Don't be silly, Bernie. It wouldn't fit in even your biggest pocket."

She had a point, damn it. "Let's steal everything in it, then."

"Same problem." She ran her lovely index finger over her lovely lips, her red nail polish blending perfectly with her red lipstick. "This place reminds me of my great-grandpa Kensington's house."

"You had a rich great-grandfather?"

"Oh, yes. The Kensingtons were super rich. One of them was a duke or a king or something."

Bernard glanced at her. Then he glanced at the mansion. King Bernard and Queen Melody. Wealth. Power. Gold and silver and tapestries and bed curtains. Servants. He liked the sound of that. But no, Melody couldn't possibly be royalty. Royalty would never end up living in Aschimos, Maryland. Hmm, well, unless they were deposed. But while that would have happened to one of *his* ancestors, surely it couldn't have to any of Melody's.

"They came to America," Melody continued. "I think it was on the Niña or the Pinta or the Santa Maria."

"I doubt anyone named Kensington was on those ships," Bernard told her.

She ignored him. "Of course, after the Revolution, none of them could be king anymore, so they got into shipping and steel. And then they lost nearly everything in the Great Depression. So you see, the history of my family is basically the history of the whole country."

Obviously. Nothing about Melody would ever be ordinary. Bernard didn't know whether to roll his eyes or stop the car and kiss her for half an hour. As it was, they arrived at the parking lot just then, so he settled for parking the car.

Lost in the past, Melody didn't notice it was time to get out. "Now, the McGirls, on the other hand, they made out like bandits in the Depression. They were bootleggers."

Which Bernard had heard a million times. He believed it. It would explain a lot. His beloved had been Melody Jane McGirl before becoming an Earls and likely had a tad more bootlegger genes than monarch genes. But whatever the percentages, they sure had mixed well. Bernard turned off the engine and opened his door.

Melody laughed. "Mom thought it was exciting marrying into a notorious family. They weren't rich anymore, but she liked to pretend."

"So that's where you get it from," Bernard said. He climbed out and circled the car to help Melody exit. The ritual was one more part of their feigned elegance, the husband opening the door for his wife and taking her hand as she rose. People often smiled at them as though they'd stepped off a movie screen from a film about a bygone era.

"Yep," she said, taking his hand. "And why I married you. You have that Kensington look. Except your nose isn't big enough to be theirs."

Presumably that was a good thing. "Noses are one thing I would never steal," Bernard quipped.

Melody snickered, hooked her arm through his, and leaned on him as they walked, she in a knee-length blue dress, he in jeans and a blue polo with a light blue blazer over. The blazer might have been overkill, but he never went anywhere without his hidden pockets, not if there might be stuff to purloin. With her free arm, Melody toted a canvas bag with the art supplies required for the class: a couple of sketchpads and two sets of drawing pencils. The supplies hadn't set them back too much, but Bernard had the receipt so he could expense them.

Between holding Bernard on one side and the bag on the other, Melody's walk was a bit unbalanced. So was his, as he tried to keep her steady. They probably looked drunk, staggering up to the mansion's side entrance. There were a few others making their way in, but nobody gave them a funny look, so they got away with it. Which was good. They were supposed to be unmemorable. They'd almost blown it right from the start.

The entrance was a pair of oak double doors with wrought iron handles set into a stone arch. Four granite steps led up to them. A little castle-shaped sign stuck in the lawn at the base of the steps warned, "Protected by Fitzroy Fortresses. Don't even think it."

Already did, Bernard silently told the sign.

The doors stood open. The passage beyond was guarded by an ornate cherry reception desk staffed by a pair of young women in red and gray uniforms. The women checked registrations as the students filed in. Most of the up-and-coming artists presented QR codes on their cell phones. A few older folks slid paper registrations across the desk. Bernard mentioned their names and said they were late registrants, whereupon one of the women tapped their information into her computer and took Bernard's payment. He didn't even wince as the two grand left his account, never to be seen again.

"You're in room two-oh-seven," the woman told him.

And then they were in, cruising a hall lined with suits of armor and weapons from the pre-gunpowder age. Every metal plate and implement was polished to a sheen, scattering light into an annoying glare. It was almost as if you weren't supposed to see where you were going, so you could bump into something, knock it over, and be sued by the owner.

"Second and third floor classes take the stairs to the left, please," a woman lost somewhere in the glow was calling. "Stairs to the left. Thank you. Yes ma'am, left. Stairs to the left. All students going to the second and third floor, go left. Thank you, sir. Take the stairs to the left."

Two-thirds of the students streamed leftward and up the grand staircase. Half of that throng, including Bernard and Melody, departed at the second floor. The rest ascended to the third, some slowing so much, they might have been scaling the slopes of Everest into the Death Zone. His arm about Melody's waist, Bernard guided her to their destination, avoiding the urge to look upward to check for cameras. There would be time for exploring later, during a break. Emerging from the stairwell, they followed further instructions from a strategically placed traffic cop, turned right, and found room 207 across the hall, directly opposite the restrooms. It was one of the largest rooms, a lecture hall with two doors and a stage with a blue curtain and rows of plush blue seating for more than fifty. Bernard and Melody took seats at the back of the center aisle, nicely camouflaged in their blue outfits. From there, they could see everything. And slip out, if necessary.

At precisely nine o'clock, the lights went down, a spotlight shone on the curtain, and someone strode out stage left, carrying himself like the President of the United States. It wasn't the President, of course. Even from the back row, Bernard could see he was maybe in his sixties, whereas the President looked more like a hundred and ten. Also, this guy was totally bald, wore gold wire-rim glasses, and smiled like a used car salesman on the cusp of a sale. Well, okay, the smile was about the same as the President's. But not the rest of him.

"Good morning, class," the man said. His voice boomed in surround-sound. "For the newcomers, I'm Gerhard Nachtnebel, Jr. Welcome to my humble abode."

Melody wrinkled her nose. "Is that a joke?" she whispered.

"Probably not," Bernard whispered back.

"Stuck up, isn't he?"

"He can afford to be."

Nachtnebel continued, "I meant to stop by yesterday, but business got in the way. You know how it goes."

Nope, none of them did. They were artists, not business tycoons.

"So, I just had to join you today to introduce your teacher for this master class, Ms. Allegra Fumagalli. Allegra is, after all, our most prominent and regular guest instructor. Her work has graced numerous galleries around the country, and she currently teaches multimedia art at Dankworth College."

Nachtnebel extended his hand stage left, but someone in the wings must have signaled something, because he dropped it and added, "Oh, yes, I forgot. We have a few newcomers this morning, so I'll recite the boring logistical stuff for their benefit." He forced a chuckle. Some of the students joined in, others groaned.

Ignoring the latter, he pressed on. "Please silence your cell phones, tablets, smart watches, and all other electronic devices that might make distracting noises. Also, please remain in the building at all times, emergencies excepted. If you must leave, you will forfeit your registration fee."

"Plan your emergencies carefully," Bernard whispered to Melody. Melody giggled behind her hand.

"Finally," Nachtnebel said, "to help us control traffic, please confine your movements to the second floor. As you exit this room, restrooms are directly across the hall. A bistro where you can purchase lunch is across and to the right, just beyond the grand staircase. The bistro is open for lunch and each morning before class for those who need their caffeine fix. Please note, facilities on the other floors are reserved for students attending events on those floors."

"Darn," Melody whispered. "We should've gotten a class on the third floor."

"Why?" Bernard whispered back. "Is the food better up there?"

She elbowed him in the ribs. Which was okay. He was used to it.

"And now, your esteemed teacher, Allegra Fumagalli." Nachtnebel motioned stage left once more.

The gathering applauded, some quiet and polite, some loud and punctuated with obnoxious cheering. A little old lady hobbled on stage, assisted by a cane. Her hair piled into a gray beehive, she wore a gray dress with silver sequins that sparkled and flashed as she moved beneath the stage lights. She might have been the slowest shooting star on record as she approached the podium, gave Nachtnebel a careful hug, and turned to her students.

"Hi," she said. Even with the mic clipped to her dress collar, she sounded far away.

Bernard tuned out the class after that. Drawing technique wasn't high on his list of interests. Now, if she could offer advice on breaking into an off-limits women's room on the third floor without getting caught, he would have been all ears. But as she couldn't, or at least didn't, he retrieved Celeste's map of the mansion from one of his hidden pockets and studied it. They were supposed to stay on the second floor. Would anyone notice if he slipped upstairs? Maybe, maybe not, but first order of business would be to check for security cameras here on the second floor and in the stairwell. It was a good bet they'd be in the same position on all floors. He also wanted to see if a security office was hiding among the classrooms.

As the morning dragged on and the real art students did the exercises prescribed by the ancient Allegra, Bernard's mind drifted until he nearly fell asleep. He started when Melody poked his shoulder.

"Draw a circle," she whispered. She made it sound like someone would die if he didn't.

He blinked himself back to full consciousness. "Why?"

"She's going to critique us."

"What's to critique about a circle? It's round."

Melody huffed. "Honestly, Bernie, you know nothing about art, do you?"

Nope, he didn't. He had no problem with that, either. But just in case, he opened his sketchbook, selected a pencil, and drew a lopsided circle.

"That's terrible," Melody said.

"Let's see you do it, then."

Melody already had. She shoved her sketchbook at him, perfect circle and all, and smirked.

"I didn't come here to make art," he grumbled. "I came here to sneak into the ladies' room."

She elbowed him in the ribs again. Okay, he deserved that one.

On stage, Allegra had collared one of the female students and her circle, which was now projected on the screen for everyone to see. The master praised its fluidity and the consistency of its thickness and so forth and so on. "However, there is a bit of a pinch right here," she said. The shadow of her finger tapped a spot near the bottom of the circle. "You turned the pencil a tad at this point. Sometimes you can achieve a good effect that way, but here we simply want the eye to follow the curve smoothly and without interruption."

The student was nodding. So were the other students. Bernard shook his head. Who cared about following a circle? That led nowhere but back to where you started.

Dismissing the student, Allegra consulted a list. "Bernard?" she called. "Bernard Earls?

Bernard slid down in his seat. "No," he muttered.

Melody pushed at his shoulder. "Go on, Bernie!"

"Low profile," he reminded her.

"Bernard?" Allegra said again, her gaze sweeping the seats, although probably with all the lights on her, she couldn't see a soul.

"Don't waste Celeste's money, Bernie!"

Of course not. He'd never hear the end of it. Resigned, Bernard rose and creaked to the front of the hall like a man twenty times his age–rather an accomplishment, as that would make him the tenth oldest man ever, counting the Bible's antediluvian patriarchs. Mounting the steps at the side, he brought his sketch book to Allegra and handed it over as though it were all the money he had. Then he shoved his hands in his pockets and looked at the floor rather than at the screen where his lopsided circle was on display for the entire class to ridicule.

Except nobody breathed a word of criticism. Not even Allegra.

"Hmm," she said.

Yeah, it was that bad.

"Hmm."

No need to rub it in, Bernard thought.

"This is interesting."

He looked up. Allegra was studying the circle with such concentration, he might have handed her a Picasso.

"It's not the assignment," she said, "but you didn't mean it to be, did you?"

Bernard removed his hands from his pockets and straightened. "Not really," he said, not because he'd meant anything at all, not because a lopsided circle could mean anything save incompetence, but because that's what the teacher wanted. He'd learned that long ago in high school. Things always went better when you gave teachers what they wanted.

"An egg. Am I right?"

Yeah, sure, obviously.

"Done with an 8B lead rather than a 2B, giving it a very soft, very dark feel, almost ominous. This egg holds both promise and threat." She looked out over the class. "I'm sure you all see that?"

The class returned a murmur of assent. Bernard wondered if he was the only one who had no idea what she was talking about.

"The gradations in pressure here, here, and here are subtle enough not to disturb the eye yet clear enough to suggest the egg is about to hatch. But what will emerge? Hope? Or doom? A fascinating little work, Bernard. Fascinating!" She handed back his sketch book. "Normally, I wouldn't let a student go without some suggestion for improvement, but it's perfect. Utterly perfect."

As Bernard shuffled back to his seat, the class applauded. So much for low profile.

He said nothing until the next student was being critiqued. Then he whispered to Melody, "What the hell just happened?"

She kissed him on the cheek. "You're a genius, Bernie! An absolute genius!"

Well, yeah, but not in art. Not so far as he'd ever known. "Thanks," he muttered. "I guess." He tried to kiss her on the cheek in return, but she ambushed him by shoving her lips in the way.

&

Circles occupied the morning. At lunch break, the class dutifully filed to the bistro across the hall to the right, where paninis and dipped sandwiches stuffed with pheasant and jackfruit and God only knew what other over-the-top ingredients were sold for over-the-top prices. Bernard made a note to save the receipts and charge Celeste for this, too. They took a table in the corner so they could have a private discussion about burgling a Nazi art stash, but Bernard had become a local celebrity, and every student—especially the female ones—sought an audience with him to get his opinion on all manner of art and artists, most of which and whom he'd never heard.

He faked it well, and Melody introduced herself to everyone—all the female everyones anyway—as his wife. The male ones had eyes only for her, which was okay in her book, leaving Bernard to introduce her as his wife. Somehow, neither sex much cared about the couple's marital status.

At least they were used to that. Far more irritating was not being able to talk about the job. Or do the recon. Bernard had noted two cameras while walking from class to bistro, one gazing down from over the passage to the grand stairs and one directly across, but with lights illuminating paintings on the wall, he couldn't see much else, and he had no time to stroll up and down looking for a security office.

Not only were they stuck in this stupid art class, making no headway, they couldn't even talk things through until, with only a few minutes left in the lunch period, they got a break from Bernard's sudden fame. He told her about the cameras, then lamented, "This isn't working out very well, is it?"

"Let's cut class," she suggested.

"What, and forfeit the registration fee?"

She touched a finger to her lips. "Oh. Right."

"I'm kidding," he said. "How do we explore the third floor without getting expelled?"

Before Melody could answer, yet another female student bounced up to their table. She was short and thin, with dark brown hair gathered into a ponytail, intense brown eyes, and clothed in a willowy white dress that seemed to float about her rather than hang from her shoulders. She gazed into Bernard's eyes for a moment, awe-struck, then turned to Melody. "Hi there!" she effused. "I'm Whisper! Aunt Deirdra asked me to get you into the class! I didn't know I was helping someone so famous! Bernard is so amazing, isn't he!"

"Oh!" Melody said. "Hi, Whisper! Thank you so much!"

"Oh, it was my pleasure! It's going to be so great watching Bernard work!"

Bernard smiled weakly. He wondered if Whisper always talked in exclamations.

Melody had slipped into Whisper mode, too. "I *love* watching him work!" she said, then she giggled a little and added, "On art!"

Whisper didn't get the joke. Or didn't notice it. "Well, I have to go! But it's great meeting you! See ya!"

"See ya!" Melody chirped. The women waggled their fingers at each other, and Whisper smiled a guilty smile at Bernard and blushed and rushed off.

Bernard shook his head. "I'm not sure Whisper is quite the name for her," he said.

"It's just a name," Melody said. "Back to the third floor. You said there were balconies, right?"

Relieved to be talking something he understood, Bernard nodded. "All over the back side of the mansion."

"Maybe you could climb up to the restroom and nab Celeste's music. Then we cut class and buy that cedar chest."

"But which balcony leads to the music, love?"

"Why do you always criticize my plans?"

"I'm not criticizing. I'm just saying—"

"I didn't criticize you for choosing this class."

"Melody, I didn't choose—"

"Maybe I'll just cut class myself and leave you here to deal with it."

There was no winning this argument. Bernard checked his cell phone. "Almost time to go back," he said.

"You go. I'll wait in the car." Melody stood and smoothed her dress.

"You're joking."

She peered at him.

"You're not joking. You're going to wait in the car."

"Yes."

"For three hours."

"If I have to."

"If you're leaving, so am I."

"And forfeit twenty grand?"

Oh, now she was going to go all logical on him.

Before he could reply, she put up a hand to stop whatever objection he might be formulating. "Go back to class," she insisted. "Don't jeopardize your art career. I'll be fine."

Stunned, he watched her stroll out of the bistro. So did half the other men in the place, but they were stunned for a different reason.

Bernard clenched his fists. What the hell was that about? And more to the point, *what* art career?

Chapter 6: Tuesday Afternoon and Evening, October 17, 2017

Melody didn't leave the building. Not yet. She regretted the deception, but sometimes Bernie could be so thick-headed. It was his fault, not hers. Had she told him her plan, he wouldn't have approved, no matter how brilliant it was. And it was, in fact, brilliant.

Upon leaving the bistro, she trotted up the stairs to its doppelganger on the third floor, where another group of students were winding up their lunch break. Many had already filtered into the corridor, some making directly for their classes, some loitering and talking and laughing. She attached herself to a small group of lollygaggers and listened to the conversation.

"I don't know how, but it didn't break," Blondie said. (Melody dubbed her Blondie because she had a stunning head of platinum blond hair.)

"Magic, probably," Dopey replied. (Big ears, see, and a kind of dopey grin. Plus, while not quite a dwarf, he *was* on the short side.)

Blondie laughed and waved her hands as though summoning a spell.

"It's all in the angle of impact," the Professor explained. (Glasses, gray beard, bald head, probably no sense of humor.) "If it struck the floor on a thicker segment, particularly a glancing blow–"

"No," Blondie interrupted. "It bounced like a ping-pong ball. It must've smacked every inch of its body on the stone flooring."

Dopey laughed dopily. "That's one lucky raccoon, then."

Melody gasped. Startled, the others turned to her, Blondie probably wondering who this interloper was and where she'd come from, the men certainly wondering if they stood a chance with her. "Did you take it to the vet?" she asked.

Dopey either laughed or cleared his throat. The sound he made was oddly like both. The Professor frowned. Blondie raised an eyebrow. "It's a glass sculpture," she said. "About four inches high."

Melody set her hand to her heart to calm it. "Oh, thank goodness."

"Yeah, my mother would've killed me if I'd broken it."

"Still," Melody said. "Better to break a glass raccoon than a real one."

"A real raccoon," the professor intoned, "would have fought back." He checked the time on his cell phone. "Speaking of back, we'd better get back to class."

The group made its way to their assigned lecture hall beyond the grand staircase. Melody followed, cell phone in hand, dropping back little by little. Along the way, she snapped photos of some of the art on the walls, accidentally capturing images of the security cameras perched above. There were only four, one above the stairwell, one across from it, and one at each end of the corridor.

The trio vanished into the second classroom from the end. Melody peeked in as she sauntered by. The tables within were littered with small chunks of stone in various stages of being carved. None looked like much other than stone that had been savaged by chisels. Hmm. Maybe it was a vandalism class. Probably that's the sort of thing you could take in a Nazi-run art school.

Melody turned and made her way back toward the restrooms, feigning confusion and examining each door she passed. Some were open, revealing classrooms, others were closed but not in the least suspicious. When she came to the women's room, she pushed on the door. It opened. Good, that was the real one, as she'd thought. She moved on past the grand stairs, past the bistro—now shuttered—

and on to the closed door at the end of the hall. She noted a security keypad beside it. That's also where she struck gold, if a pair of restrooms adorned with "Out of order" signs could be considered gold. Under normal circumstances, such a find would be a catastrophe.

They were the last doors on the left. Crossing her arms over her chest, Melody turned her back on the women's room, gazed at her feet, supremely flustered, and leaned on the door. Nope. It didn't open. Then she trudged to the men's room door and repeated the procedure. That one didn't open, either, which was good. If it had, she'd have been required to barge in, violating all rules of propriety, even if it was secret Nazi art stash instead of a real men's room.

Melody activated her phone's camera app and pretended to browse messages, which wasn't easy to do on a camera app. Turning sideways, she snuck a photo of the door's lock. Then she shuffled back to the women's room and snapped another. Dropping the phone into her purse, she turned to go and ran smack into a burly fellow in a blue uniform. He had his hand on a flashlight clipped to his belt. Probably he thought that made him look more menacing, particularly in the absence of a gun, which Melody noted he didn't have. He couldn't shoot anyone, but he sure could club them!

"Can I help you, ma'am?" the guard rumbled.

Where had he come from? He stood a head, maybe two heads taller than Melody, although thank God he only had one head. She giggled a little. If Celeste had her way, he might have had two. Or zero. She didn't know what she'd do if she bumped into a two-headed man. Or a no-headed man. Probably scream. "I don't know," she said. "Can you?" She giggled again.

His brow wrinkled. "I imagine so. That's my job. Part of it, anyway."

"What's the other part?"

"Throwing out troublemakers."

"Oh, you're a bouncer."

He didn't like that designation. He pinched his lips. "You being a troublemaker?"

"Don't worry, you won't have to bounce me."

He peered at her, clearly not sure of that. And then he got the double entendre and flushed in embarrassment. "Uh..."

Melody set her hand on the poor guy's forearm. She would have touched his shoulder, but it was almost too high to reach. "See, I'm a very cooperative woman."

He looked at her hand and bit his lip. Poor fellow.

"I'm trying to leave. I just can't find my way out."

The guard took a step back to disengage from her touch. He squinted down the hall, no doubt wondering how anyone couldn't find their way out of such a simple place. Then he pointed at the stairs. "That way and down two floors."

"Thank you. You're the nicest bouncer I've ever met."

As Melody made her way out, she could feel the guard's eyes on her. Just for the fun of it, she added some extra wiggle to her walk.

$$\&$$

Once more, Melody didn't leave the building, but this time she harbored no regrets. The guard was just a guard, and what he didn't know wouldn't hurt him. Instead, she slipped into the drawing class without attracting attention and settled next to Bernard. He blinked at her. She smiled.

"I thought you were waiting outside," he whispered.

"Change of plans. I went to the restroom instead."

"How's that a change of plans?"

Melody eased her phone out of her purse, called up the photos, and passed the device to her husband. Bernard studied the images. He zoomed in on the cameras, zoomed in on the locks, studied some more.

"Well?" she asked.

"Not bad," he admitted. "Not bad at all." He kissed her on the cheek.

On stage, Allegra Fumagalli called, "Bernard?"

With a sigh, Bernard grabbed his drawing pad. "Time to have my straight lines critiqued," he told Melody. "This is where my reputation is destroyed."

Once next to the podium with his latest artistic achievement displayed on the screen for the whole world to mock, he stuffed his hands in his pockets and waited. Melody pondered his work, a set of seven lines, all roughly parallel, none of them even close to straight. She wondered how best to frame it. Chrome? Wood? Black plastic? No, no, not black. Red. Definitely red.

"Once again," Allegra said, "you defy both instructions and convention to achieve a profound effect. A maverick, Bernard, a true maverick. You begin with the 2B, but instead of decreasing one hardness with each subsequent line, you oscillate with 5B, 3B, 6B, 4B, and a curious interpolation of HD before returning to 2B. You make no attempt to keep the lines straight or parallel, yet their very irregularity mirrors the sequence of leads, creating a striking unity in chaos. You no doubt look upon this as a completed work, not just an exercise. What's the title?"

Bernard cocked his head and studied the projection. "Melody," he said.

"Ah," Allegra mused. "Melody. Yes. A tone poem in graphite."

Melody nearly melted with joy. What an amazing man she'd married!

𝄞

"Thank God day one is over," Bernard grumbled as they cruised the state routes back to Aschimos. "I thought I'd never get past all those women."

"Most men wouldn't complain about that," Melody teased.

"Most men aren't married to you, love."

"I should hope not. I don't have time for anyone but you."

That lightened his mood. And despite his fears, the class hadn't been a total washout. Melody had found the mysterious restrooms and catalogued the security cameras and locks. Curiously normal locks, from what he'd seen. Likely pickable. There were the cameras, but deactivating those would be child's play for Shawn. That only left the guard. As with Celeste's adventure, he'd appeared out of nowhere. Bernard needed that explained, and quickly. That should be top job tomorrow. But how?

A monster SUV zipped by on the right and changed lanes, nearly clipping his bumper. He leaned on the horn about ten seconds longer than strictly necessary. In the cacophony, a thought struck him, which was infinitely better than having a monster SUV strike him. "Allegra Fumagalli didn't call on everyone in class, did she?"

"Nope," Melody said. "She picked a few people at random each time."

"I got lucky twice, huh?"

"I guess she likes you."

"Great. I gotta be there, then, but maybe you don't."

Melody pouted. "You want me to stay home?"

"No, no, love. I mean, you can do some snooping during class time."

She brightened again. "I love snooping!"

Bernard laughed. "I know."

"What do you want me to do?"

"Figure out where that guard came from. But be careful. We don't want to arouse his suspicions."

"Don't worry. He's not very arousable. Or at least, being aroused embarrasses him. Plus, he likes me."

Well, sure. Everyone did.

Setting a finger to her lips, Melody frowned. "But what if Allegra *does* call me?"

Melody wouldn't get that unlucky. That was Bernard's forte. Still, best to be prepared. "I'll make up some excuse for you," he assured her. "You draw some triangles or something and leave them with me. If she wants to see your work, I'll present it for you."

"Okay. I'll do every shape I can think of tonight."

Which would still be dicey. What if Allegra wanted them to draw something real, like the heads of the people sitting in front of them? No use worrying about it, though, and shapes would be better than nothing. Bernard could fake the rest. The key thing was, they had to discover where that guard had come from and why, and Melody was the best equipped to find out.

&

Back home, Bernard and Melody flopped on the couch. Once more too tired for cooking, Melody used her Pizzapalooza app to order a pepperoni, pineapple, and jalapeño pizza. Their Persian cat Fifi appeared and sprawled in Melody's lap, purring like a motorboat and rolling all over her human. The terminal cuteness of the two females in his life absorbed Bernard's attention for a time.

It was a pleasant absorption, but it came with a price. Detached from the cares of life, his devious brain cooked up something useful for him to do. You'd think it might be on his side, being his own brain and all, but no. It was as bad as his father in that regard. Dad always did have an uncanny ability to sense when Bernard was doing nothing–which in his youth was a fair percentage of the time, so maybe it wasn't so uncanny after all—and direct his son's energies toward some chore. Likewise, Bernard's brain. In short order it served up a problem.

To wit: what if, for any of about a billion reasons, he couldn't access the fake restroom? For one thing, security might regularly patrol the area. If they were smart, they'd mix up their procedures, change their patrol times, pop in at random. And they'd be monitoring the cameras. Could Shawn knock out the video without someone suspecting chicanery? He needed a plan B. Fortunately, Melody had suggested one. The balconies.

Reluctantly, Bernard unflopped from the couch, unrolled his roll-top desk, and squared his laptop for action. He flew through the drone footage one more time, focusing on the rear of the mansion and the balconies with their wrought iron curlicues and Adirondack chairs and little tables and potted plants. The bonsai garden distracted him for a few minutes. How did they grow trees that small? Down the rabbit hole he went, discovering via web search that bonsai trees were just trees, dwarfed and shaped through pot culture, pruning, pinching, and wiring. Bonsai was half horticulture, half art. Living sculpture. Or just plain magic. Bernard would be lucky to keep a cactus alive, much less a tree, and even should he manage it, the plant would be in constant need of a massive haircut.

Enough, his brain scolded. Fascinating, but not the job at hand. Back to work.

The drone footage wasn't enough. He needed a closer look at the balconies and their glass doors. Easy peasy. The bistro had a balcony which was open to customers. If they sat at a balcony table, or one near the balcony, he could study its details at leisure.

Well, no, not so easy. The balcony seats were always the first to be taken at lunchtime.

Fine. As soon as the lunch bell rang (metaphorically speaking), they'd rush out and grab a balcony table. One of them could hold it while the other got the food. While dodging adoring fans. Why did his lopsided circles and crooked lines command such admiration?

Focus, Bernard, said his brain. *Stop lollygagging.*

Fine, whatever. Melody would figure out the guard during the morning session. They'd make a mad dash for the bistro balcony at lunch. While eating, he'd eyeball the locks and check for other security measures. Assuming the details fell into place, he'd recruit Shawn for the tech work that evening, then on Thursday they'd perform the heist and vanish forever from the art world. And good riddance to that!

There were questions, yes, but he had a plan. "We'll do it tomorrow," he told himself.

Except he must have said it out loud. "I had my heart set on tonight," Melody said. She winked at him just as someone hammered on the door. She gently removed Fifi from her lap. Fifi meowed in complaint.

"I meant..." Bernard began but didn't finish, because what was the point? Melody already had the door open to receive dinner.

The pizza delivery guy, a geeky college-age fellow, smiled and started to hand over the box. Bernard watched from a distance as the geek's face slipped from a customer-friendly smile to shocked senseless to full-on hormone rush.

"Thank you!" Melody said. She took the box from his trembling hands and closed the door in his face. Gently, of course, and only because he didn't move his face when he should have. Bernard figured he'd still be out there at midnight, trying to recover from the shock of Melody's beauty. Meanwhile, she sashayed back to the living room, right up to Bernard at his desk, and sat in his lap.

She opened the box and wafted the pepperoni-pineapple- jalapeño aroma under his nose. "What something hot?" she purred.

"Before or after pizza?" he asked.

She kissed him on the nose. Together, they adjourned to the table. Melody put on a show of setting out their best cheap ceramic plates—okay, their *only* cheap ceramic plates—plastic tumblers filled with root beer, and paper napkins. Then she brought out a thick red candle, set it in the center of the table, and lit it with a barbeque lighter.

Bernard found it tricky to eat while they were gazing into each other's eyes, but Melody made it look second nature. She didn't even lose her sappy smile, not even while chewing. He'd forgotten all about guards and balconies and stolen opera scores by the time she asked, "So what's the plan?"

It took him a minute to realize she wasn't talking about romantic pizza dinners at home or their follow-ups. "You figure out the guard routines during the morning session. I'll check the bistro balcony security at lunchtime. That should give me what I need to plan my entry."

Melody giggled.

"What?"

"What do guards and balconies have to do with *that*?"

"Not *that* that. The other that. The locked restroom." He paused for a bite of pizza. "And that will be that."

"That's a lot of thats." She selected another slice, lingering over the choice like it was a matter of life and death. "But that's *not* that. We can't cut class for the rest of the week."

Bernard hadn't thought about that particular that. He didn't relish the thought of spending the rest of the week drowning in praise for his inability to draw a straight line, but she was right. Vanishing at the same moment as a stolen relic would attract attention. "I suppose we'd better finish out the week," he said, resigned to his fate.

"Don't sound so sad," Melody said. "You might have a career as a famous artist." She nibbled at her pizza, either delighted by the thought of being married to a famous artist or just enjoying the mingled flavors.

"I think I'll stick to what I know."

"Oh yes? And what's that?" She batted her eyelashes at him.

They ended up with a lot of leftover pizza.

Chapter 7: Wednesday, October 18, 2017

Over breakfast–everything bagels, garden veggie cream cheese, and coffee with a spritz of hazelnut flavoring–Melody filled three pages in her sketch book with shapes and doodles and pretty fair drawings of headless people, although unlike Celeste's, hers had clothes on. She started with triangles, since Bernard suggested it, then moved on to pentagrams and hexagons, parallel lines vanishing into the distance, fanciful mountain sketches in which every mountaintop seemed to be swaying in the wind, a few trees, a bird, and a quick rendering of Fifi curled into a ball. The latter was drawn from life. Fifi was indeed curled into a ball on one of their spare dining room chairs, from whence she occasionally eyed Bernard's bagel with malicious intent.

Melody gave the whole shebang to Bernard with the explicit instruction, "Don't lose it. It's priceless."

Which it would be should Allegra Fumagalli call on Melody while Melody wasn't in attendance. So long as he had her work, Bernard could say she'd gone to the restroom and present the sketches on her behalf.

It would be the truth, too. Upon arrival at the Nachtnebel mansion, she made a beeline for the real women's room on the third floor. There she would hide until classes started, leaving Bernard to fend for himself. They would rendezvous at the bistro later. That simplified matters, save one thing. Bernard spent the whole morning on edge, half expecting Allegra to call upon his wife and half wondering if Melody had been taken into custody and tortured. And no, that wasn't paranoia. Nazis, remember? They would do that.

In the end, Allegra didn't call on Melody. Nor did she order the production of triangles, pentagrams, swaying mountains or balled-up cats. Rather, she assigned houses, and not just any houses but houses stored in their memories. Naturally, Bernard's memory failed him. He couldn't picture a single house, not even the one he'd grown up in. His pencil—a 5.4G or whatever the hell it was—hovered over his drawing pad and drew nothing, because his brain gave his hand nothing to draw. For thirty minutes it served up dismal blankness. Then the master began calling names.

The first student to be critiqued presented a drawing of a farmhouse surrounded by tall trees and backed by a wheat field. Allegra praised a few points, suggested a few improvements, and summoned her next victim. That student had drawn a little suburban bungalow. The third, a skinny young woman who looked like she wasn't quite through high school yet, presented a McMansion surrounded by a stark, desert-like landscape. Allegra quite liked the desolation engulfing the illusion of wealth. "You've been studying Bernard's work," she said. The student nodded with such enthusiasm it was a wonder her head didn't fall off.

"And speaking of that," Allegra said. "Bernard?" Her voice quivered with anticipation.

With a sigh, Bernard traced a big, empty square on the page, then he shuffled to the front, handed over his failure to the critical firing squad, and shoved his hands in his pockets. After being so highly praised yesterday, it embarrassed him to be exposed as a fraud.

Allegra put his square on display. Silence gripped the lecture hall. Her eyes roamed the square. She said nothing. Nor did anyone else. You could have heard a dust speck strike the screen.

Bernard studied his shoes. They were nice shoes. Black. Pointy. Polished. Much better than his square. Maybe he should have drawn them, instead. One sort of lived in one's shoes, right? So one *could* call shoes a house, no? Or at least a basement?

"I'm speechless," Allegra said, proving she wasn't.

Bernard was.

She turned to the class. "Anyone care to comment?"

He shook his head. Here it came.

Nobody moved at first, then people began to squirm, and at length a tentative hand rose.

Allegra pointed to the hand. "Yes. Michelle, isn't it?"

A lean brunette rose from her seat. And rose. And rose. She rose in slow motion to an incredible height, maybe an inch or two taller than even Celeste. And then she spoke. Sort of. Her voice came from someplace very far away. "Well. Well. Um. Well."

Bernard stole a glance at her. Her twenty-something face broadcast utter misery. She was rather appealing that way. A guy could feel compelled to rescue her from her afflictions, whatever they were. Fortunately, Bernard didn't feel compelled. Melody was the only woman he cared to rescue, and most of the time she didn't need it. If anything, she rescued him.

"Please," Allegra prompted. "Be completely honest."

"Okay," Michelle began. "Well. I just feel so horrible for Bernard. I mean, this...this...this emptiness. It must come from a really deep place. This isn't a house. This is his life. His whole life. I almost feel compelled to rescue him from his afflictions. Whatever they are."

Bernard's jaw dropped.

"It's true, Bernard," Michelle assured him. "It's true. I really do. You poor, poor guy." She gave him a sad smile and sank back into her seat, her eyes fixed on him maybe for the rest of her life.

Allegra drew a long, deep breath. "Anyone else?" she asked, but who could possibly have anything to add after that? "Very well. Thank you, Bernard. Thank you." She passed his work back to him and set a gentle hand on his forearm before allowing him off stage. He slunk back to his seat in the rear. He could feel every eye in the joint follow his retreat into the darkness from which he'd come.

Oh, God. Lunch break would be *horrible*.

𝄞

𝄞

Melody emerged from the third-floor restroom ten minutes after class started. The corridor stood empty save the artwork on the wall, the security cameras, and her. Without the noise of the students, it felt serene, like a cathedral, except the ceiling wasn't that high and there weren't any icons or candles or incense. She wished she'd brought some with her. Candles and incense, anyway. She didn't have any icons squirreled away in their apartment, and she sure wasn't going to pilfer any, not from a church. That would be just plain wrong.

She tiptoed along the corridor, taking her time, soaking up each painting as she passed by. She didn't recognize any of them. Most of them were still lifes set in—

Still lifes?

Still lives?

Hmm. Probably still lifes. Still lives sounded like the lives of people who weren't going anywhere.

Most of the paintings were still lifes set in depressingly dark surrounds. What was the point of that? Art should make you happy, shouldn't it? Even that one with the naked lady sleeping on a couch in the background was all dark. Nearly monochromatic, in fact. Melody thought the poor girl should move to a brighter locale, maybe Florida, where she could at least get some sun. Besides, she was perfectly dressed for tanning, which you couldn't at all do in a dark room. She ought to be on a beach. Yes, a nudist beach.

Melody's mind was only half on critiquing all that horrible art, though. The other half was busy monitoring every door in the hall, waiting for the guard to emerge from somewhere. She had a bit of a wait, twenty minutes or so. And then, precisely on the half-hour, the door at the end of the hall near the fake restrooms opened and disgorged the security guard who had stopped her yesterday. He entered in stealth mode, silent as a burglar. Melody knew from personal experience how silent *they* could be. The door, too, made no sound as it opened and closed, nor did his footfalls as he began his rounds.

He wasn't looking for her. In fact, he was more concerned with the paintings on the walls, which was strange. Museum guards tended to watch people, not artwork. This guy must not have been trained very well, or maybe nothing ever happened here, so he could afford to enjoy the art.

A quarter of the way down the hall, he realized with a start that he wasn't alone. And then he wasn't silent anymore. "Hey!" he called. He sounded irritated, like she had somehow messed up his enjoyment of the depressing paintings. Maybe he was a masochist.

"Hey!" Melody chirped, more than making up for his lack of friendliness. "Nice to see you again!"

He lumbered to her. Being so big, he probably couldn't move much faster, although football players were that big, and they could certainly move, at least when they weren't busy running into each other. He hooked his fingers on his belt and gave her an intimidating glare.

Melody wasn't intimidated. If anything, her smile brightened. For one thing, he was an unarmed guard, with nothing but a flashlight and his thumbs clipped to his belt. "Fancy meeting you here," she said.

"Nothing fancy about it," he snapped. "You lost again, or what?"

"What."

"I said, you lost again, or what?"

"Yes. What."

His eyes narrowed. "What?"

"Exactly. What." Melody turned to the nearest painting. This one featured a bunch of black grapes, a dark red apple, and a collection of dark green greens in a dark green bowl, all off-center on a dark brown table with black curtains in the background. "Do you like this one?" she asked the guard.

The guard huffed. "I don't come here for the art."

That was clearly a lie, but whatever. "Oh, I see." Melody slipped him a coy smile. "You're here to meet women."

He nearly choked.

"I hate to disappoint you," she said, "but I'm married."

"Now look, lady—"

"My husband's here, in fact, in class. So you'd best behave yourself."

"You're the one needs to behave. I'm just doing my job."

"And what exactly is that, Mr...." Melody leaned close to his chest to inspect his nametag. "Mr. Brian Garfinkel."

He made a face. "Garfunkel."

"Oh! Like Simon and Garfunkel. Are you related?"

"No. My parents just liked 'em." He was still making that face, so maybe he didn't like them, himself.

"Maybe I should just call you Brian," Melody suggested. Best not to call him by a name he hated. "I'm Melody."

"Yeah?"

"Yeah. So, Brian, what is your job, anyway?"

Brian took a step back, eyed Melody's face—and other attributes—and shook his head. "I told you yesterday."

"Yes, helping people and throwing them out." Melody set a finger to her lips. "That seems contradictory."

Managing to find Melody's face again, Brian did his best to look helpfully severe. "I only throw out troublemakers."

"Good thing I'm not a troublemaker, then. But tell me, Brian, why…" Melody glanced around as though someone might overhear them. Unlikely, since it was just the two of them. She stepped close and lowered her voice to a whisper anyway. "Why would you be walking around here when there's nobody to help or throw out?"

"I gotta make my rounds," he snapped, not caring that the nonexistent crowds might hear. "It's my job."

"But how do you help people and throw them out if you only make your rounds when nobody's there?"

"Not just when nobody's there! On a schedule! And sometimes somebody *is* there, like you!" He jabbed a finger at her. The poor fellow was getting so worked up, he could barely keep from slobbering.

"I see," Melody assured him. "You're making your rounds because of me. That's sweet." She smiled sweetly.

"You got nothing to do with it, lady. It's a schedule. I come through here every half hour, whether you're here or not. 'Cept lately, you always are!"

Melody bent aside to peek around his oversized form. She frowned at the door at the end of the corridor and the numeric keypad on the wall beside it. She'd noticed that detail yesterday. She turned and frowned the other direction, where there was nothing but classrooms and the bistro and the stairs and the real restrooms. She waggled a finger back and forth between the corridor's two ends. "Every half hour? How does that work? It's a mile down and back."

He was gesturing now, not really at anything but sort of all over in frustration. "It's not a mile! Not even close!"

"But it must take you more than half an hour to—"

"No! It takes four minutes and thirty-eight seconds, lady! I got it down to a science! Four minutes and thirty-eight seconds, 'cept when *you're* here!" He jabbed a finger at her again, almost making contact someplace a gentleman shouldn't.

Melody slapped his hand away. "Behave yourself Brian, or you'll have to throw yourself out." Now, that was an amusing image. She laughed.

Huffing, Brian hooked his thumbs over his belt again and did his best to behave, or at least calm down. "Look, lady—"

"Melody," she insisted.

"Fine, Melody, whatever. Look. You need to leave."

"But my husband is in class still. We were going to meet for lunch."

"Fine. Know what? March yourself down there to the bistro." He pointed, in case she didn't know where it was, which was rather pointless pointing, because how could she not? "Stand right there by the door," he instructed. "And don't move 'til Mr. Melody shows up and takes you into custody."

Melody could have commented on that insinuation, but probably it was best to overlook it. "I'm not meeting him there," she said. "I'm meeting him on the second floor."

"Then what the—"

At this point, Brian selected an expletive Melody found wholly unnecessary. She refused it access to her highly cultured brain.

"—are you doing up *here*?"

She smiled her sweetest, most innocent smile. "Talking to you, of course."

"Gah!" Brian clapped his hands to his temples.

"I should be going, before you have a total meltdown." She waggled her fingers at him and made for the grand staircase. Just before descending, she looked back. He was still there, hands to his head, a catatonic look on his face.

Poor fellow. He'd become a dark, depressing still life.

𝄞

"So what you're telling me," Bernard began, but he didn't finish. That was in fact the fifth time he didn't finish, and for the same reason as the other four.

A female student from the master class slipped up to their table, leaned on it, and crouched down to gaze into his eyes. He could feel the empathy in her every breath. "If you ever need someone to talk to..." she whispered.

"I have someone to talk to," Bernard answered. He'd given that answer four times already. He sounded like a robocall. Maybe he'd been reduced to the level of a bot. "See this lady here? She's my wife, Melody." He pointed.

The woman didn't even glance at Melody. She sighed and rose. "Wife. Yes, I understand. Here's my card." As if by magic, a business card dropped from her hand onto the table, and she hurried away.

Bernard gave the bridge of his nose a pinch, just to make sure he wasn't a bot, then tucked the card into his trouser pocket for later disposal and began again. "So what you're telling me..."

A shorter, darker version of the previous woman leaned on the table and crouched down to gaze into his eyes. "Bernard," she whispered. "You poor thing. If you ever need someone to talk to..."

The robocall replayed. "I have someone to talk to. See this lady here? She's my wife, Melody."

This woman dared to look at Melody, regarding her with evident hostility before returning to the object of her pity. "If you ever need someone to *listen*...” She slid a business card to Bernard and retreated.

Watching her go, Melody’s eyes acquired a sinister gleam, something that almost never happened.

Once he’d tucked away that business card, Bernard exerted a mighty effort to break out of bot mode. “Brian patrols the third floor every half hour, but never on the second floor, not him, not another guard, nobody, is that right?”

“Yes!” Melody cheered, pumping a fist in the air. The sinister gleam vanished.

Bernard took her enthusiasm as both the answer to his question and elation that they’d finally made it past, “So what you’re telling me is...” In which case, that one word established two key facts. First, the third floor was indeed special, as Celeste had inferred. Second, the guard’s patrol schedule was fixed. He didn’t vary it. Which made him, or whoever supervised him, an idiot. “Each pass takes four minutes and thirty-eight seconds?”

“Yes!”

“Unless you’re there.”

“Yes!”

“And he enters from the private wing through a door that requires a numeric code for entry.”

“Yes!”

“Beautiful work, love. Absolutely beautiful.”

Melody batted her eyes at him. “Oh, Bernie, you’re so—”

“Bernard,” a husky feminine voice interrupted. Its owner crouched by the table as though she’d just been beamed down from space. She all but fell into Bernard’s eyes. “I know what it’s like. If you ever need to talk...” She cast a cold glance at Melody. “...*really* talk, call me." She slipped a business card at him, rose, and swayed off toward lunch.

In fair imitation of a mother grizzly protecting her cubs, Melody growled, "If one more woman says that, I'll pour iced tea down her cleavage."

"That would be fun to watch," Bernard teased.

"Except you'll have your eyes closed."

"Naturally."

"What did you *draw*?"

Bernard showed her. "It was supposed to be a house I remember," he said. "But I couldn't remember any."

Melody took the sketch pad in hand and mulled it over. "No wonder they feel so bad for you," she murmured.

"Not you, too."

She handed it back. "It's your fault, Bernie. You forgot the roof. Now every time it rains, you'll get soaked!"

He loved that interpretation. "I'll keep an umbrella handy," he promised.

Whisper rushed up to the table and gushed, "Bernard! That was so amazing! You should have seen it, Melody!"

"I just did!" Melody told her.

"Don't you dare drop me a business card," Bernard warned.

Whisper laughed. "Why would I do that?"

"Every other woman in the place wants me to know she's there if I need someone to talk to."

Whisper laughed again, which Bernard supposed was justified. "Every other woman in the place is psycho!" Then she leaned close and actually did whisper, although not without the exclamation point. "But if you do need someone to talk to, let me know!"

She rushed the door.

Melody cast Whisper's retreating back her darkest glare.

Bernard rubbed his eyes. "At least she didn't give me her card," he said.

𝄞

Allegra Fumagalli did Bernard a huge favor that afternoon. She didn't call on him. Why wasn't clear, but he supposed she didn't want to further intrude upon his misery. Once in one day might have been enough. She had them draw pets this time. Dogs. Cats. Iguanas. Whatever. Bernard tried to draw Fifi, but the poor critter ended up looking like something sucked up by a vacuum cleaner and spit out again. Which was okay, since it was one Bernard Earls masterpiece the world would never see.

But then...

"Melody?" the master called. "Melody Earls?"

Every eye in the place turned to the back of the room. Melody rose like a queen preparing to issue a decree. When she slipped past Bernard into the aisle, all those eyes followed her progress to the stage. This wasn't the bouncy Melody filled with love of life, the McGirl Melody Bernard knew so well. This was the Kensington Melody, descended from dukes or kings or whatever. Bernard wondered why everyone didn't kneel. He sure felt like kneeling. But he soon discovered why.

Surrendering her rendering of Fifi to Allegra Fumagalli, Melody waited, head high, so calm and still she might have been a marble statue. White Carrarra marble, imported from Tuscany. The finest on Earth.

Fifi reposed on the screen, curled into a cute little ball, drawn in quick, simple lines, lacking detail but so peaceful she almost put Bernard to sleep.

"I see," the master intoned with such gravity it was a wonder the stage didn't crumble beneath her. "Yes, I see." She gave Melody a sidelong glance, as though she'd caught her student in the act of murder. "Anyone care to offer an opinion?"

Michelle's hand shot up, then she rose and rose and rose, showing no hesitation this time. "It's a self-portrait." Icicles hung from her words. "Pampered, content, living off the..." She pinched her lips tight. "That is, well-supported by her *husband*." She spat out the last word.

Murmurs of assent raced around the lecture hall. Melody quietly seethed, but she did it so well, only Bernard could tell. Allegra handed the drawing back to her student, her narrowed eyes practically aflame with retribution. Melody returned a cold smile and turned to go. A quiet but clear hiss erupted from somewhere.

Bernard had had enough. Before Melody could take her first step, he sprang to his feet and issued a decree of his own.

"You morons! That's our cat! Our cat Fifi! It's a damned good drawing, too, lifelike and artistic and a million times better than anything I ever drew, and Melody is my *wife* and my business partner and my inspiration and my whole damned *life*! Go to hell, all of you!"

He snatched up his drawing pad and pencils and Melody's pencils and dumped them into the canvas bag. Gripping the bag's handle like a war club, he charged the stage, took Melody's hand, and in as dignified and royal a manner as he could muster in his state of agitation, escorted her from the room, the second floor, the mansion. He opened the back door of his powder blue Lincoln Zephyr, threw in the bag, which dumped its contents all over the seat. Drawing the deepest breath of his life, he helped Melody into the passenger seat.

Dewdrops sparkled in her eyes. "Oh, Bernie," she said. She wrapped her arms about him and pulled him down. "You're the best husband ever." She kissed him for about ten minutes. At least, it felt like ten minutes, or maybe forever, yet for all that it was too, too short. Once their lips undocked and Melody was settled in the car with the door closed, Bernard glanced up at the third floor. Someone was up there on the end balcony at the back of the building, watching. He was uniformed. Might have been that guard, that Brian Garfunkel.

Bernard sighed. So much for being inconspicuous.

𝄞

And so much, Bernard mused on the drive home, for this class, for any hope of being readmitted to the Nachtnebel mansion, for stealing the twice-stolen *Rienzi,* or for banking Celeste's twenty g's. Worse, they'd likely be out the registration fee. Celeste would demand a refund of all expenses. He hadn't just blown the job. He'd sunk the *Titanic.* He'd never thought of himself as an iceberg, but the way they'd treated Melody—the teacher, the class, the lot of them—they deserved it.

He stole a glance at her. She was frowning at her lovely red fingernails, lost either in thought or remorse. "It's okay," he said. "There'll be other jobs."

"Huh?"

"This one wasn't worth it anyway."

"Wasn't worth it! Bernie! My cedar chest!"

So that's where her mind had gone. Not surprising, really. It was a nice cedar chest, and Melody had a keen eye for sparklies of all shapes and sizes. Maybe she's been a squirrel in a previous life. "We'll get it. It might just take a bit longer."

She dropped her hands into her lap. "Don't tell me you're giving up. Not after I did all that work."

"I'm sorry, love, but they won't let us back in, not after that."

"Yes, they will. They have no choice. They owe me."

They sure did, but Bernard doubted they'd see it that way.

Melody twisted sideways to look him in the eye. In the ear, anyway. His eyes were on the road. "Tell me your plan," she said.

He tossed her his most dashing smile while almost keeping his eyes on the road. "I'm taking you out to dinner."

She blinked. Then she kissed him on the cheek. "That's sweet of you, but how does that get you into the fake restroom?"

"Forget the fake restroom. It's history."

"Is not. Tell me your plan."

She wouldn't ever let it go, so he told her. "It would've been simple. I'd hide on the third floor like you did. I'd wait until–"

She giggled. "You can't do that!"

"Why not?"

"I hid in the women's room!"

"I mean, I'd hide in the men's room."

"Oh. That's fine, then. Go on."

"I'd wait until Brian finishes his first pass, then I'd pick the lock on the fake restroom and slip in. I'd have plenty of time to search for this *Rienzi* thing. I could take all day if need be. Then I'd time my exit so Brian wasn't there. I'd have a twenty-five-minute exit window every half hour."

"Perfect," Melody said. "But what about the cameras?"

"Ah, that's where Shawn comes in." Bernard mentally slapped himself. He was starting to talk like this was going to happen. "Where Shawn would have come in. But now..."

Melody put a hand on his shoulder and massaged it. "Don't worry. Everything will work out."

"But Melody–"

"Don't be such a pessimist, Bernie. Things always work out."

"For you, not for me."

"I'm involved." She tweaked his ear.

Put that way, it sounded like a sure thing. But it wasn't. He'd insulted the teacher and her entire class. "Allegra Fumagalli's probably told Nachtnebel to blacklist us."

"Because of a little temper tantrum?"

"That wasn't a temper tantrum. It was a nuclear blast."

"Bernie, listen to me. You're an artistic genius. You're a martyr for your art. You're *supposed* to behave that way. Trust me, they can't wait to see you again."

A genius and a martyr. He liked fifty percent of that, anyway. "But love, if you're right, I'll have to be in class. I can't find *Rienzi* if I'm in class."

"Draw something tonight, give me your sketch pad, and leave the rest to me."

Which sounded strangely reasonable. Not in any ordinary sense, but with Melody, a miracle was bound to happen. "That sounds strangely reasonable," he affirmed.

"You bet it is. Let's do dinner and then see Shawn."

Bernard checked the dashboard clock. It was barely three-thirty. "It's a bit early for dinner."

"It's never too early for dinner if it's yummy enough."

"What's yummy enough?"

"Shrimp primavera." Melody licked her lips in anticipation.

Bernard set course for Pasta Paradise, their favorite Italian chain restaurant.

Chapter 8: Late Wednesday, October 18, 2017 and Straight on to Morning

After a way too leisurely dinner stretched to incredulity by a grand finale of triple chocolate lava cake sundaes—good thing they were still almost young enough to eat like that and get away with it—they arrived at Shawn Ueltschi and Felicity Barnswald's apartment. It was just before seven under a darkening sky.

Actually, it was Felicity's apartment. Shawn had sort of maybe kind of moved in a couple months ago while maintaining his own place. (Shawn had tech smarts, but finances must not have been his forte.) Felicity's abode was all reds and pinks and floral designs, with a modest Barbie collection posed inside a cheap display cabinet. Bernard had never quite squared the feminine décor with Felicity's personality.

"Guys!" she squealed when she opened the door. "What a surprise! Hey Shawn, guess who's here?" She bellowed the latter over her shoulder before stepping aside and waiving them in.

Bernard motioned Melody to lead the way. Shawn poked his head out of the kitchen. His dark brown hair had gotten a bit longer recently. It waggled in greeting until he pushed it out of his face. "Hi, guys!" he gushed. "What're you doing here?"

Before Bernard could answer, Melody bounced over to him. She gave him a hug and a peck on the cheek, which turned his face a distinct red. "Bernie has a job for you!" she said.

True, but hardly the best way to bring up the subject. Shawn morphed from red to white while gagging as though he'd swallowed a whole grapefruit, peel and all. An entirely justified reaction, since the last time Bernard offered Shawn a job, the kid only escaped prison because Fitzroy Fortresses was too embarrassed to admit that their brand-spanking new unhackable system had been hacked by a college nerd. Instead of prosecuting, they hired him.

Melody escorted Shawn to the living room and settled him on the sofa. Felicity shot Bernard a pinched but otherwise inscrutable look before cozying up to Shawn and purring something possibly sweet and comforting in his ear. Whatever it was, it neither sweetened nor comforted him. Bernard and Melody appropriated the facing chairs and waited for Shawn to recover.

"Don't say a word," Felicity told her guy. "I'll handle this." Turning on Bernard, she asked the most important question. "How much does it pay?"

"Let's discuss details first," Bernard said.

"Water," Shawn croaked.

Felicity started to rise, but Melody waved her down. "I'll get it," she said. "You three talk business. Well, you and Bernie. Shawn can use sign language until I get back."

Shawn made a gesture that might have meant, "With ice." Or maybe, "I'm gonna throw up." It was hard to tell.

"Oh good," Felicity said. "A consultation. Shawn's consultation fee is a thousand an hour."

The woman was nothing if not persistent. "Not a consultation," Bernard said, "just a simple electronics test for a Fitzroy customer. At least, I assume it would be simple for someone of Shawn's talent."

In the kitchen, a cabinet door closed and the ice maker spit cubes into a glass. Shawn shivered as though the ice had been poured down the back of his shirt.

"An evaluation, basically," Bernard added. "To ensure the customer's staff is prepared for eventualities."

Felicity took Shawn's quaking hands into her own and rubbed some warmth into them. "Sounds like ten hours work to me. That's ten thousand dollars. Up front."

Forget the son of the Nazi. Celeste would shoot Bernard herself if expenses reached that level. "How about fifty?" he countered.

"Fifty thousand? Wow!"

"No, just fifty."

Felicity pouted. "That won't even cover the EKG Shawn's gonna need."

"I'm sure Fitzroy offers good health insurance."

Shawn gestured again, but it was undecipherable this time, and anyway Melody had returned with his water. He took a sip, then another, then a long pull, then managed to find his voice. "I can't play with a customer's system." he said. "I can't even tell anyone outside the company about his system. I suffered eight hours of corporate training on that point alone."

Bernard had no desire to jeopardize Shawn's job. For one thing, Melody would never forgive him. For another, a skilled inside man was hard to find, especially at a rate Bernard could afford. Unfortunately, he couldn't eliminate all risk. At most, he could minimize it. "I don't need system information," he said. "I just need four cameras to freeze or loop or whatever for a few minutes. Can you do that?"

Shawn opened his mouth to object.

"For five hundred dollars, he can," Felicity said. At least she'd come down on the price.

"How about one hundred?" Bernard countered.

"Two."

"Fine, two. How about it, Shawn?"

Shawn blinked at Bernard, blinked at Felicity, blinked at Melody. Melody smiled encouragement. Felicity squeezed his hand. "Uh," he said. He lifted his glass to his lips.

"Great," Bernard said. "The homeowner's name is Gerhard Nachtnebel, Jr."

Shawn spit a tidal wave of ice water over Felicity, who shrieked and jumped to her feet.

"Oh, Shawn!" Melody cried in sympathy. "Lemme get some paper towels."

"Oh, *Shawn*?" Felicity bellowed. "What about *me*?"

Bernard refrained from further negotiation while Melody mopped up. It took rather a while, involving not only dabbing at faces, finery, furniture, and the floor, but also escorting a put-out Felicity to her room so she could change. Since Shawn's finery only consisted of jeans and a faded *Jurassic Park* t-shirt, he elected to suffer the damp. The men waited, twiddling their fingers and making faces at nothing. Fifteen minutes later, the women returned.

"So," Bernard said.

Shawn put up a hand to stop him. He opened his mouth. He closed his mouth. He opened it again and didn't close it until he found the strength to utter one crucial word: "Maniac."

Bernard had been called a lot of things in his life, but that wasn't one of them. He was the sanest person he knew.

"I'll say," Felicity agreed. "He should be paying you a lot more."

Shawn shook his head more violently than necessary. "Not Bernard. Mr. Nachtnebel. He's a maniac."

Bernard supposed that might be the logical outcome of being the son of a Nazi. Still, he didn't want to prejudge the man. He'd seemed okay when introducing Allegra Fumagalli. Besides, one of Bernard's own great uncles had secretly kept three wives, or so a family legend went, but a predisposal to polygamy hadn't manifested in the presumed cad's descendants. Indeed, they didn't talk much about it, aside from trying to figure out how they were all related.

"Just so we're on the same page," Bernard said, "what kind of maniac?"

"He shot at two of his landscapers. And a roofer. And a pizza delivery guy."

Why would Nachtnebel be ordering pizza? Or waiting at the door to take delivery? Sounded like urban legend, but whatever. "Anyone injured?" Bernard asked.

"No, but they could have been."

"Was he cited for it?"

"I don't know. All I know is, the maintenance guys are afraid of him."

Bernard wondered how Shawn, a software engineer, knew the maintenance guys. Seemed like a totally different department. But again, whatever. "You won't be visiting him," he said in his most reassuring tone. "He won't know your name or your face or anything."

"What if he tortures you?" Shawn asked, voice quaking. "What if you squeal?"

Bernard looked at Melody. Melody shrugged. "Okay," Bernard said. A bit of paranoia was natural. He himself had worried over the possibility of torture when Melody was pumping intel from Brian Garfunkel. "Three hundred."

The addition of hazard pay didn't cheer Shawn, but Felicity snapped it up. "Deal," she said. "Don't be a wimp, Shawn."

"A live wimp is better than a dead daredevil," Shawn muttered.

"You're neither dead nor a daredevil," Bernard said. "Evel Knievel would have yawned at this job."

"And gotten more than three hundred for it," Felicity pointed out.

"Who's Evel Knievel?" Shawn asked.

Bernard took Shawn's lack of culture as a yes. Possibly a rash assumption, but he'd had enough of this discussion. "There are four cameras on the third floor of the west wing," he said. "Tomorrow morning, I'll send you a text. I'll just say hi. When you get it, do your stuff. Send me a hi back. Keep them frozen or whatever for three minutes." He paused to ponder the timing. One end of the hall to the other, pick the lock, get inside. "No," he decided, "four minutes. Then reset them. Later, I'll send another hi, and we'll do it again. Two quick passes. That will be that."

Shawn shuddered.

"Come on," Bernard urged. "It's just a test."

Felicity wrapped her arms around Shawn and whispered none too quietly in his ear. "Four hundred, baby."

"Three," Melody whispered in his other ear.

Felicity looked ready to bite somebody. "Oh. Yeah."

"Fine," Shawn said. "But that's it. That's the last thing I do for you."

"Sure," Bernard said. And it would be. Unless he needed something else.

&

The howler monkey was back. Its howl assaulted them the moment they emerged from the stairwell and grew in intensity with each step toward their apartment. Through gritted teeth, Bernard asked, "Doesn't the little beast go home once mommy's off work?"

Melody planted her hands over her ears. "Maybe mommy's working late."

"Maybe mommy should get a job in California."

Melody was aghast. "And leave Chris-Chris here full time?"

"That's not what I meant."

"Thank God."

They paused at Mrs. Clarke's door. The howl howled on. "Should we make sure he hasn't murdered grandma?" Bernard asked.

Melody risked uncovering one ear to set a thoughtful finger to her lips. "I'm sure he hasn't. But maybe he stunned her. She might be lying on the floor, unconscious."

"Yeah, that decibel level could do it." Bernard knocked on the door. Loud and long. The door shuddered under the impact.

The howl dropped to almost conversational level, then the door opened and Mrs. Clarke smiled up at her neighbors. "Are you two checking up on me again? How sweet of you."

"Think nothing of it, Mrs. Clarke," Bernard said. "It's just, we thought Chris-Chris would have gone home by now."

"Ordinarily, yes, but he wanted to stay the night tonight. So I'm making popcorn and we're going to watch *The Loud House*."

"You're already living in that," Melody said. "Maybe you should watch *SpongeBob* instead."

Mrs. Clarke smiled again. "I'd invite you in, but there will be popcorn everywhere. You probably don't want it down your shirts and in your shoes."

"Yeah, we'll pass on that adventure," Bernard agreed. "Well, have a good night. I hope he lets you sleep eventually." *Not to mention us*, he added to himself.

Waggling her fingers, Mrs. Clarke eased the door shut. The decibel level increased as soon as the deadbolt clicked shut.

"Popcorn in our shoes." Melody grimaced. "Yuck."

Bernard took her hand and guided her to their door. As he unlocked it, he said, "But down your shirt could be interesting."

"That's all you ever think about," Melody said.

"What's that?"

She kissed him on the cheek. "Food."

In the actual event, it proved hard to think of food. Not that Bernard would have after that big Italian dinner, but Chris-Chris didn't wear out his lungs until just after midnight, by which time Bernard was ready to trade in his life of ethical crime for mayhem. Melody coped by burying her head under her pillow, but that didn't cut it for Bernard. The noise infiltrated the polyester stuffing. Besides, he couldn't breathe when he was under there. He stomped to the living room and watched *Indiana Jones and the Temple of Doom* to get some relief from the racket. He would have asked Melody to join him, but she hated the film's violence. And the bugs.

Once the movie had ended and the joyous shrieks of toddlers had faded away, he fell asleep on the couch. He woke to a warm pressure on his chest and a sense that he might still be suffocating under that pillow. He grabbed whatever was weighing him down and almost dumped it on the floor.

Almost. He realized at the last second it was Melody. "Rise and shine!" she chirped.

"Ugh," he acknowledged. He released her.

She settled on her knees on the floor beside him. "Time to get ready for class. I'll make breakfast. You get yourself together and draw some great art." A quick peck on the cheek, and then she was off to work her culinary magic.

Bernard sat, put his head in his hands, and shook it. "What time is it?"

"Six forty-two," she called from the kitchen. "You overslept by twelve minutes."

"And underslept by three hours." He dragged himself to the shower. By the time he was cleaned up and dressed and at the table, Melody had served scrambled eggs, pre-cooked sausage, wheat toast with strawberry preserves, and coffee. Bernard's sketchbook and pencils awaited beside his plate.

He had no idea what to draw and told Melody so.

"Allegra's doing personal stuff," she said. "Houses. Pets. I'll bet people are next. Draw someone important to you." She straightened, turned herself to catch morning light streaming through the glass balcony door, and lifted her lips into an enigmatic Mona Lisa smile.

Bernard sucked in his breath. She was perfect. He could never draw *that*.

"Well?" Melody prompted. "Go on."

Okay, if she insisted. He grabbed a pencil and drew. The lines spilled out, splashed onto the paper, flowed into an oval with lips and a nose and eyes and eyebrows and hair, a mad rush of inspiration bringing Melody to life on the page, and when he was done and his eggs were cold and he looked at what he'd created...

"Oh my God," he groaned.

Melody relaxed and picked up her fork. "What?"

"Oh my God."

"That good?" She leaned over, eager.

Bernard slapped the sketch book shut.

"Hey! Let me see!"

"No."

"What do you mean, no? Let me see!"

"You'll divorce me."

Melody's laugh was a summer breeze chasing off the autumn cool, but it didn't change Bernard's opinion of his work. "I'm not kidding. It's terrible."

She downed a forkful of eggs, then frowned at her plate. "Hey," she said. "These are cold." She gathered their plates and took them to the microwave. Back with the reheated meal, she reached for the sketchbook. Bernard pressed his hand to it to keep her from taking it, but she wrenched it away before he could stop her. After opening it and leafing to his latest creation, she set a finger to her lips, cocked her head, made a little sound that could have been praise or condemnation or anything in between.

"Sorry," Bernard said.

He tried to take the sketchbook from her, but she moved it away from his grasping fingers and spent another minute in silent contemplation. Then, closing the book, Melody slid it back to him. She gazed into his eyes, her expression unreadable, which was rather a change for her. Melody wasn't much good at hiding her feelings. Not from him, anyway.

Might as well get it over with. "Admit it," Bernard insisted. "It's terrible."

"Bernie," she said as though tiptoeing by a sleeping guard dog. "You have no sense of art."

No kidding. He poked at his eggs with his fork.

"But you're a genius at creating it."

"Stop teasing. It's not funny."

"I'm not teasing. That's the most beautiful image of me I've ever seen."

That was hard to believe. The most beautiful image of Melody was Melody herself, and she knew it. Not that she was vain in the usual sense. She just possessed superhuman self-confidence.

"And do you know why?" she asked.

Having misplaced his words somewhere, Bernard shook his head.

"Because it came from your heart."

Maybe. It certainly hadn't come from his hands. "Even so," he said, "I don't think the class should see this. They'll interpret it in some twisted way that makes you the villain in my life."

"Nonsense. And even if they do, so what? I know the truth. Let me handle that, and you break into the bathroom."

Bernard didn't know whether to be encouraged or to have a bad feeling about this day. Somehow, he managed both.

Chapter 9: Thursday, October 19, 2017

Despite yesterday's eruption, they were admitted to the mansion without question, just as Melody had predicted. They split up on the grand staircase, Melody exiting at the second floor and Bernard ascending to the third as though he belonged there. Nobody noticed, which was odd because once she was in the hall making for class, a lot of people noticed Melody. Okay, no, that wasn't the odd part. People always noticed Melody. You don't not notice a woman that lovely and with that much spring in her step, a woman who radiated such love of life and who life loved right back with such enthusiasm. But this morning, she received attention not so much for all she possessed, but for the one thing she didn't, at that moment.

"Where's Bernard?" a young man asked. He slipped to her side and whispered the question, almost in her ear.

Melody smiled at nothing. "Oh, he'll be along."

The fellow scanned their surround. He wasn't bad looking. Not as dashing as Bernie, but handsome in a *GQ* sort of way. Tall, fit, lean in the face, hair cropped short on the sides and a bit piled on top. He was wearing black jeans and a dark green button-down shirt, open at the collar and untucked at the bottom. "But he's not here now, huh?" he asked.

"Not yet." Melody turned her smile on him, and he just about melted into a puddle.

Somehow maintaining solid form, he swallowed and said, "So, uh, you want to sit with me today? I mean, you and Bernard. If he shows up. Or if not, just you. I hope he doesn't. Uh, doesn't mind. Not doesn't show up. But if he doesn't..."

Melody patted the poor fellow's shoulder. "That's sweet of you," she said, "but I need to sit in the back, as usual. So he can find me. If he's late."

"Oh. Well. Okay. But, but, but, why?"

"He'll want to find me, don't you think?"

"Who wouldn't? But, I mean, he could find you anywhere, I'm sure. Why the back?"

"We might need to make a quick exit." Which was true. If anything went wrong, escape could be imperative. Not that anything would, except, oh dear, with Bernard things *did* go wrong with some frequency. She bit her lip. Why did she let him go up there by himself? He might need her luck today. In person, not a whole floor away.

The young man missed that train of thought. He was puzzling over a problem of his own. Finally, his expression lit up. "I know," he said. "I'll sit in the back, too."

Real genius, he was.

"Oh, yes!" Melody brightened before morphing into crestfallen. "Wait, no. I really do need to save a seat for Bernie."

"Oh. Oh, yeah, I guess...well, maybe another time?"

"Maybe," she said. "I'm really sorry."

They entered the classroom, and her disappointed pseudo-suitor shuffled down the aisle to his usual place, wherever that was, oblivious to the fact that even if Melody did save Bernie a seat, there were plenty to spare nearby. She almost felt sorry for the fellow. It had been an unfair contest from the get-go.

Before class got underway, another male straggler straggled in, glanced at Melody, did a double-take, and slipped into the seat next to her. "Hey," he said in greeting.

"Hey!" she replied. "Enjoying the class?"

This fellow was shorter and not quite so handsome, but he had a dazzling smile. He stared into her eyes, clearly enjoying

                    Rooftop Sonata

something, until he remembered his manners and stopped staring. Mostly. "So, where's Bernard today?"

"Oh, you know." Melody turned and gazed longingly out the door. "He's just running a bit late."

"You want me to keep you company until he gets here?"

"That's sweet of you, but no. I need to finish up some sketches. And anyway, if he does show up, you're in his seat."

"Oh, oops." The fellow jumped up as though the seat had given him an electric shock. "Maybe I'll see you at lunch? If he doesn't make it by then?"

"Sure, that would be nice." Melody batted her eyelashes at him. After that, it was a wonder he could find his way down the aisle.

Allegra Fumagalli made her entrance before further men could try to take Bernard's place. The instruction this morning was exactly as Melody had predicted: draw someone you know, someone important to you. Melody took her time composing a portrait of Bernie complete with the look of calculation he always wore when figuring out how to steal something. It wasn't likely she'd be called, not after yesterday's brouhaha, but she wanted it to be perfect for Bernie. Maybe she'd even frame it. Maybe it would be auctioned off for a million dollars, and they could retire from their life of creative procurement and be just plain creative thereafter. She liked the thought of that. Just the two of them, drawing portraits of each other and maybe occasionally Fifi, getting filthy rich from doing little more than staring at each other.

Alas, her fantasy was interrupted by Allegra calling, "Bernard? Are you here today, dear? Bernard?"

Melody tucked Bernie's sketch book under her arm and rose. She glided to the stage and presented his drawing of her. "He's running late this morning," she explained. "But he asked me to bring this, in case you called on him."

With a contrite smile, Allegra took the sketchbook as though it was made of pure gold. She gently placed Bernard's drawing on the projector. A collective gasp rustled the gathered students. The master gazed at the portrait of Melody, and gazed, and gazed. She said nothing, neither asked anyone's opinion. When she looked up, a tear trickled down her cheek. She removed the sketchbook from the projector and with great reverence handed it back to Melody.

Melody couldn't help it. She bowed as she received it.

"This," Allegra said, "is pure love rendered in graphite."

"That's what I told him." She laughed an embarrassed laugh. "He thought it was terrible."

"Of course he did. Genius is never satisfied. Monet destroyed some of his own works." Allegra gave Melody a pat on the shoulder and waved her off the stage.

Melody returned to her seat and spent the rest of the morning wishing Bernard was there. She couldn't wait to tell him he was officially a genius.

𝄞

Bernard wasn't feeling like a genius just then. The plan had gone off without a hitch until the important part. He timed his emergence from the men's room just after the guard, Brian Garfunkel, had finished his nine o'clock rounds. Before stepping into the hall, he texted his *hi* to Shawn, who a minute later texted *hi* back, then Bernard strolled to the fake women's room and went to work on the lock. By their arrangement, from the moment of Shawn's text he had four minutes to get there, pick the lock and duck inside before the cameras resumed normal operation. Exclusive of the travel time, he should have been done in three, maybe two, but the lock refused to unlock. With time running out, Bernard trotted back to the men's room. He made it with two seconds to spare

Shawn would be waiting for a second signal, the signal Bernard was ready to escape the treasure trove, but that was no good now, so Bernard risked a wordier text. *Problem. Try again 9:35.*

Shawn responded with a "yuk" emoji.

At 9:30 on the dot, Brian slipped through the connecting door and walked his rounds. He was as good as his word, taking just four minutes and thirty-eight seconds, most of which was spent looking at the paintings as he passed them by, then he was gone. Bernard had no idea how they could be that fascinating day after day, but whatever. He texted Shawn another *hi.* A minute later, Shawn replied. Bernard returned to the fake women's room and tried his luck again, once more getting nowhere. What the hell?

Retreating to the men's room just in time, he sent yet another off-plan text: *Hit a snag. Gotta think. More shortly.* Shawn sent an angry emoji this time, and Bernard shut himself in the handicapped stall to do his thinking.

That took time, as he wasn't a complete expert on locks. He'd done some reading, sure, and he could make short work of most keyed locks, but he was far from a locksmith. Still, something niggled at him, some reason why a keyed lock might not be pickable. The explanation took its sweet time coming, like a name he'd forgotten and couldn't come up with until hours later, usually when he was half asleep, except he wasn't half asleep now. He was too agitated to snooze, and anyway, he was holed up in a restroom. Not the best ambiance for a nap.

At length, his brain served up the answer: deadlock.

Damn it.

Some devices, such as the night latches employed by hotels to prevent staff from intruding on customers, could be deadlocked from the inside. Nobody on the outside could open a deadlocked lock, not even with a key. If the fake restroom was deadlocked, someone must be in there, and he'd simply need to wait until they came out. Unless another entrance was lurking somewhere.

He recalled Celeste's map from memory, or as much as he could summon. Here on the third floor, the off-limits restrooms huddled beside the door connecting the mansion's public and private wings. Oddly, there was nothing like them on the first and second floors, but otherwise they seemed ordinary.

No, not quite. There was something else. Both seemed too small to serve as storage for a secret stash of stolen art. Bernard had speculated they might be one big room, but could one entrance be deadlocked and the other not? Unlikely. The locks must be the same, installed for some reason other than keeping Bernard Earls out. More likely, they were to keep out anyone with keys—such as guards—whenever Gerhard Nachtnebel, Jr. was running his greedy little fingers through his secret treasure.

Still, it was worth checking. Opening the restroom door a crack and taking surreptitious peeks into the hall, Bernard waited until ten o'clock. Brian appeared on schedule, made his rounds, and slipped out four minutes and thirty-eight seconds later. What was the guy, a robot? Bernard texted Shawn another *hi*, and a minute later Shawn's *hi* came back. It sounded awfully clipped, although Bernard had no idea why. It was just two letters in a text message, like all the others. But he could tell. The kid was going to murder him.

Bernard made for the fake men's room door and went to work. It proved futile. He retreated to his hiding place one more time and sent Shawn a final text: *Nope. Done for today.* Shawn declined to reply, even to the extent of an emoji. Probably they didn't have one that covered his complex of fear, anger, and relief.

For the next hour and a half plus, Bernard hid in the men's room, unable to come out lest he be spotted on the security cameras. For the first half hour, he worried over the job, particularly over the loss of twenty thousand dollars plus expenses. But deadlocks were deadlocks, which left him dead in the water. Since that line of thought led nowhere but depression, he downloaded the game *Pigeon Wings* and played that. By the time lunch break arrived and students flooded the halls, making it safe for him to emerge, he was getting pretty good at it.

𝄞

"*Pigeon Wings?*" Melody covered her mouth and snorted. She sure was doing that a lot lately. Twice in one week. "What kind of game is that?"

"Flying," Bernard said. "Racing. Shooting. You're trying to stop the evil Duke Dexter from destroying Megalopolis."

She snorted again—three in one week; maybe she should see a doctor?—then fanned herself. It must've been the funniest thing she'd heard in a long time, even funnier than MoneyMonkey. Modern technology was nothing if not amusing.

They were seated by a window in the bistro, next to the balcony door. While describing the game, Bernard was holding a clear plastic cup of lemon iced tea and studying the room's security system. Motion sensors were mounted in strategic spots on the ceiling, obviously disabled now, what with students ordering and eating lunch and bankrupting themselves in the process. The food prices were ridiculous. He could have put a down payment on a house for as much as his pulled pork and grilled pepper slaw sandwich had set him back. Good thing Celeste was covering their lunches, although she didn't know it yet. So long as he procured *Rienzi*, anyway.

Under control again, Melody nibbled at her sandwich, chicken with chutney on a ciabatta. "What do we do now?" she asked between bites.

"I'm considering your idea. But I'm pretty sure Shawn will go into cardiac arrest, and Felicity will send us the medical bills."

Melody waved that off. "Put it on Celeste's tab. What was my idea, again?"

"The balconies."

"Oh, right. That was a great idea, huh?"

"In hindsight, yes."

She gave him her look of rebuke. "It's not hindsight. You haven't done it yet."

Bernard took a drink. "I mean, since I couldn't pick..." He glanced around. Nobody was paying attention to them. Not yet. But best to be safe. "You know."

Melody winked at him.

He nodded at the balcony door. "The door's nothing special, and Shawn can deal with the electronics. I need to check external surveillance. I can't be seen swinging from a bal—"

"Bernarrrrrrrd," a soft voice squeaked.

Great. Another fan. Bernard looked up into the crystalline blue eyes of a curvaceous woman with green, orange, pink, and yellow hair. The swirling colors nearly hypnotized him, which might have been the idea. Maybe she was like one of those deep-sea creatures that use light to lure their prey close enough to devour. "Uh," he said. "Yes?"

"Your portrait of Melody is the most moving drawing I've ever seen." She sighed in ecstasy. Rather over the top, that was.

"Thank you," he muttered. "The real thing is even more moving." He poked a finger in the general direction of Melody.

The intruder glanced at Melody, gave her a small but civil nod, and returned her attention to the greatest artist she'd ever met. "I was hoping you might draw me."

Since that was likely to be a recipe for disaster, Bernard shook his head. "I'm sorry, but I can't take commissions right now. I'm rather busy with—"

"Oh please, just a quick sketch? It doesn't have to be anything fancy, not like the one of Melody. Nothing that special. Just something quick?"

Bernard put up a hand to stop her, but it didn't stop her.

"Just maybe a half-hour session? I'll come to your studio and lie back on the couch and you can do a quick little sketch?"

"Can't," he said without thinking. "Too dangerous."

She blinked at him. "Dangerous?"

Oops. He tried to backpedal, but he couldn't find the pedals. He sort of sputtered instead.

"Oh," she said with a sly smile. "You mean me lying naked on your couch while your wife's around? Aw, hell, I'm sure she's used to it. You must have done lots of nudes." She turned to Melody. "Am I right?"

Melody's expression broadcast murder, but somehow the woman didn't get it, not even when she said, "The only nude he's doing is me."

The interloper grabbed an empty chair from the neighboring table and sat. She planted her elbows on the tabletop and her chin in her hands and smiled at Bernard. "I'll pay whatever you want."

How did he get into these spots? Bernard pulled out his cell phone to check the time. "Listen, maybe we can discuss it later. It's almost time to–"

"Oh, no you don't." She laughed. "I'm Olivia, by the way. Olivia O'Leary. And I'm a woman on a mission."

Bernard didn't see how lying naked on his couch while he sketched her badly and Melody fumed constituted a mission, but he wasn't getting out of this unscathed. Fortunately, inspiration struck. "My studio," he said, "is in a place called Ford's Ford. Ever hear of it?"

"Nope."

"It's just outside D.C. Kind of pricey area. Really bad traffic."

"Horrible traffic," Melody added. "Even chauffeurs don't like to drive there."

Olivia's eyes sparkled. "Give me a date and time and address, and I'll be there."

Bernard didn't have the address memorized, and he had no idea how Celeste would take to his making an appointment to use her place without her consent, but under the pretext of making a calendar entry, he pulled up the info on his phone and relayed it. "Saturday, ten A.M.?"

Olivia made a note on her own phone. "Perfect. I can't wait to have my very own Earls original!" And off she bounded, the happiest woman in the world.

Melody eyed her husband. "Bernie," she growled.

"I know, I know," he said. "I'll draw with my eyes shut. But who knows? Maybe that'll be an improvement."

𝄞

The afternoon session passed in a blur. Bernard's mind wasn't on art. Not on drawing, anyway. There *was* an art to burglary, particularly when complicated by deadlocks and balconies and maniac Nazis. But that wasn't something he could put on display for the class.

His current magnum opus required determining which balcony, if any, gave access to the fake restroom. Naturally, no ordinary restroom would have a balcony. Not much call for one, was there? Nor, now that he thought about it, would a storage room need one, not under normal circumstances. But this was a treasure room disguised to look utterly ordinary. It might well have a balcony, if for no other reason than to avoid drawing attention to itself. A balconyless spot on a heavily balconied wall would stand out. He'd have to check the drone footage again. Or maybe Shawn could give him the layout. Once he knew which balconies were which, he could traverse from the third-floor bistro to his target. Unless the balconies were covered by exterior cameras, in which case Shawn again.

While he thought, he doodled in his sketch book, barely knowing what he was drawing. Another problem occurred to him, one of greater moment: timing. One day remained in this class, just one, which meant he must either nab *Rienzi* tomorrow or beg Celeste for more tuition funds. Either way, it would be dicey. Deadlines were almost as bad as deadlocks. They stifled his creativity, or at least his ability to get paid.

"Bernard?" The willowy voice didn't quite register. Melody nudged him. When he looked up, Allegra Fumagali was waving him to the stage.

"Uh-oh," he muttered.

"What?" Melody muttered back.

"I don't even know the assignment."

"Stop worrying, Bernie. Take your sketch book and go."

He shuffled to the stage, book in hand. Melody was probably right. He could do no wrong in this class. He could hand over a blank page and be praised to heaven and back.

Allegra received his doodles with reverence. "Wow," she breathed. "How do you always manage to outdo yourself?" She put his work on display, whereupon her happy sigh echoed around the room, taken up by student after student.

"Just lucky, I guess," he said without conviction. This had to be Melody's divine influence. It defied explanation otherwise.

"Lucky," Allegra said. She laughed. So did everyone else. "No, Bernard, no. You must have a deep well of suffering to draw from. Or maybe you're more in tune with your sorrows than the rest of us. Look at this." She waved a hand at the projected drawing.

Bernard looked. He couldn't make head or tail of what he'd doodled. It wasn't exactly unified. It looked like a hodgepodge of balconies, all out of alignment, tilted this way and that, while some poor unfortunate dangled from one of them. The cockeyed lines warped the entire image into something eerily like a Picasso. Not cubist, but cubish. Maybe Bernard had invented a new genre of art.

Allegra returned the drawing. "See me after class," she whispered.

Could master class students earn detention with bad art? Or by being insufferable show-offs? Bernard returned to his seat, burdened by a feeling of disastrous karma. "She wants to see me after class," he told Melody. "I'm doomed."

Melody touched his cheek and kissed him. "You're such a pessimist. She probably wants to commission a portrait. Two in one day!"

Great. He might have a promising career as an artist, but it would ruin his burglary business.

After Allegra dismissed the class, Bernard and Melody waited until the room cleared. The master descended from the stage and toddled toward them. They met her halfway. She gave Melody a civil nod, then turned to Bernard. "You are without doubt the brightest student I've taught here at the Nachtnebel Arts Foundation. To be honest, most of the artists who pass through these halls are mediocre at best. A few do show promise. But you, Bernard, you have a genius rarely seen."

Not detention, then. So far, so good. Must indeed be a commission. How much should he charge? He had no idea. Best to let her start the negotiations. "Thank you," he said.

Allegra put her wrinkled hand on his shoulder. It was a bit of a stretch for her. "Listen. There's a special event taking place on Monday. Mr. Nachtnebel is offering a rare tour of his private collection to select members of the arts community. I think you should attend."

Bernard almost gaped, which would have been bad. "Private collection?"

"He doesn't do this often. It's a rare treat. Very few are allowed in. No photography, of course, and no sketching, but an artist like you will absorb so much from it."

He wouldn't mind absorbing that *Rienzi* manuscript, if it was on display. Or at least getting a look at it, so he'd know what to pilfer when he saw it again.

"I'll get you in," Allegra said.

"I'm honored. What about Melody?"

She turned and gave Melody a considered once-over. "Hmm, yes, I suppose you do everything together."

"As much as possible," Bernard acknowledged.

Melody put a hand to her mouth and giggled.

Luckily, Allegra had already turned back to Bernard and didn't notice. "All right, you can both attend. Be here Monday at eleven. The showing will take an hour, after which a luncheon will be served. Black tie."

"I don't have a black tie," Melody said. "I do have a lovely white dress with a black bow."

Allegra raised an eyebrow. "That should do."

And so it was settled. Once in the car on the way home, Melody started giggling again. "What now?" Bernard asked.

"I'm sorry," she said. "I couldn't help it. It was such a funny image."

Bernard hadn't gotten any images except the target of their efforts.

"When she said we do everything together..." Melody giggled again.

"I'm sure she wasn't thinking of *that*, love."

"That?"

"That."

"Oh, *that.*" Another giggle. "I wasn't, either. I was thinking about climbing balconies together. And yelling like Tarzan."

"Oh," Bernard said. "Naturally. That."

"Yeah. That."

Speaking of that, Bernard needed another session with Shawn, fast. It was already approaching six o'clock, and the traffic was beyond horrific, which was the norm for rush hour D.C. He activated his phone and said, "Call Shawn Uletschi."

The device had to think about that for a moment, but finally it got it. Sort of. "Calling Sean Maletzi," it said. Bernard could barely remember who owned that name. Someone he'd done a job for eight or ten years back, probably, but if so, why was the guy still in his contacts? Probably because Bernard wasn't much good at fiddly maintenance stuff like removing unnecessary names from his phone.

He canceled the call and tried again, dragging out the last name. "Call Shawn You-let-ski."

This time the call went to the right person, or at least the right person's voice mail. "Hey, it's Shawn. Leave a message. Thanks."

Beep.

"Shawn, it's Bernard. We need to drop by tonight. Call me and let me know a good time." He disconnected, then said, "He should be home by now. Where is he?"

"Oh," Melody said, "they probably went out. Or maybe they're cuddling on the sofa, watching a movie."

Bernard squinted at a pair of oncoming headlights. "I'm not sure Shawn knows about cuddling."

"Don't be silly, Bernie. He's only half as clueless as he used to be."

"Half, huh? That leaves plenty of room for ignorance."

"Felicity's taught him, I'm sure. Just like I taught you."

"I don't remember you having to teach me much."

Melody grinned and gave his shoulder a love tap. "I taught you everything you know."

He would have objected. He'd known everything to start with. Most everything. Some of it, anyway. He'd almost had a girlfriend in high school. "Regardless," he said before his self-image could further deteriorate, "We'd better head over there and hope they're home."

As if by magic, his cell phone jangled, and how about that, it was Shawn.

"Give me some good news," Bernard told his unwitting accomplice. "Tell me you're home."

"Nope." Shawn's voice sounded strangely hollow, as though he was calling from within a vast cavern.

"What do you mean, nope?"

"I mean nope."

Bernard's fingers tightened on the wheel. "What are you doing, then?"

"Meeting Felicity's mom. And her stepfather. And her father and stepmother. And her brother and stepsisters, and–"

"No offense," Bernard interrupted, "but I'm not interested in family reunions. I have one more task for you."

"I told you, I'm done with that." Shawn's voice grew distant on the last two words, intercut by other distant voices.

Bernard shook his head. The kid had a lot to learn about conducting business on a phone.

"Sorry, I was just introduced to one of Felicity's stepsisters' boyfriends."

Presumably that wasn't what it sounded like, but Bernard couldn't resist asking. "How many boyfriends does she have?"

"Huh?"

Bernard's fingers tightened further. He hoped the steering wheel could take it. "Never mind. We need to meet. Tonight."

"No way. Forget it."

"No choice, Shawn. The test ran into some problems. I had to devise a new one."

"You haven't even paid me my four hundred yet."

Great. Felicity's influence was rubbing off on him. "Three," Bernard corrected.

"Fine," Shawn snapped, "but interest starts accruing if it's not in my account by midnight."

"Don't worry. I'm driving now, but as soon as I get home, I'll MoneyMonkey it to you."

Melody giggled.

"Who's that?" Shawn yelped.

Bernard wanted to squeeze his eyes shut, but that made driving tricky, so he didn't. "My wife. You remember her, right?"

"Oh. Yeah." Shawn sounded so relieved, he might have just had a death sentence commuted to a reward.

"Don't be so jumpy. Everything's fine."

"That's not what you said a moment ago."

Okay, now the steering wheel was in jeopardy of being ripped right off. Bernard took a few deep breaths to calm himself.

"Anyway," Shawn continued, "we won't be home until ten o'clock."

"We'll be waiting," Bernard told him.

"No. I gotta get up for work in the morning."

"Look, it won't take long, all right? I just need to discuss a small change to the plan."

"The plan was for me to be done after today."

Bernard glanced at Melody. She was inspecting her finger-nails, but she clearly sensed his frustration. "I'll bring some cookies," she said. "What kind do you like?"

For some reason, Shawn had no reply to that.

"Chocolate chip it is," she decided. "And vanilla bean ice cream."

Shawn relented, but not without a fight. "It's going to cost something extra."

"No," Melody said. "I think vanilla bean is the same price as regular vanilla."

"I mean this extra task, whatever it is."

"Sure," Bernard growled. "Fine. Whatever. We'll negotiate that tonight."

"And then I'm done," Shawn said.

"Of course."

"Don't call me about this again."

"Of course not."

"I mean it."

"I know." Which wouldn't stop Bernard from calling about it again, should the need arise, but for now, they had an accord. "Enjoy the reunion, Shawn."

Shawn didn't bother indicating how that was going. He disconnected before Bernard could request anything further.

Chapter 10: Late Thursday, October 19, 2017

Melody had Bernard stop at the grocery store and pick up a plastic clamshell box of bakery chocolate chip cookies and a carton of vanilla bean ice cream, except the store was out of vanilla bean, so they wound up with plain vanilla.

"Boooooring," Melody said.

Bernard had never been able to tell the difference himself, but it was the wrong time to mention that. "Shawn won't notice," he said. "He only notices computer stuff."

"He noticed Felicity," Melody countered.

"Only because you pushed him toward her."

"I didn't push. I nudged."

In Shawn's case, that was like the difference between vanilla bean and boooooring vanilla, but again, not worth mentioning.

They arrived at Felicity's apartment building ten minutes early, so they waited in the car while the minutes crept by. The night had a cool, comfortable feel. The brighter stars winked on and off and on and off as a scattering of yellowed clouds drifted through the light pollution. Melody sighed. "Beautiful, isn't it?"

"Not bad," Bernard agreed. He turned his gaze on something even more beautiful. If she noticed, she didn't comment. "We should take a vacation once this job is done. We can afford it, finally."

She beamed at the stars, such as they were. "That would be fun. Where should we go?"

"Someplace dark where we can see the stars for real."

Still gazing heavenward, Melody reached for him, draped her arm around his shoulders, and pulled. They tilted toward each other until their cheeks nestled together. "Where would that be? Last time we talked about stars, you said the only dark places were the Australian outback or North Korea."

True. He laughed at the memory of them standing in the summer heat outside Paul Revere Plaskett's mansion, gazing up at the glowing clouds. Images of light pollution from space revealed the interior of Australia and repressed North Korea to be among the darkest places on Earth. But there were others. "West Virginia would work," he said. "Up around Spruce Knob, the state's high point. Astronomy clubs take their telescopes there, I hear. There's a state park nearby with campsites."

"Oh, I see. You don't want to stargaze. You want to get me in a tent in the dark." She kissed his cheek.

He took her into his arms and pressed his lips to hers. "Of course I do," he whispered, and then he kissed her again, for a very long time.

Alas, it couldn't go on forever. Somebody rapped on the passenger window and sprayed a cell phone flashlight in Bernard's face while yelling through the glass, "Hey buddy! How you doin'? Can you help me? I'm about outta gas, and I gotta get to Shock Trauma in Baltimore. My father was just in a real bad accident. They medivacked him. He might die at any second. Could you lend me five bucks for gas?"

Bernard squinted and pushed the button to lower the window just far enough to allow sound waves through. "If you don't get that light out of my face," he said, "you'll be medivacked next."

The flashlight turned off. In the glow of the parking lot's lighting, a terrified man gaped at him. From the fellow's expression, the world was scheduled to end in less than thirty seconds. "Five bucks? I don't have much time, I gotta get to Baltimore and—"

"You sure don't have much time," Bernard told him. "Not after you interrupted something that beautiful."

"You can make out with her anytime. My father's dying! Could you lend me five—"

"If I was your father, I'd take a belt to you for scamming people. Get lost." He pushed the button and raised the window.

The scammer's face transitioned from panic to anger, and he made a rude gesture. Just in case Bernard couldn't see it, he turned his cell phone light back on and illuminated his fingers. One finger, anyway. And then he was gone.

"That wasn't very nice," Melody commented. "Shining that light on us like that."

"Not at all," Bernard agreed. "Not to mention that stupid story."

Across the parking lot, the light flashed on as the scammer tried to con someone else out of five dollars.

"I wonder how much he makes?" Melody asked.

"Probably more than we do."

"Tacky, though."

"Very."

Melody grabbed Bernard and kissed him again. "Good thing we're not tacky. Let's go see Shawn."

"Let's." Bernard exited and rounded the vehicle to help Melody out, then they walked arm-in-arm into the building, confident in the knowledge that they, at least, were classy criminals.

𝄞

"No," Shawn said. He pointed his index finger at Bernard to make the point. Like the rest of him, it was skinny and geeky, a finger used to rapid-fire typing on a keyboard but little else.

At least he hadn't used the same finger as the five-dollar guy. *Five-dollar guy*, Bernard thought. *That's a good name for him.* "It's what you already did, just different devices," he told Shawn in his most soothing, reasonable, convincing voice.

Which failed to either sooth or convince Shawn, nor, apparently, did he find it at all reasonable. "Except you want a map, too. I know what you're doing. You're trying to pull another weasel job, only this time, the consequences are death."

Bernard felt his soothing, reasonable, convincing demeanor fracture, but he held it together with mental duct tape. "What do you actually know about that weasel job?"

"It involved a silver weasel."

"In other words, nothing. First, it wasn't a weasel, it was a pine marten. Second, I did the Plasketts a favor. They ended up with three pine martens instead of one. Third, I got you a great job and launched your career."

"Bernie," Melody chimed in, "is a true philanthropist."

Shawn pointed at Bernard again, but before he could speak, Bernard pointed at Melody and said, "See?"

Felicity, meanwhile, had been watching the exchange in uncharacteristic silence. She had served everyone peach iced tea plus a dish of boooooooring vanilla ice cream and chocolate chip cookies. Now she had a half-eaten cookie in her left hand, a half-full glass in her right, and a dish of ice cream balanced on her thighs. She couldn't point at anyone, but she did shift her gaze to Bernard and, at long last, interjected an insightful comment. "Five thousand."

Bernard looked at the ceiling. Maybe the Angel of the Lord would come down and smite her for greed? Nope, didn't happen.

Shawn clapped his hands to his head. "No, Felicity! No! Not for five *hundred* thousand!"

"Fine," Felicity snapped. "Half a million, then."

Melody put a hand on Felicity's shoulder. "Honey, half a million *is* five hundred thousand."

Felicity scrunched up her face and thought about it. "Oh, right. A million, then."

"Bernie doesn't have a million."

Felicity delivered a savage bite to her cookie.

"Shawn, look." Bernard scooted forward in his chair. He held up his hand and began ticking items off on his fingers. Part of him wondered how fingers had suddenly become so important to this business. "One. The original test didn't work. My fault. There were complications I hadn't considered. You did your part, thought, so the three hundred for that is yours."

"You didn't MoneyMonkey it to me yet," Shawn grumped.

No, he hadn't, because he hadn't had time to ask Celeste for expenses. But he could do that later. He had enough to cover it himself until then. He pulled his cell phone from his pocket and monkeyed with the money.

Melody snickered. "MoneyMonkey," she whispered at Felicity, and Felicity chortled, too. Shawn's cell phone dinged.

"Done," Bernard continued before the women's amusement turned into a distraction. "Two. I have a job to do. One way or another, it's got to be done."

"That's your problem," Shawn said.

"Three. I can't do it without you, which means it's your problem, too. But you'll get paid."

"And shot."

"Five thousand," Felicity added.

Shawn straightened. He looked like a guard in a prairie dog colony. "I am *not* getting shot for five thousand dollars!"

Felicity opened her mouth, but Bernard waved her to silence. "Did you see that?" Felicity demanded of Melody.

Melody couldn't have missed it. "Behave yourself, Bernie."

"Four." Bernard had four fingers up now, all of them quivering in anger, but with all the distractions, he couldn't recall what his fourth point was. "Four," he repeated.

"Four thousand?" Felicity suggested.

Bernard gave up and dropped his hand. "Four hundred," he said. "That's more than last time, for exactly the same job."

"Except the map."

"It's not a map, it's just how many balconies from the bistro to the bathroom."

"Why does a bathroom have a balcony, anyway?" Shawn asked.

It was at least a reasonable question. "I don't know," Bernard said, "but I need that number, okay?"

"Then it's not the exact same job."

Bernard gave up one more time. "Okay, okay, five hundred."

"I am *not* getting shot for five hundred–"

"Damn it, nobody's getting shot, Shawn!"

In one smooth movement, Melody rose, slipped to Bernard's side, and cradled his reddish face to her bosom. Shawn suddenly found something engrossing to study on the ceiling. Felicity ground her teeth in an infelicitous manner. "Take it easy, Bernie," Melody whispered. "Shawn's just on edge."

"More like terrified," Shawn mumbled. "Nachtnebel is a maniac. Plus, the company will fire and prosecute me if they find out."

Bernard still had his cell phone in his hand. Melody eased it away from him and called Celeste. She put the call on speaker and set a finger to her lips to signal for silence. Everyone but her might have stopped breathing.

"Bernard," Celeste said. "How's it going?"

"It's me," Melody chirped. "Bernie's busy right now, but he asked me to tell you we need to put a subcontractor on retainer. Is that okay?"

"I thought you put lawyers on retainer," Celeste said. "Don't tell me he's in *that* much trouble."

"Nooooooo," Melody said. She laughed. "Could you send us, oh, I don't know, maybe two thousand?" She made it sound as inconsequential as two cents.

"These expenses are getting expensive," Celeste said in a dark tone Bernard hadn't previously heard from her.

"We probably won't use it all," Melody said. "We'll return the leftovers."

"I have a fridge full of those. But all right. Just don't make me regret it. You'll regret it."

Melody laughed again. "Oh, Celeste, would we do that?"

"I'm serious, Melody. You tell Bernard that."

Bernard nearly spouted a rebuttal, but Melody touched her fingers to his lips. He crossed his arms over his chest and swallowed his indignation. "Don't worry," she told their employer. "We're professionals. If we can't finish the job, you'll get your money back."

Bernard wondered how he'd swing a payday loan when he didn't have a payday. But the promise worked. Celeste said she'd MoneyMonkey the money, Melody giggled again, and that part was settled.

"By the way," Melody told Celeste, "Bernie got a commission to paint a portrait. Could he use your studio Saturday morning at ten?"

He'd forgotten about that. This might not be the best time to ask about it, either. In the silence that followed, Bernard imagined Celeste wondering what kind of double-cross they were prepping.

"How did that happen?" she finally asked.

"Would you believe it? It turns out Bernie's an artistic genius."

"No, I wouldn't."

Bernard didn't blame her.

"Well, it's true," Melody said. "Just ask Allegra Fumagalli."

Celeste mulled that over. "I just might do that," she decided. "Why my studio?"

"We don't have one," Melody explained. "And he needs a professional place to work. This lovely young lady student wants to pose nude for him."

Felicity's eyes nearly tumbled out of their sockets. Shawn turned beet-red and gagged. Bernard remained stone-faced.

"What's this student's name?" Celeste asked.

"Olivia O'Leary."

"Oh, her."

Now Melody's eyes widened. "You know her?"

"Not directly. We took some of the same classes. She's a perpetual student. Always will be. Not much talent. But that makes sense, at least. Just don't leave Bernard alone with her."

Melody glanced at Bernard. Bernard wondered how he'd gotten into this. *Rienzi*, Nazis, art classes, commissions to paint naked women, all of it.

"Is that a yes?" Melody asked.

"Why not," Celeste agreed. "Get here half an hour early. You can let the...model...in. I'll hide upstairs, in case she remembers me."

Call done, Melody turned to Shawn. "There. We have two thousand to work with. Bernie paid you three hundred. We'll give you another seven now, and that leaves a thousand for future needs. Deal?"

Bernard almost choked on the rampant inflation. "How can you do math at a time like this?"

She gave him a demure smile. "I maybe failed algebra, Bernie, but not arithmetic."

All eyes turned to Shawn. He folded his hands in his lap and studied his knuckles. He might have been counting to make sure they were all there. "This is really important to you, isn't it?"

You bet, Bernard thought. *Twenty thousand dollars important.* But as he couldn't say that without winding up Felicity again, he just nodded.

"All right." Shawn sank into the sofa. He looked like a lost puppy. "I'll text you the balcony information first thing in the morning. The exterior cameras cover ground floor access, but nothing higher up. I can handle the balcony door alarms, but they can't be manipulated the same way as the hall cameras. I only have a two-minute window for maintenance deactivation. After that, somebody's likely to notice. From the time I signal, you've got two minutes to do whatever you're doing, then they come back online, ready or not."

"Two minutes," Bernard agreed. If the balcony door on the fake restroom was anything like the one in the bistro, He'd have it jimmied in no time. Those doors hadn't been designed with security in mind. Fitzroy had marshalled their tech to cover that, and Shawn was covering Fitzroy. But Shawn was worried, so he added, "This is all just a test. It's okay if it doesn't work." Which was true and false. It *was* a test, sort of. But if it didn't work, Bernard had no idea what to try next. He only had one thing going for him in that case: another thousand to dangle in front of Shawn.

Chapter 11: Friday, October 20, 2017

They woke to a thoroughly yukky morning: cold, grey, wet. They could hear the patter of tiny raindrops on the window. Bernard didn't want to get out of bed. After silencing the alarm, he wrapped himself around Melody and pulled her close. She snuggled up to him and sighed, warm and happy.

Alas, it didn't last. A banshee howled somewhere in the building, followed by a thundering not unlike a rhinoceros at full charge—not that Bernard had ever felt such a thing, but he imaged it must be like that—and then hammering on a door, maybe theirs, maybe some else's. Then all grew quiet.

"Chris-Chris is here," Melody mumbled in Bernard's ear.

"We need to do something about that monster," Bernard told her.

"He's a little kid, Bernie."

"I'm sure we can find a gag in his size."

Melody pushed herself away and sat, dragging the sheet and blanket with her. So much for warm and happy. She gave him the evil eye. "You can't gag a little kid."

"Watch me."

"It's impossible. You'd never catch him."

There was that, of course.

Since they were awake, they stumbled to the shower, which made the situation a bit more tolerable, and then dressed and got breakfast, this time just generic corn flakes with sliced bananas, probably also generic. Bernard didn't see any stickers on them, any-way. While they ate, he doodled in his sketch book. He wasn't sure what he was drawing. Trees, maybe, but not like any trees he'd ever seen, scraggly and twisted and filled with creepy critters perched on their branches, unnatural crosses between birds and squirrels and iguanas. If this was art, he'd be a billionaire.

After breakfast, Bernard gathered the equipment required for balcony acrobatics: climbing rope, a climbing harness, carabiners wrapped in a hand towel so they wouldn't clank when he walked, and a laser distance measurer. He stuffed the stuff into a canvas bag identical to the one in which they carried their art supplies and, just in case anyone peeked, settled his drawing pad on top.

By the time they left for class, the rhino across the hall had morphed into a howler monkey again. Pondering life as a billionaire artist, Bernard asked Melody, "Ever think about working from home?" He locked the door.

"Not anymore," she replied.

The drive to the Nachtnebel mansion was uneventful if slow, given that Marylanders couldn't drive in rain. Or snow. Or sunshine, half the time. They crept along a good fifteen miles per hour under the speed limit, when they were rolling at all. "Ever think about moving to another state?" Bernard asked Melody.

"Hawaii?" she asked with a gleam of hope in her eyes.

"Too expensive."

"Then why did you ask?"

"Just making conversation."

"You need conversation lessons, Bernie."

"At least I don't need art lessons."

They continued in silence after that. Bernard fought the traffic and Melody glared at the rain as though trying to will it away. He was surprised she didn't succeed, given—he mused with considerable affection—how much God loved the little kleptomaniac.

They had left early enough to arrive fifteen minutes ahead of class, even given traffic and weather. The bistros were still open for the caffeine junkies in the audience. Melody took charge of Bernard's drawings and made her way to class, while Bernard slipped to the third floor for latte and attempted burglary. His phone dinged while he was waiting for his coffee, announcing a one-character text from Shawn: *3.*

Bernard carried his drink onto the balcony, where he gazed over the soggy landscape, growing equally soggy in the process. You'd think someone would have noticed, but no. Neither students nor staff paid him the least attention, maybe because people don't pay attention, maybe because this was Bernard, and as a great artist nothing he did surprised anyone. That could be a useful cover. Maybe the universe was finally giving him a break.

He scanned the wall of the building, where balconies were arrayed like cereal boxes in a grocery store. Three, Shawn had said. Three balconies from here to the so-called restroom. He tried to convince himself it would be easy. After all, he'd scaled a balconied building or two before. But this was different. He'd never tried to cross to an adjacent balcony separated by so much empty air. Now that he was about to, the gap felt as wide as a football field.

Not that it was. Keeping his back to the door, he took his distance measurer in hand and, steadying it atop the railing, trained it on the balcony next door. The device served up the distance: about ten feet. *Doable*, he told himself. With luck, he wasn't lying.

Bernard checked for stray eyeballs. Most everyone had left the bistro save the staff, and those who remained were focused on finishing up and getting out. He set his cup on the floor and got into his climbing harness, hoping nobody would notice. That would have been awkward, since the device strapped over his shoulders, about his waist, around his thighs. Great for safety, but it looked horribly kinky. That done, he secured the rope to the harness and, measuring it out against his arm length, tied in carabiners at the eight and twelve foot marks. The first he clipped to the railing. The second he clipped to his harness for temporary storage. He tucked the remaining carabiners into a secret pocket, then folded up the bag and stashed it in another.

All set.

He hoped.

After a final check for curious bystanders, he clambered over the railing and down, carefully lowering himself until he was suspended by the rope. Then he swung back and forth, back and forth, using his body to pump up the amplitude like a kid on a playground swing until he rose close enough to the adjacent balcony to grab the bottom of the rail. He clipped the second carabiner there and hauled himself up far enough to peek through this balcony door. A black curtain covered it on the inside. Perfect. He scaled the railing and swung himself over.

One traverse done. Two to go.

After a brief rest, he repeated the procedure and arrived on the second balcony, where the door was also covered by a black curtain. What was that about, anyway? While he recuperated, he pondered the art class beyond that curtain. Probably it had to do with lighting. Maybe they were painting night scenes. Whatever. One balcony to go.

He made the final traverse, then he was standing on the presumed restroom balcony, with a trail of rope marking his passage. This door, too, was obscured by a black curtain. He revised his guess. It wasn't for art. This was where the vampires slept. No, that was just exhaustion speaking. It had taken twenty minutes to get this far. The exertion had left him shaky and a bit weird in the head, but if he escaped with *Rienzi* in his pocket, it was worth it.

Next job: the door. Slim Jims at the ready, he sent the Shawn a *hi*. A moment later, Shawn replied with *hi*. He had two minutes to get inside. He set to work.

Thirty seconds passed. A minute.

The lock refused to open.

A minute fifteen. A minute thirty.

The lock stayed locked.

 A minute forty-five.

Bernard cursed the cursed lock. Interior security would come back on in fifteen seconds. With insufficient time remaining, he minutely inspected the lock. It looked ordinary. Why wouldn't it pop? Maybe it was him. Maybe the traverse had tired him more than he realized. Fine, he'd try one more time. He texted Shawn again. Shawn replied. Bernard started over. The seconds ticked by. Still the lock refused to open.

Something awful occurred to him. He inspected the whole door this time, not just the lock. On the surface, it was the same as the bistro patio door, but then he spotted what was wrong. The sliding panel and the fixed panel were flush with each other. This door *couldn't* be opened. It was a fake. The whole thing was a fake. The lock must be unopenable, too.

Nachtnebel really, seriously didn't want anyone getting in there. Celeste had been right, at least insofar as something important being squirrelled away in this room.

There was nothing for it. Bernard put away his tools and made the grueling traverse back to the bistro balcony, retrieving the evidence of his passage as he went. Half irritated that he'd been defeated again, half elated that *something* of value lurked back there, he stuffed his gear back into the bag and pondered his options. Well, no, he didn't, because there weren't any. If he couldn't open the hall door and couldn't gain access via the balcony, he was defeated.

Worse, between registration and Shawn's fees, which Celeste would want refunded, he'd be out three grand. More, counting supplies and lunches.

This, he told himself, *is what comes of greed.*

He didn't know how he'd break it to Melody, but best to get it over with. He tugged on the bistro balcony door.

It didn't open.

He tugged again. Nothing.

He leaned into the glass and cupped his hands around his face to block out the glare. The lights were off, the shop empty, shut up tight.

Of course it was. Once classes started, there would be no customers. He'd been so focused on the traverse that he hadn't even considered that. He almost slapped himself, except it would hurt, and he'd had enough pain for one day. On top of it all, now he was stuck on this stupid balcony in the rain. He could pick the lock, but he'd trip an alarm in the process, and he shouldn't risk a detailed text to Shawn.

Hell with it. Bernard lowered himself to the floor and sat cross-legged in the drizzle, brooding over the sodden grounds and bonsai garden and grayed-out woods in the distance. It reminded him of that Samuel Weston painting they'd failed to steal for Mr. Freaking Jacobi.

Hmm. Maybe he should try his hand at painting.

&

Once again, Melody was on stage with Bernard's work. Once again, Allegra Fumagalli had projected her precocious student's art, to the astonishment of all. The wild disarray of nightmare trees—if trees they were—in which dark fantasy creatures lurked, waiting to drop upon some unsuspecting passer-by held everyone in breathless, speechless awe. Not even Allegra could find her voice. Minutes passed. Melody was pretty sure at least a few of those unbreathing people should have passed out by then from lack of oxygen, but somehow they didn't. Maybe they were aliens. Allegra, too. That would explain a lot.

Finally, the master inhaled. She turned to Melody. She tried to speak two or three times before any words formed. Melody wanted to ask which planet she'd come from.

Finally, Allegra found her voice. "I envy you so much, Melody."

"Me, too," a female student lost in the crowd said.

"Me, too," another chirped, and another, and another, and pretty soon all the women were sighing, "Me, too!"

Melody couldn't blame them, poor girls. She was married to the most amazing man in the world. Who wouldn't envy her?

"Bernard is an artistic genius of the first rate," Allegra continued. "He's the sort who will die in poverty but be remembered throughout all history."

That didn't sound enviable at all. What was the point of being remembered if you had to spend your whole life without nail polish and fancy dresses and cedar chests? Cedar chests, anyway. Melody had a dresser overflowing with nail polish picked up while shopping for dresses picked up while trying on dresses. Those had cost her nothing at all. But face it, it was hard to stuff a cedar chest into your handbag.

"I'll tell him you said that," Melody said. "He'll be stunned." He sure would be.

Allegra returned the drawing without further comment. Melody slipped back to her seat in the rear and tuned out the rest of the class. She amused herself by drawing a page full of little aliens, some with seven fingers, some with eight arms and three legs, some with heads twice the size of their bodies and large, bug eyes. And, oh, all sorts of creative forms. Maybe she should swap out her supermodel career for life as a sci-fi cover artist. Hmm.

By lunchtime, she had assembled quite the alien menagerie. Her mind had slipped from drawing to movies, science fiction movies in particular, and she was working out ways to cast all her critter creations in a blockbuster film. A sci-fi romcom sounded fun. Unfortunately, before she could develop a plot, class was dismissed for lunch. Bernie would be waiting for her in the bistro. With any luck, he'd have *Rienzi* in hand, or rather in his pocket, since having it in his hand would be tantamount to waiving it under Gerhardt Nachtnebel, Jr.'s nose while screaming, "I stole it! I stole it!" Not smart. And Bernie was smart, even if not lucky.

With that troubling thought filling her mind—the not lucky part, not the smart part—she hurried to the bistro, where she discovered just how unlucky he'd been.

&

Officially, the bistros opened exactly at noon when classes were dismissed for lunch, so the doors would be thrown wide just before the students arrived. But things hadn't gone officially today, not on the third floor. The staff came on duty at eleven thirty to prep food, drink stations, condiment supplies, cash drawers, everything. Halfway through the process, a young staffer named Amara happened to glance out the balcony door and about jumped out of her red and white striped uniform when she saw a remarkably good-looking bum seated on the concrete deck, cross-legged, back heavy against the wrought iron railing, frowning at his twiddling thumbs.

Amara alerted the rest of the staff with a forceful, "Um." She pointed out the window for emphasis. Alas, nobody was alerted. They chugged along, readying the bistro for the throng of famished students soon to arrive. She'd have to handle this on her own. Questions whirled through her brain. Who was he? How did he get onto the balcony? Was he dangerous? Drunk? High on God knew what? Probably the latter. Artists got up to all kinds of things like that. Oh, wait, an artist. Maybe this was performance art.

The guy just sat there, twiddling his thumbs, oblivious to her presence.

Okay. Whoever he was, he couldn't stay out there, and the patio had to be opened, anyway, even though nobody would want to eat in the rain. She tiptoed over, clicked the latch, and tugged the door an inch aside. At the sound, the bum stopped his thumb-twiddling thing and exhaled so heavily, it was a wonder the balcony didn't collapse under him.

Amara wished he'd make eye contact, so she could see the state of his pupils if nothing else, but he didn't look up. The first move belonged to her. "Hey," she said. It came out somewhere between a squeak and squeal.

"Hey," the bum replied. He uncrossed his legs but didn't rise. "Are you the manager?"

"N—n—noooo?" Why did she have to sound so scared? It wasn't dignified. She straightened and tried again. "No." There, that was better.

He lifted his eyes.

The misery in them nearly melted Amara's heart. And wait, she knew this guy, knew exactly who he was, which made it all the worse. Students on the second floor had been talking about him all week. "You're Bernard?" Damn her traitorous voice. Why had it come out a question? She knew it was him. She didn't have to fear him. And yet, something was wrong here. For one thing, why was he on the third floor instead of the second?

"Yeah," Bernard acknowledged. With help from the railing, he clambered to his feet like a man three times his age. He graced her with a sad, sad smile.

"Why are you out here? On the third floor? In the rain?" She wasn't sure which of those was more wrong.

"I got locked out."

Amara's hand flew to her mouth. "Oh my God! They locked the door while you were still out here?"

"Seems so."

"Oh my God, O my God, I'm so sorry!"

Bernard shrugged. "You didn't lock it, did you?"

To bc honest, she might have. She'd been having one of those weeks. They'd rotated her through every bistro in the building, what with people calling in sick and that new guy showing up late every day since he started and then being fired, and, well, just every crazy thing you could imagine. But wait, no, after breakfast today she'd been cleaning the tables on the other side of the room. It couldn't have been her, not today. "No, no, it wasn't me, I'd never do that to you, not to you!" As if she might do it to someone else. Get a grip, girl, get a grip!

Amara stepped aside and waved Bernard in. He shook the water from himself, picked up his art bag, shook the water from it, and stepped inside just as an ancient fellow tottered up behind her. The newcomer stood a head taller than Amara but looked comically thin. A stiff breeze could have blown him away. He scratched what little gray hair remained above his ear and wondered, "What's going on here?" He sounded as befuddled as Amara had ever heard him sound, which was saying something.

"Oh, Mr. Smithers! Bernard got locked out!" Amara blubbered. "On the balcony! Out there!" She pointed, in case it hadn't been clear. This day wasn't going at all right. Maybe she forgot to take her medication. Wait, no, she wasn't on medication. But after this, she might need some.

Bernard puffed himself up. "And I don't appreciate that," he told the thin one.

Smithers worked his jaw in annoyance. "I don't either. Who's responsible for this? Was it you, Amara?" He tried to menace Amara with narrowed eyes and a wicked scowl, but he just looked like a giraffe annoyed because all the leaves at his height had already been eaten.

No matter, Amara was plenty worked up on her own. "No! I was cleaning tables! Over there!" She pointed again. "I don't know who locked the door!"

"Well, rest assured, I'll get to the bottom of this. Give this man a free lunch." To say Smithers whirled and stalked off doesn't do justice to the motion. Bernard and Amara both leaped forward to catch him as he rotated in slow motion and tilted so far off his centerline that it could only have been a miracle he didn't fall. But surprisingly, he didn't need their help. He completed his turn, arranged his feet under him, and stalked off. By the time he made it behind the counter, he'd apparently forgotten about getting to the bottom of anything. He vanished into the back, never to be seen again.

Amara turned to Bernard, every muscle in her body taut. Which was ridiculous. He'd been nothing if not kind, beneficent in fact, given the circumstances. Why was she still on edge? "Um," she said.

"All's well that ends well," he told her. His smile warmed her, relaxed her. It was pure magic. The whole world righted itself in his glow.

"Free lunch?" she asked.

"Thank you."

"My pleasure."

"Can Melody have one, too?"

Melody, Melody? Oh yes, his wife. Lovely, friendly lady. Always happy. Amara liked her. "Sure," Amara said. "What the boss doesn't know won't kill him."

"He'll have a long life then," Bernard quipped.

She laughed and somehow found herself escorting him arm-in-arm to the counter. He'd be first in line when the doors opened.

&

"I've been thinking," Melody said.

Uh-oh. No telling where that would take them.

"About what?" Bernard asked. They were back home, sharing a dinner of take-out tacos and nachos, a meal he found oddly addictive. Maybe it was the week he'd just had. Maybe he needed extra salt and sugar and fat in his diet to make up for, well, everything.

Melody licked her fingers. She made it look so dainty. "Maybe you should get stuck on restaurant balconies more often. It sure was an easy way to get free food."

"It wasn't that easy, love. It involved climbing over railings and swinging in space. And I had to sneak our freebies down to the second floor when Amara wasn't looking."

"Oh, come on, they do that all the time in movies."

"What, swing in space or sneak food out of bistros?"

"Swing, silly. Indiana Jones only had a whip, and he look what he could do."

"He also had special effects and stunt men. It's a lot harder without those."

Melody unwrapped another taco. "I don't see why you're complaining. Those were *great* roast beef sandwiches."

"Yes, but that might be all we get out of this job."

She nibbled at the taco, snagged a corn chip and swirled up some cheese, rolled her eyes in delight as she consumed it. "You'll think of something," she assured him. "You always do."

Her confidence in him was endearing, but it wouldn't get him anywhere near *Rienzi*. He scooped up some nachos, too. The chips were turning soggy. He rather liked them that way, sometimes. "Looks like I'll have to bribe Shawn again. If I can."

"The door in the hall is locked from in the inside," Melody mused. She picked up her cup and swirled the ice.

"Basically."

"And the patio door isn't a door."

"Nope."

"Then there's another way in." She slurped down some cola. "Maybe the air ducts."

Bernard blinked at her. "Air ducts?"

"Yeah, like in the movies."

"Melody, we aren't in a movie. Not Indiana Jones, not any movie."

"Why not?"

"Why *not*?"

"Why not?" She took another nibble of taco before adding, "We *should* be in a movie. Life's better in movies. Much more organized, at least, and with a happy ending." Before Bernard could point out the latter wasn't always the case, she added, "So long as you watch the right movies."

"Gerhard Nachtnebel, Jr. wouldn't wriggle through an air duct," Bernard pointed out. "Not even in a movie."

"Then there's another door," Melody said. "Has to be. Just find it."

"That's why I need Shawn."

Melody studied her half-eaten taco as though the key to the universe was folded within.

Something occurred to Bernard. "Wait a minute, are you saying our life isn't happy?"

She shrugged, put the taco down, picked up her cup.

"You're happy, right?"

She swirled her ice and took another drink.

"You're *unhappy*?"

Melody grinned and winked at him. "Nope."

Bernard gave up. He turned his attention to the last of his meal.

Melody giggled. "Gotcha, didn't I?"

"That wasn't funny." Which it wasn't, not entirely, but he found himself laughing anyway, and then Melody was laughing along with him, and the future and even this job didn't seem quite so bleak anymore.

Chapter 12: Saturday, October 21, 2017

One great thing about Saturdays: you could sleep in. And another: no art classes at the Nachtnebel Arts Foundation. No need to draw horrible sketches, no blather about the genius of your horrible sketches, no hordes of adoring female students drooling over you.

Melody rolled over and into Bernard and nibbled on his ear. That was another great thing about Saturdays. Just Melody and he, cuddled up in bed, nothing to do all day but...

A terrifying screech rattled the windows. Bernard bolted upright. Melody about hit the ceiling.

There it was again, the blood-curdling sound of something being butchered alive.

Melody flopped on her back and stuffed her head under her pillow. "Chris-Chris," she said. It sounded like she was talking through a monster marshmallow, but Bernard got the words.

"It can't be," he said. "It's Saturday."

"Maybe his mom works weekends."

"When *isn't* his mom working?"

"How should I know? C'mere." Melody tossed the pillow aside, grabbed Bernard, and pulled him down on top of her, but to no avail. With each subsequent screech, he became more agitated. Nothing she did could compete with the racket. Until, without warning, the monster across the hall fell silent, and all was bliss once more.

"Finally," Bernard said, taking Melody in his arms again. "Now, what were you—"

The alarm went off.

"What the hell is *that* for?" Bernard bellowed as he scrambled to silence it.

"We gotta go to Celeste's," Melody reminded him.

"Why?"

"So you can draw a naked lady with your eyes closed."

Oh, God, that was right. Olivia O'Leary wanted her very own Bernard Earls sketch of herself in her birthday suit. "I can't do it," he grumbled. "You won't let me look, and she won't be satisfied with random smears of graphite."

Melody rolled out of bed and took his hand. "Oh you of little faith in yourself," she said. "Let's go."

Cleaned up and fed, they drove off to their appointment with destiny, or whatever it was. Soon they were at Celeste's gated and tree-festooned home. Celeste greeted them at the door, her curves seductively draped in a not entirely loose candy-striped dress. Literally. She looked like a candy cane minus the hook. Bernard wondered if Melody would wear such a thing. Which was silly, because of course she would. He made a mental note to add it to her birthday list.

Celeste was all business, though. Straight off, she showed Bernard how to operate the call box and gate, adding, "You probably can't hear a thing. Something went wrong with the wiring."

"No kidding."

She didn't notice the sarcasm. "Yeah, a while ago." She counted on her fingers. "Wow, eight years ago. I didn't realize it had been that long. But that's okay. I don't get many visitors. You know the way to the studio. I'll be upstairs. Just shout when you're ready to go."

That was the last they saw of her that morning.

Bernard and Melody took themselves to the studio, where he surveyed the light as though he knew what he was doing, then positioned a couch, then had Melody do a test recline. "Should I take my clothes off?" she teased.

"I think I can manage this part with them on," he replied. "Later, though, when we're home..."

He nudged the couch this way and that until he had it just right, or what he thought was just right. Then again, his artistic fame was built upon being oblivious to artistic principles, so how would he know? Why did he bother? Why had he even agreed to this?

Who knew. Not him, that was for sure.

At precisely ten o'clock, the call box buzzed and a static-shrouded voice attempted to announce the arrival of someone. It could only be Olivia, so Bernard buzzed her through without question and waited at the open door while an ancient red Camero rattled up the drive. Melody took one look at the car and nearly swooned. Old, sure, but exactly her style: sporty and red.

And then Olivia climbed out, wiggling and jiggling atop a pair of white stilettos, her rainbow hair bouncing about her shoulders, a white clutch in her hand, her dress thin and white and totally unsuited to the cool weather. Indeed, it was translucent, showing off far too much of what lay beneath. Which was nothing but Olivia.

Bernard focused on her hair. That was the only safe part of her.

Melody raised a critical eyebrow at their guest, then she leaned into Bernard and whispered, "I'm gonna find her a coat," and vanished into the house.

Olivia flashed Bernard a seductive smile. "I'm here," she breathed.

"I noticed," he replied. He stepped aside and motioned her in. "This way." He led her to the studio couch. "Before we start," he started, but when he turned to face her, she had started, too. Her dress already piled about her feet, she sat, kicked it away, and undid her shoes. Then she lay back on the sofa, one arm tucked under her hair, her body undulating over the cushions like swells on a wind-swept ocean.

Bernard swallowed. Twice. Maybe three times. Melody would smother Olivia with that coat, if she ever returned with it.

"Don't say a thing," Olivia said. "Just draw."

Bernard fumbled a stool into position, fumbled a pencil into his hand, all but dropped his sketch book while trying to find a blank page. Then he drew. He couldn't avoid looking, not if he was to portray her in even mock semblance, but once he got into a rhythm, he discovered that, oddly, she was just another object, like a roofless house or a tilted balcony or a twisted tree filled with weird creatures, just something to inspire the motion of the pencil in his highly unskilled fingers. He drew and drew. Lines unfurled across the paper, lines and blotches and shading and negative spaces, and Melody didn't return, and Olivia didn't move, not even to bat an eyelash, and he drew and drew and before he knew it, he was dashing off a signature. He set the pencil aside and turned away, utterly drained, mentally, emotionally, physically. He couldn't even tell her he was done.

"You can look now," she said, her voice practically in his ear.

"No," he said. "I can't."

"I'm dressed."

He turned, and son of a gun, she was. Or anyway, as dressed as she had been when she came in. Her chest was eye-level and inches from his face. He leapt to his feet.

"I can't wait to see," Olivia breathed.

Oh. Right. Bernard carefully tore the page from the sketchbook and presented it to her. He didn't look at it himself. Probably it was as much a mess as his sketch of Melody, probably more of a mess, but nobody seemed to care that he couldn't draw a dot without botching it, so it didn't matter.

Olivia gazed at the drawing, eyes wide, not even breathing. And then she chirped, "Oh. My. God. This is sooooooo amazing." She dipped her hand into her clutch and withdrew it, holding a green piece of paper. She handed the paper to Bernard. He took it without looking. Then she kissed him on the cheek and said, "Thank you so much!"

"My pleasure," he mumbled.

"We should do this again sometime."

"Again?"

"Without the art." She kissed him again, closer to his lips, and batted her eyelashes.

Bernard stepped back. "Olivia..."

"Oh, fine," she said. "Be that way. Bye!" She skipped–actually skipped–out of the studio, and before the front door banged shut, she uttered a squeal of delight.

For all of ten seconds, there was dead silence. Bernard felt like something had fallen out of the sky and clonked him on the head, but when he looked about, there were no meteorites or airplane parts or even chunks of plaster on the floor. There was something in his hand, though. Something green.

A hundred dollar bill.

He stared at it as though it was a moldy chunk of cheese. But no, it really was a hundred dollar bill.

"Bernie?" Melody's hand touched his shoulder. He looked up. She locked eyes with him, worried.

Well of course she was. Her husband had just been alone with a naked lady who had come on to him. He took her hands and squeezed them. "Um," he said. He wanted to apologize, but nothing followed.

"Bernie?" she said again. "We have to talk."

He forced out his confession. "I'm sorry. I didn't close my eyes."

"Don't be silly. Nobody can draw with their eyes closed." She pulled one hand free, touched his cheek, and smiled, but her lips quivered as though she was holding in a scream. Something dreadful must have happened, more dreadful than him looking on another woman in the altogether.

"What's wrong?" he asked.

She chewed on a nail. When she answered, her voice was the barest of whispers. "I think we're working for an assassin."

$$\&$$

They didn't speak of it right away. Bernard called up the stairs to tell Celeste they were leaving, then they boarded the Zephyr and made for home. Only once they were well away from Ford's Ford did Melody open up.

"I wasn't looking for a coat," she began. "That was just an excuse. I was snooping."

"Naturally." Bernard gave her a playful wink.

She didn't even crack a smile. "I found Celeste's office in the back of the house, so, you know."

He did indeed. To Melody, an office full of personal goodies was like a nail polish boutique. "So that's why you weren't keeping an eye on me."

Focused on the road, he felt but didn't see her eyes roll heavenward. "Honestly, Bernie, you think I don't trust you?"

He shrugged. "No, but you always tell me to close my eyes."

"That just shows I care."

He wasn't sure how, but whatever.

"Anyway," Melody continued, "now that you're a great artist, you'll probably be drawing naked ladies all the time. I'll just have to live with it."

He hoped not. With luck, he'd portrayed his first and last naked lady. Well, Melody excluded. That would be okay. "What about this office?" Bernard asked to get off the subject of art.

"I found a file folder full of photos."

A nicely alliterative discovery. "Of what?"

"Guys. Mostly old."

"The people or the photos?"

"The photos," Melody said. "Some of the guys, too, but not all of them. There were handwritten notes on the back. Of the photos, not the guys. Names. Death dates. How they died. Bernie..."

Bernard hazarded a look at Melody. Her eyes were wide.

"The names were all German. Some of them were wearing Nazi uniforms. And they were all murdered."

"The names or the men?"

"Don't joke! This is serious!"

Granted. Until now, Bernard had worried about being shot in the head by a Nazi, or the son of a Nazi, anyway. He hadn't considered being shot in the head by Nazi hunter. But that made no sense. How could Celeste possibly be a Nazi hunter? Weren't those all ancient Jewish men bent on bringing war criminals to justice in court? And how could a stolen opera figure in a Nazi hunter's plans?

He reached out and stroked Melody's hair. "Don't worry, love," he said. "Whatever Celeste's up to, I doubt it spells trouble for us. We're just delivering a product."

Melody took his hand in hers and squeezed, but he could tell she didn't believe it. Not for a second.

$$\text{\textflatsharp}$$

The monster was in mid-rampage when they arrived home. Between Melody's disquiet and the screeching—there must have been a whole flock of pterosaurs in Mrs. Clarke's apartment—Bernard lost it. He gave their neighbor's door a beating. The door took it quietly, unlike Chris-Chris, who screeched on and on and on.

Eventually, the portal inched open. "Oh, Mr. Earls!" Mrs. Clarke said. "Are you coming or going?"

"I can't tell," Bernard grumbled, but he couldn't grumble too severely. Poor Mrs. Clarke was trapped inside with that racket. Her suffering must be theirs times twenty.

"I know what you mean. I'm not even sure I slept last night. Chris-Chris is such an early bird. And a night owl. Sometimes I wonder when he sleeps. Of course, when he does, it's like he's been hit on the head."

If Chris-Chris hadn't been a little tyke—and if Mrs. Clarke hadn't been such a sweet lady—Bernard might have considered that option. Alas, circumstances limited his course of action to diplomacy. "Why is he here?" Bernard asked. "It's the weekend."

"His mom got called into the office. Some big emergency. I don't know what." Mrs. Clarke glanced over her shoulder as an ear-piercing squeal erupted. "I'm afraid I'm about at my wits' end. I'm not as young as you, Mr. Earls."

Mr. Earls wasn't sure *he* was as young as Mr. Earls anymore.

Melody took his hand and squeezed. Normally that comforted him, but not where Chris-Chris was concerned. "Will you be okay?" she asked.

"Who?" Bernard asked. "Mrs. Clarke, or me?"

She elbowed him. "Mrs. Clarke of course."

Mrs. Clarke sighed. "I guess I have to be."

"Keep your phone handy," Bernard said. "Call 911 if it gets bad." Time to retreat. He took Melody's hand and tugged her toward their apartment.

Melody tugged back. "We can't abandon Mrs. Clarke," she said. She gave him a severe look. Then she smiled at Mrs. Clarke. "I have an idea. Halloween is coming up. How about we take Chris-Chris to get a pumpkin. That will give you a little break."

Bernard about fainted from fright. "*Take* him! But, but, but..."

Melody nudged him in the ribs again. "Oh, Bernie, don't be such a baby. It's just for a little while, and he'll love it."

Mrs. Clarke looked simultaneously delighted and horrified. Bernard wasn't sure how she did that, but it was an impressive face. "Oh, Mrs. Earls, I couldn't ask you to do that."

"You're not asking, Mrs. Clarke. We're offering. Aren't we, Bernie?" A quick glower accompanied the last three words, precluding any response but an affirmative. Bernard nodded in terror. Melody continued, "I know a farmstand where they sell pumpkins, gourds, corn stalks, decorations, everything. Chris-Chris will love it."

"That's what I'm afraid of," Mrs. Clarke said. "But if you want, and if he wants to go, I won't stop you." She turned. "Chris-Chris!" she called. "Chris-Chris! Come here, sweetie! I have a surprise for you!"

Chris-Chris had a surprise for them, too. He charged up the narrow foyer, screaming like an enraged cheetah, a toy light saber in one hand and a molded triceratops in the other. He ran smack into the door, beat it with both the weapon and the dinosaur, and then froze, looking up into Melody's soft eyes and Bernard's mile-wide ones. He took a step back and tucked his possessions behind him as though these strangers might steal them. Truth be told, Bernard wished he had a light saber of his own. For protection.

"Chris-Chris," Mrs. Clarke said in her most soothing voice. "This is Mr. and Mrs. Earls. They live across the hall from me. They're friends."

Chris-Chris shook his head. Nope. Not friends. No way.

"They're going to buy pumpkins for Halloween. Would you like a pumpkin?"

Chris-Chris nodded. Slightly. Yep. Pumpkin. But not from them.

Melody squatted in front of the boy and smiled that smile nobody could resist.

Chris-Chris gave resistance a good go.

"Want to come with us and get a pumpkin?" Melody asked.

Chris-Chris shook his head.

Then he touched the triceratops to his lips while he thought about it.

Then he dropped his toys, rushed Melody, and about knocked her over with a giant hug.

"Yaaaaaaay!" he shrieked. Right in her ear.

$\flat$

Melody couldn't hear much after that, not for the next half hour anyway, but she put her handicap to good use. Whenever Chris-Chris asked a question or wanted something, she tossed the matter to Bernard for resolution. And there were a lot of requests. Window down. Window up. Candy. Cookies. Ice cream. Water. Window down. Soda. His T-rex, which had fallen on the floor alongside his triceratops and hat and lollipop. Window up. Bernard was about ready to defenestrate the kid, or maybe jump out himself.

Pity. It was a nice day otherwise, with cool air and warm sun, a crystalline sky, light breeze. Lowering the window for Chris-Chris made it a touch chilly, but you rather wanted the windows down on a day like this. A tang of woodsmoke drifted in from somewhere, tickling Bernard's nose. Melody drove this time, but not her Corvette. They couldn't install both the child seat and her husband in there. She'd nabbed Bernard's keys instead, insisting it was her turn to drive. No doubt it was a scheme to escape the duty of managing their precious cargo. She cruised the four-lane state highway like a Nascar driver, weaving through the traffic in Bernard's Linclon Zephyr, Chris-Chris strapped into a child seat in the rear, Bernard twisted about and grunting while trying to retrieve the denizens of Jurassic Park from the floor behind him.

"This isn't how I pictured the afternoon going," he grumbled. There, that object in his hand, was that the T-rex or the lollipop? Both must be equally sticky by now.

"How did you picture it?" Melody purred.

"I can't tell you. A child is present."

"It's okay. He only understands growls and howls."

True, but it was the principle of the thing. Bernard handed Chris-Chris whatever he'd grabbed, who took it with a squeal followed by a demand: "Chocolate shake! Chocolate shake!"

"He understands junk food," Bernard commented. "How did we get roped into this?"

"We didn't get roped. Mrs. Clarke couldn't possibly lasso both of us."

"You know what I mean."

"We volunteered. It was very sweet of us." Melody smiled her sweetest smile.

"Or demented." Bernard snagged the hat from the floor and handed it to Chris-Chris, who snatched it away, dropping T-rex—so that's what the last retrieval had been—in the process.

"Rexieee!" he screamed.

Bernard retrieved Rexie from the floor. Or was that the lollipop?

And so forth and so on, until they arrived at Sunnyhill Farms, a modest farmstand surrounded by a massive dirt parking lot rimmed by orange pumpkin mountains two heads taller than Bernard. Those piles looked dangerous. Pull the wrong pumpkin, and you'd be buried under a gourd avalanche.

A throng of people flowed through the market, carrying pumpkins, decorative gourds, grinning cardboard skeletons, multi-colored corn, and produce of every kind. Most of them were happy, laughing, having the time of their lives. A few looked less pleased. Bernard identified with the grumps. He and Melody corralled Chris-Chris between them, each holding one of his hands. It kept him from running off, but not from launching himself into space and swinging between them. And man, was he ever heavier than he looked.

After tossing the car keys to Bernard, Melody took charge of the operation. She guided them to orange hill after orange hill, picking up and putting down pumpkins, asking the kid's opinion. "Bigger!" he shouted each time. "Bigger!" They must have inspected every pumpkin in the place twice if not three times before she finally settled on a trio of hefty fruits. Bernard got stuck carrying two of them. Melody took the third. That left zero hands to restrain Chris-Chris, but he decided those pumpkins needed close guarding to prevent theft and stuck close to them.

How ironic, Bernard thought. *If anybody here would steal them, it would be us.*

Once the future jack-o-lanterns were paid for and stashed in the Zephyr's trunk, they hit the road, Melody again driving. Bernard had planned to wrest the wheel from her, but she'd picked his pocket while he was loading the produce and once more had control of the keys. It was beyond lunchtime, so they stopped at a Burger Bazaar, where they ordered Ginormous Cajun Fishalayas for themselves and a Cheesy Kiddie Burger Box for Chris-Chris. With a chocolate milkshake. Which the kid tried to dump on his head, but Bernard caught him in the act and prevented catastrophe. The back of his car, though, would never be the same. It was covered in crumbs, French fry shreds, and lollipop goo. At least this would soon be over.

Once again, he really shouldn't have thought that.

&

Melody distributed the three pumpkins thus: one for Chris-Chris to take home, if he ever went home again; one for Mrs. Clarke, to brighten her day; and one for Bernard and herself. Dropping off the latter at their door, they took the other two into Mrs. Clarke's apartment and placed them with due ceremony on the dining room table. They looked festive against the dark wood, and Mrs. Clarke did indeed beam with pleasure, for all of a minute. Then her joy turned to consternation.

"Oh my, I just thought of something," she said. She wrang her hands. For real. Bernard didn't think anybody actually did that.

"What's that?" Melody said in her most soothing tone.

Chris-Chris roared down the hall, Rexie in one hand, the triceratops in the other, and plunged into the guest room, where it sounded like a duel to the death ensued.

Mrs. Clarke held out her hands. They quivered a little. "I can't possibly carve a pumpkin anymore."

How, Bernard wondered, could she be such a good cook if she couldn't wield a blade?

Melody, though, purred sympathy. "Don't worry," she said. "Bernard is a master pumpkin carver. In fact, he's an artist."

He leaned into her and whispered, "Don't start with the art thing."

"Everyone in class says you are," she whispered back.

"Everyone class is psychotic."

She nudged him in the ribs. "Let's get to work. Chris-Chris! Pumpkin carving time!"

Somehow still alive, Rexie and triceratops roared out of the bedroom and back to the table, dragging Chris-Chris along for the ride.

Fortunately, the little demon had more artistic sense than Bernard and was happy to have his jack-o-lantern feature triangle eyes, a triangle nose, and a grin with triangular teeth. Bernard could draw and cut those without trouble. And of greater moment, without losing a finger. Mrs. Clark was another story. She sketched a goofy-looking face with tiny pupils inside of large eyeballs inside of huge eye sockets, and a lopsided grin filled with teeth so perfect, a dentist would admire them. Carving proved a challenge, because the teeth and the eyeballs were—by Mrs. Clarke's explicit instructions—to be made by stripping the pumpkin of its orange rind, revealing the pale meat of the fruit.

Worst of all, Bernard did a creditable job, which led Mrs. Clarke to exclaim, "You're a genius, Mr. Earls! A true artist with a knife!"

Good thing he loathed violent crime. Her accolade might have been mistaken for something else. "I'm not an artist, Mrs. Clarke. I just have a steady hand."

"Listen to that," Melody said, leaning toward Mrs. Clarke as though sharing a confidence. "He's so modest."

While carving was in progress, Chris-Chris staged a dinosaur battle that ranged all over the apartment and drew in additional contestants, including a molded iguana, a stuffed panda, a soldier action figure, and a naked, decapitated fashion doll in a dump truck. Bernard thought the kid was probably too young for the latter. The naked fashion doll, not the dump truck. Somehow, Mrs. Clarke cajoled him to join them for jack-o-lantern lighting. They turned out the lights, closed the curtains, lit the candles, and gazed in wonder at their creations.

Chris-Chris managed four seconds of wonder before emitting a high-pitched scream and running off to rejoin the battle.

Mrs. Clarke sighed. "I love him to death," she said. "But I do hope I get tomorrow to myself."

So did Bernard.

For the third time, he really shouldn't have thought that.

&

Back in their apartment, Bernard deposited their pumpkin on the table. Dinner time was approaching, and he had zero desire to perform further feats of artistry. Carving could wait until tomorrow. Right now, he had to convince Shawn to break the rules yet again. It wouldn't be easy. Bernard broke the rules all the time, so it didn't seem a big deal to him, but Shawn had more scruples, or at least better reasons to play by the book. A good nine-to-five job. Felicity. Not getting shot in the head by the maniac son of a Nazi.

Okay, Bernard shared that last reason, along with (apparently) not getting shot in the head by his own employer, but Melody reveled in rule-breaking, at least when it involved light fingers, and the prospect of a nine-to-five job revolted Bernard. He loved the freelancer lifestyle. So he put the question to Melody: "How do we get Shawn to turn over the floorplan?"

"Oh, that's easy," Melody replied.

Bernard waited, but she didn't expound. "Yeah?"

"Yeah."

Still no details were forthcoming. "How?"

"Invite them over for food and games."

Okay, Bernard was lost, but he was used to that. "Let's do it, then," he said with more enthusiasm than he felt.

Melody called Felicity's cell number and put it on speaker so Bernard could hear. ("But don't say anything," she warned. "You'll just mess it up."). After some quick pleasantries, she got down to business. "Why don't you guys come over for dinner? I'll throw together something and Shawn can bring his *Star Trek Wars Trivial Pursuit.*"

"*Star Trek*?" Felicity asked. "Or *Star Wars*?"

"Both. Tomorrow's Sunday. We can stay up late."

"So long as Chris-Chris does, too," Bernard mumbled.

"Quiet," Melody whispered back.

"What was that?" Felicity asked. "I didn't catch it."

"Nothing, just Bernard. You know him."

"Oh, yeah, him."

The women giggled together, and that was that. The plan was in motion.

"What do you mean, you know him?" Bernard asked.

"Just girl talk," Melody replied.

In that case, he didn't want to know.

Melody slipped into the kitchen and got to work, and by the time Shawn and Felicity arrived, she'd prepared tuna salad and pineapple sandwiches cut into neat triangles, a plate of veggies with a tub of ranch dressing in the middle, and lemon iced tea.

Shawn was suitably dressed in one of his faded *Star Trek* t-shirts and an old pair of jeans, while Felicity had dolled herself up. She wore a pink dress with yellow flowers and had her hair pulled back in a ponytail secured by a pink scrunchie.

"Thanks for having us over," Shawn said. He placed the games on the table. When he spotted the food, his eyes glittered.

"Don't mention it," Bernard said. "We figured after a week like this, we could all use a break."

"Our week was fine," Felicity informed him. "We made a thousand dollars." She selected a sandwich and sampled it. Her eyes rolled in delight. "Oh, Melody, this is *amazing*!"

Melody beamed. "Thank you! I got the recipe off the Internet. It's the first time I've tried it."

"I'd tell you about my week," Bernard said, "but you don't want to know."

"I do," Shawn said.

"No, you want to play trivia games."

"But—"

"Baby," Felicity scolded. "Let's not talk shop right now. Time for that later." She raised an eyebrow in Bernard's direction. Clearly, she suspected what was coming. That woman was too clever for her own good. But she was right. They needed to lull Shawn into a false sense of security first. They set up the game and ate and played, around mouthfuls of food answering deep questions like "What type of dog was the inspiration for Chewbacca?"

Shawn won three games out of three in what Bernard figured must be record time, a mere three hours. By then, Melody had served up glasses of cheap white wine, which was fine because everyone in the party was accustomed to the cheap end of the spectrum by necessity.

"Ah," Bernard said as he sampled the bouquet. "Domaine de la Romanée Conti Montrachet 2000. An excellent choice, my love."

Melody giggled and clinked glasses with him.

Felicity eyed her drink with suspicion. "Domain what?"

"Domaine de la Romanée Conti Montrachet 2000," Bernard repeated. "Quite the steal at a mere ten thousand. I didn't ask how Melody managed that."

Alas, Shawn had already taken a sip. He spat it all over the game board. "*What?*"

"Hey!" Felicity grabbed a napkin and mopped up the droplets. "You just spewed five hundred dollars' worth! Stick out your tongue. I'll wring out the napkin onto it."

Ambushed by laughter, Melody nearly spilled her own glass. Bernard deftly relieved her of it. "Calm down," he told his guests. "You know we can't afford anything close to that."

Shawn had grabbed another napkin and was dabbing the faded remains of the starship Enterprise on his t-shirt. "Then why did you say it?"

"Get with the program. If we can't have luxury, we can at least pretend."

Once the merriment subsided and everyone had drained one glass and was working on a second, Bernard was ready to broach the subject of the next assault on the mansion of the maniac spawn of a Nazi, but Felicity beat him to it. With a wink at Melody, she said, "Let's hear about your rotten week, Bernard."

Bernard told them all about the fake restroom, the dead-locked door in the hall, and the fake balcony door. Well, not *all* about it. He didn't bother explaining why someone might have a fake restroom, although both Shawn and Felicity looked plenty confused on that point. Fortunately, it's not as easy as you might think to formulate a rational query on such a subject, so Bernard talked right by it, focusing on the need to find a way inside.

"Uh," Shawn finally asked. "Why?"

In fact, that had a lot to do with why someone might have a fake restroom, but Bernard had a deflection prepared: "It's a test," he said.

"Your weasel test almost got me arrested," Shawn pointed out.

"But it didn't," Bernard countered. "It got you a great job, instead."

"Now look–"

Dollar signs glittering in her eyes, Felicity cut in. "What do you need us to do?"

We, huh? She hadn't put it that way before. Interesting. Bernard set his glass on the end table and leaned back, channeling some high-powered CEO about to give marching orders to a global company. "I've been tasked with finding a way in, if one exists."

Felicity beamed at Bernard. "Sounds expensive." She focused her radiance on Shawn and whispered, "Sounds expensive, baby."

Shawn made a face not too remote from a pug glowering at a moldy bone. "You're saying you want the floorplan."

Bernard shrugged. "That could help, I suppose." He sounded so noncommittal, he almost believed he didn't care.

"No way. All of Fitzroy's most sensitive stuff is stored on an internal network. It's not connected to the Internet, and all the print jobs on that network get logged." He took a modest gulp of fake high-end wine. "Way, way too dangerous."

"Good," Felicity said. "Ten thousand."

Here we go again, Bernard grumbled to himself.

Melody leaned forward. "Honey," she told Felicity, "we don't have that kind of money."

"You had it for the wine."

"That was just Bernie daydreaming."

The women glanced at Bernard, Melody with an affectionate smile, Felicity with cold calculation. "So's this," Felicity said, "if he doesn't pony up."

"Shawn," Bernard said. "You don't need the Internet or a printer, just a pen and some paper."

Shawn blinked at Bernard. "Huh?"

"Make a written copy of the floorplan. The relevant parts, anyway. I don't need the whole thing."

"Write?" Shawn gasped as though Bernard had suggested killing somebody.

"Yeah, didn't they teach you that in school?"

Maybe they hadn't. Shawn made that pug face again. "That's totally retro," he mumbled. "But I guess that could work. So long as they don't search me when I leave for the day."

Everyone stared at him. Why, Bernard wondered, would they search him? Was that even legal?

"They're very military," Shawn explained. "Their site security is based on DoD protocols."

Which was going to cost Bernard something extra, he supposed. "Okay, how about another two hundred." That gave him room to negotiate with Felicity.

"Five thou," she countered.

Room that he needed. "Three hundred."

"One grand?"

"I'm running out of spare change as it is," Bernard said. "Four hundred?"

"Fine, five hundred, but not a penny less."

"Deal."

Shawn didn't look too upset this time. Maybe he was getting into the spirit of the adventure. In fact, when he met Felicity's sparkling eyes, he almost smiled along with her. Almost. But then, the pug face resurfaced. "Wait a minute," he said.

Bernard slumped. "What now?"

"What's *in* that restroom, anyway?"

"Melody my love," Bernard said in his most gracious tone. "How about some more wine for our distinguished guests?"

Chapter 13: Sunday, October 22, 2017 flyover, then Monday at ground level

Sunday was glorious. No noise from across the hall. No noise from next door. Sparkling blue sky, neither too cold nor too warm. Just right, like baby bear's porridge in the Goldilocks tale. Bernard and Melody slept in, took their time getting out of bed, and having nothing to do, luxuriated in a day of family time which, since they had no children, primarily involved activities better left to the imagination.

Monday, though, was another story. The howler monkey was back at six thirty A.M. sharp. After Bernard peeled himself off the ceiling, metaphorically speaking, and after Melody consented, a half hour later, to crawl out from under the pillow her head had burrowed beneath, they rose (sort of) and stumbled through breakfast and a shower and dressing, by which time the howler monkey had morphed through elephant, T-rex, lion, murder victim, and something oddly like a hyperthyroid choo-choo train.

"That kid has talent," Bernard grumbled as, against his will, he donned his best suit and a black tie. He didn't mind dressing up, but it was way too early for formal gear. The private viewing at the Nachtnebel mansion started at eleven, and even given the hour, hour and a half drive there, they had time to kill. But they wanted to get on the road before Bernard came any closer to killing something other than time. Like a hyperthyroid choo-choo train.

"Voice talent," Melody agreed. "He might have a great career in radio advertising."

"If he does, I'm never tuning in again."

"Then how will you get free music?"

"There are apps for that."

Melody had just finished tying the black bow on her skin-tight white dress and was examining herself in the full-length mirror on the back of the bedroom door. "They have ads," she pointed out.

"So does the radio."

"But you can change channels until you find music."

"Fine. I'll swear off music forever." Bernard presented himself to her for inspection. "How do I look?"

"How do *I* look?" Melody did a runway turn for him.

"Like the most beautiful thing in the universe, which you are. How do I look?"

"You don't think it's a bit much?"

"Why would I think that?"

Melody gave herself another once-over. "People are supposed to be looking at the art."

"Oh, they will be."

She reached back for his hand. He gave it to her, and she pulled him to the mirror. They stood, side-by-side, arms about each other. "Hmm," she said.

"What's wrong?"

"Nothing."

"That's what I thought."

Across the hall, Chris-Chris shrieked like he'd been dropped off a tall building. The shriek lasted and lasted and lasted, so the building must've been the Burj Khalifa in Dubai, although how a kid that little could be heard from the other side of the world was a mystery. Well, no, it wasn't.

Melody pursed her lips. "It's just...maybe we're *too* perfect."

Bernard kissed her on the cheek. "Of course we are. Let's go before we ruin it by suffering permanent hearing loss."

They stepped into the hall at a quarter to nine, well ahead of schedule. Bernard had barely locked the deadbolt when Mrs. Clarke's door opened and emitted a terrifying growl. Bernard and Melody about jumped out of their clothes, which in Melody's case would have been quite a feat given how that dress hugged her body.

"Oh, Mrs. Earls!" Mrs. Clarke wailed. "I was just coming to see you."

That she had addressed Melody wasn't lost on Bernard. This was going to be terrible.

Melody gently folded Mrs. Clarke's hands in hers. "What's the trouble?" she cooed.

"It's Chris-Chris. I hate to admit it, Mrs. Earls, but I think I'm about to go mad!"

"You aren't the only one," Bernard muttered. He must've spoken louder than he thought, because Melody fired a warning glance across his bow. He zipped his lip.

"He is quite loud this morning," Melody sympathized. "But there must be something we can do. What usually calms him down?"

Duct tape, Bernard thought.

"I really don't know," Mrs. Clarke said. "I can't take much more of this."

Melody gave Mrs. Clarke a hug. "Maybe you should call his mother."

"I tried, but it goes to voice mail. She might be in a meeting. She spends most of her day in meetings."

"What about his father?"

"He's in Alaska."

"Oh my. When's he coming back?"

"He isn't. He ran off six months after Chris-Chris was born."

Smart move, Bernard didn't tell them.

Unfortunately, Melody sensed it and grazed him with her darkest look. "Isn't there anyone who could take him for a while? Just to give you a break?"

Mrs. Clarke didn't answer with words, but the look she gave Melody suggested her hope rested entirely upon two people. Only they, out of the entire population of the world, could rescue a feeble great-grandmother from her hyperactive great-grandson.

"We can't right now," Melody said. "We're just on our way to a black tie event." She turned and fiddled with Bernard's tie for emphasis.

"Oh," Mrs. Clarke said. "Oh, my. I hadn't noticed you were all dressed up. Silly me. What sort of event is it?"

"An art exhibit."

"Oh. Oh dear. You're right, we shouldn't let Chris-Chris anywhere near one of those."

At least she hadn't lost *all* her marbles. Not yet, although Bernard wondered how much longer she could maintain a grip on the few that remained.

Stepping backwards through her door, Mrs. Clarke sighed and looked at her shoes. "I don't know how I'll manage, but I guess I must."

Melody took her hands again. "I expect we'll be home before three o'clock," she said. "Maybe we could take him for a while this afternoon. To give you a small break, anyway."

Mrs. Clarke melted with relief. "Oh, Mrs. Earls," she beathed. "You're a saint, an absolute saint."

Bernard had had enough of sainthood. It was too hard on the ears, for one thing. But Melody nearly killed him with her next warning glance, so he said nothing.

When Mrs. Clarke was once more closed in with the howler monkey, who had expressed his joy at being reunited with his great-grandmother by emitting a particularly piercing howl, Melody slipped her arm around Bernard and escorted him down the hall to the stairs.

Although it likely wasn't safe to speak yet, he risked it. "That was kind of you," he said.

"Uh-huh," she muttered.

"Reckless. Nearly suicidal. But kind."

"Uh-huh."

"But let's not think about that until later."

"Uh-huh."

They descended the stairs, emerged into the brilliant morning sun, and made their way to Bernard's Zephyr. He helped her in, then assumed the driver's seat and started the engine.

"Bernie?" she said.

"Yes, love?"

"Why didn't you talk me out of it?"

"You would've elbowed me."

She inspected her perfectly polished red fingernails. "But now we *really* have to suffer."

That was an understatement. Maybe he should have accepted the pummeling. Except for one thing. "I never win an argument with you. Not that kind, anyway."

"Oh. Right." Melody dropped her hands into her lap and looked out the window. "Sometimes I hate being so perfect."

"I know," Bernard said in his most consoling tone. "It's a burden we both must bear."

$\oint$

Once more unto the evil arts empire, if evil it was. At the least, it was built upon ill-gotten gains. Bernard wondered why he could never pull off a stunt like that. His own ill-gotten gains always went to keep the roof over their heads and food on their table. Why was it always the people with Nazi fathers who ascended to the summits of wealth?

The invitees gathered at the public entrance on the west, where the morning shadows chilled them. The weather app called for temperatures near seventy later on, but low sixties prevailed at the moment, with a stiff breeze stiff that made it feel far colder. Twenty-five people had congregated, fifteen shivering women in beautiful dresses much like Melody's and nothing but elegant wraps to keep their shoulders warm, ten men in suits that looked snappy and felt cozy. Clearly, fashion continued to oppress women, despite whatever strides society might have taken toward equality. Bernard pulled Melody close and did his best to transfer heat to her without raising eyebrows.

The doors opened at nine o'clock sharp. The guests filed in, passing the cherry reception desk and gathering in a messy semi-circle about a woman in the Foundation's red and grey uniform. Last week, she'd been one of the ticket takers. Another female employee closed and locked the doors behind, preventing stragglers from gaining admittance. Bernard hadn't checked the class schedule, but the mansion brooded in silence, so Nachtnebel must have been taking a day off from harvesting registration fees.

The uniformed women smiled in silence. After three minutes of that, Bernard began to wonder if they'd turned to stone. If he rapped on one of their foreheads, what would it sound like? Fortunately, before he could perform the experiment, a door on their left opened, and the great man himself strode through.

Close up, Gerhardt Nachtnebel, Jr. looked no different than from far away. In his sixties, bald, bespectacled, light glinting from those gold wire frames. He smiled and shook hands with a few of the guests, including Allegra Fumagalli, who Bernard hadn't previously noticed. She was the shortest in the group and thus well hidden.

Once Nachtnebel had greeted his most special guests, he addressed everyone.

"Welcome! I'm excited to see you all here today. I don't often conduct tours of my private collection. What you are about to see includes treasures so valuable, it would be imprudent to reveal them to the public. Therefore, I must ask you to sign a non-disclosure agreement. Also, no photography or video recording of any kind is permitted. We ask that you check your cell phones with us before we begin. Phones will be placed in lockboxes, and you will be given the keys. No sketching, either. I won't confiscate your pens, but don't let me catch you drawing."

He chuckled at that last remark, and most of the others snickered along with him. Melody looked puzzled. Bernard could almost hear her asking, *Who would draw with a pen? You can't erase your mistakes.*

They were herded into the room from which Nachtnebel had appeared. It barely contained them. Probably it was pressed into service for small group instruction on other occasions. A dozen desks with attached chairs were arranged in three rows of four, something like a high school classroom. A bank of cell phone lockboxes stood along the back wall. It wasn't fixed to the wall, so Bernard wondered if it had been brought in just for this occasion. He couldn't imagine why students' phones would have to be locked away during class.

The guests exchanged their phones for keys and were handed documents and black pens. They each found a desk, read through the fine print—it was all fine print—and signed. The terms were simple if verbose. It was, in essence, a legal gag stuffed down their throats to prevent them from revealing to anyone, under any circumstances, for the rest of their lives, what they were about to see.

Perfect, Bernard thought. Nachtnebel was about to rub their noses in daddy's stolen goods, exactly as Bernard had hoped. He signed without hesitation. Melody took a few moments to process everything, then she signed, too, a gleam in her eye. Bernard knew she was dreaming of that cedar chest she'd been drooling over.

Formalities dispatched, Nachtnebel led the group up the grand staircase to the third floor, then marched them to the door connecting the public and private wings of the mansion. He turned to face them like Gene Wilder as Willy Wonka about to admit the children to his factory. The fake restrooms sat inconspicuously on their left.

"Beyond this door..." Nachtnebel thumbed over his shoulder. "...lies my family's residence. My private collection is housed there, to ensure security. Nobody entering the public areas of the mansion has access to it."

That was for sure. Bernard had already tried. Twice.

"I should warn you that some of what you will see may shock you. These are art treasures long presumed to be lost. You may wonder why I don't reintroduce them to the art world. It's quite simple. Although they came to me legitimately, they have a checkered history. It would be difficult to reveal their existence without incurring massive legal liabilities."

He winked. The rascal actually winked. Bernard grudgingly gave him full points for chutzpah and hoped Natchnebel would be insulted by such application of a Yiddish term.

Blocking the keypad with his body, Nachtnebel entered a security code. The door clicked open. He led them into his private residence, but not too far, only to the first door on the left, same side as the fake restrooms. Another keypad secured that door. Once through, they found themselves in a space about the size of three ordinary bedrooms. Track lighting illuminated paintings adorning the walls and *objets d'art* perched on white pedestals that were molded like Doric columns. The guests dispersed through the little gallery, gasping and oohing and aahing.

Bernard and Melody circulated, too, pausing for a suitable time to study each item. Not being half a percent the artist Allegra Fumagalli thought, Bernard recognized nothing, not a painting, not a sculpture, nothing.

"Boooooooring," Melody whispered in his ear.

"You can say that again," he whispered back. "No *Rienzi*. No music at all."

One detail wasn't boring. Not an item in the collection but a door. A door on the west side of the room, painted the same dull white as the walls, so unremarkable as to be nearly invisible save the security keypad by its side. Bernard mapped the layout in his head. What could be beyond the white door? Unless it was a storage closet—and why would that be secured?—it could only be the fake restrooms. This was the other way in Melody had deduced. She'd been right: the deadlocked restroom doors and the false patio door screamed the existence of another entrance, and here it was.

But how to get in? Bernard's eyes wandered the paintings and, just by accident, the security cameras above. There sure were a lot of them. All angles were covered, including that white door. Another job for Shawn, although Bernard had no idea yet what that job would be. The gallery had no windows, so no possible balcony entrance. If a balcony was out there, it would be another fake. Shawn might be able to get him the security codes, but waltzing into the private residence would be risky. He needed to ponder this.

The guests spent an hour marveling at Nachtnebel's treasures before their host herded them back to the public wing and into the bistro, which had gone formal with white table clothes, flowers and candles, water goblets filled with mineral water, bone China place settings, and silver utensils. Real silver. Bernard wouldn't have minded pinching four sets of those. They could use them when Shawn and Felicity came over for dinner. But no, that wouldn't have been prudent. Guests eating with their fingers would be noticed.

They were seated with Allegra Fumagalli and three total strangers. One was an older fellow in a burgundy suit and loud shirt which somehow managed to clash with his black tie. Bernard would have to ask Melody how that could happen. Wasn't black supposed to go with everything? The other two were a pair of forty-something women in black dresses with white bows, the mirror image of Melody's outfit. Allegra introduced the trio as Simeon Frankenberry, Chloe Cail, and Adsila. Just Adsila, which Allegra pronounced "add-SEE-lah."

"How pretty!" Melody said. "I've never heard that name before."

The complement all but melted Adsilah. "It's Iroquois," she said. "It means blossom."

"Oh, are you Iroquois?"

"Maybe a few percent. Nobody knows for sure. There's a story about one of my ancestors getting horribly lost and almost dying in a dense forest in Pennsylvania before he was found by Iroquois hunters and taken to their village. Supposedly they nursed him back to health, he fell in love with one of the young women in the village, and they had about a dozen kids. But some in the family say it's total fiction." Adsilah shrugged. "I picked Adsilah for my professional name because I thought it was cool."

"And do the rest of you use pseudonyms for your artwork?" Bernard asked. It seemed a good ice-breaker, but as soon as it was out of his mouth, he realized his mistake.

"Who would pick Frankenberry as a pseudonym?" Simeon grumbled. "It's bad enough as a real name."

Bernard took a sip of his water.

"Wouldn't be so bad," Simeon continued, "if they hadn't invented that ridiculous cereal. Even without that, you wouldn't believe the number of times I've been called Frankenstein."

"People can be so annoying," Melody sympathized. She gave Bernard a sharp glance.

"You *could* use a pseudonym, Simeon," Chloe said. "I've given you about a thousand to pick from."

"Each as bad as Frankenberry."

"You're just a curmudgeon, that's your problem."

"Of course I am, and my art reflects it. At least my own name fits my persona."

Allegra watched the exchange, amused. When things finally quieted down, she said, "I do so love the company of other artists. Makes one feel young."

Bernard got an entirely different feeling, but he kept it to himself. Anyway, he had work to do. "What did you all think of the exhibit?" he asked.

Melody yawned and patted her mouth. Nobody but Bernard seemed to realize that was what she thought of it.

Allegra picked up her glass. "I was interested in *your* impressions, Bernard."

He hadn't come to form impressions. He'd come to steal something. "I'm admittedly not well-studied in art history, so I didn't recognize anything. I sensed, though, that the exhibit was part of something larger. Part of a performance, maybe. Suspense. Menace. Even, if I may put it this way..."

He raised an eyebrow at Allegra. She motioned him to continue. "Evil."

Everyone shivered. The word almost sent a chill down his own spine.

In the silence that followed, servers came to the table and set Caesar salads before each of them, then withdrew.

Chloe leaned forward and whispered, "Everyone knows it's stolen art. Gerhard's father was a Nazi soldier. That's why he made us sign that nondisclosure agreement. There are rumors, but if it got out exactly what's stashed in there, there'd be an uproar. He'd be investigated, might even to go prison. At the very least, he'd lose the collection."

"Ah," Bernard said. "That explains why he shot at his landscapers. And a roofer. And a pizza delivery guy."

"Shot at them?" Allegra laughed loud enough to draw attention from the other tables. "Where did you hear that?"

"Rumors."

"No, Gerhard's a sweetheart. I doubt he even owns a gun."

Simeon harrumphed.

"You think he'd shoot at someone?" Adsilah gasped, but not in horror. More like delight.

"Oh, hell yes," Simeon said. "Look at that guy funny, and he's likely to take you out. Besides, that roofer wasn't a roofer. He was a thief, trying to break in from above." He pointed upward. "There are maintenance accesses up there. If it were my place, I'd sure shoot anyone who tried to get in that way. Or any other way, for that matter."

"Don't be ridiculous," Allegra said.

"I mean it. I would."

"I know *you* would. But not Gerhard. Besides, how would a thief get up there in the first place?"

Simeon looked like he was about to take a bite out of someone's nose. "How would I know? I'm not a thief."

Bernard made a mental note to ask Shawn about those maintenance accesses. He'd seen them during the fly-by on the Foundation's website but hadn't given them much thought.

Because Simeon had a point. Bernard was a thief, and even he wasn't sure how to get up there.

Not yet.

Chapter 14: Later Monday, October 23, 2017

Chris-Chris was in full T-rex mode. They could hear the roar as soon as they entered the stairwell on the first floor.

"Why hasn't anybody called the cops?" Bernard asked Melody.

Melody gaped at him. "That would be terrible, Bernie! Calling the cops on a little kid just because he thinks he's a dinosaur!"

"He's not a kid, he's a menagerie of all organisms living and extinct that ever made a sound over a hundred twenty decibels."

"He's just a little boy."

"A little boy who's violating every noise abatement ordinance in three states."

They trudged up the steps, avoiding discussion of what would happen next courtesy of Melody's rash offer to take the little beast under her wing for a while. Okay, God knew Mrs. Clarke needed a break, but it wouldn't be much of a break. She'd have to vacate the premises, and probably the county, to escape the racket.

They halted before Mrs. Clarke's door, petrified by the terrible screams within. Something was being dismembered by the T-rex. Chris-Chris was managing both sounds all by his lonesome. The kid would have a great career with a Hollywood sound studio, if he lived long enough.

"Okay," Bernard said, resigned to his fate. "Let's get him out of here."

Melody raised her hand to knock. "Out of the apartment or the building? Or Aschimos?"

An idea sprang from the dark recesses of Bernard's devious brain. "Sunshade Park. Isn't there a playground there?"

"Oh yes, that would be perfect. Nobody ever goes there."

Exactly. Tucked between a small industrial park and derelict shopping center abandoned by all tenants save one—a fairly horrid but stunningly cheap pizza joint—Sunshade could only be accessed from a side street that led from nowhere to nowhere else. Bernard wasn't sure why they'd hidden a public recreation area there, but at least Chris-Chris could scream his head off without bothering anyone. Anyone but his chaperones.

Melody knocked. The dinosaur battle raged on. Mrs. Clarke didn't appear. She knocked harder without result. Bernard took over and pounded on the door, which did the trick. Mrs. Clarke opened it a crack, gazed in relief upon her saviors, and undid the chain. "Oh, Mr. and Mrs. Earls. I was afraid it was the police."

"Just us," Melody assured her. "We'll take your little bundle of joy to the park."

Mrs. Clarke put her hand to her forehead. "Thank goodness. His mother should be here around four thirty. If you can last an hour and a half and have him back by then, you'll have my eternal gratitude." She left the door open while she fetched Chris-Chris. Her voice was drowned in the maelstrom of sound stirred up by her great-grandson, but the message must've gotten through, because the death duel morphed into cheering. The kid rushed into the foyer and threw himself at Melody, wrapping himself around her knees. She only stayed upright thanks to Bernard's steadying hands on her shoulders.

Thereupon followed the longest ninety minutes of Bernard's life. The drive to the park felt like a cross-country road trip, what with the dinosaur battle in the back seat. Once at their destination, they pointed Chris-Chris toward the playground, where foam rubber mulch formed a springy bed beneath swings, a slide, monkey bars, a carousel, a seesaw, and a climber built like a castle with round and rectangular holes, ladders, and tunnels. The kid performed his entire repertoire of savagery at the top of his lungs. Nobody heard. Nobody but Bernard and Melody, who sat on a bench near enough to keep watch, but not near enough to go more than half deaf.

Bernard occupied himself with work to take his mind off the screeching and snarling. "The more I think about it," he told Melody, "the more I think the roof is the solution."

Melody frowned at the trees edging the park. "There isn't a roof," she said. "Just leaves."

"At Nachtnebel's place."

"Oh. Why not just go through the connecting door?"

"Someone might see. Shawn can deactivate the cameras, but he can't stop nosey family members wandering the halls. And don't forget Brian Garfunkel. We know his schedule for the public wing, but we don't know what he does with the rest of his time."

"Probably watches GoofTube videos," Melody suggested. "But that roof. That looks tricky. Can you climb it?"

"Most likely. The service entrances are up there. I just need to figure out how. Once we're done babysitting little Lucifer, I'll study that drone footage. Plus, I'm willing to bet those doors are easy pickings. The harder they are to reach, the less likely they'll be heavily secured."

Melody dug in her purse and came up with some spearmint chewing gum. She offered a stick to Bernard, then popped one in her mouth. "You hope it's hard to get up there so it will be easy to get inside?"

Bernard leaned back and savored the mint flavor. "Something like that."

"Men make no sense."

He wasn't going to rise to that bait.

Chris-Chris let out a Tarzan cry, followed by a lion roar, a howler monkey howl, and a T-rex "time for dinner" bellow.

"However hard it is," Bernard said, "it'll be a piece of cake after this job."

Melody shook her head. "I won't have energy to bake a cake when we get home. Let's pick one up at the store."

"Chocolate?"

"Chocolate."

"Ice cream?"

"Moose tracks."

"Deal." Bernard offered her his hand. She shook it, then he lifted it to his mouth and began kissing her, from her fingers, over her wrist, up her arm to her shoulders, and finally her cheek and her lips. All thought of roofs, stolen art, Nazis, and dinosaurs faded into oblivion. There was nothing but the two of them for thirty-two seconds, thirty-two glorious seconds that seemed like eternity.

Then a screech owl screeched in their ears, and they nearly did a synchronized backflip off the bench.

"Ewwwww!" Chris-Chris cried. "Stop that!" He stood two feet in front of them, little fists planted on his scrawny hips, matronly rebuke in his little brown eyes.

Bernard scowled his father's warning scowl. "Don't knock it until you've tried it."

Melody elbowed him. "Bernie! He's too young to try it." She leaned forward and touched Chris-Chris on the shoulder. "Sorry. We didn't know you were watching."

"I'm *always* watching you, Wazazazki!" the kid screamed, then he bolted for the playground, flailing his hands over his head, squealing at the top of his lungs. A flock of starlings abandoned the treetops in alarm, swirling away over the industrial park like a roiling black cloud.

"Who's Wazazazki?" Bernard asked.

Melody shrugged. "Probably someone in a kid's movie."

Checking the time on his cell phone, Bernard sighed. "Forty-three minutes and twenty-seven seconds to go," he said. "After that, I can kiss you again."

"No," Melody corrected. "After that, we get the cake and ice cream, then we have dinner and dessert."

"And *then* can I kiss you?"

Melody slid against him and rested her head on his shoulder. Chris-Chris must have forgotten to watch Wazazazki just then, because he didn't object. "For starters," she said.

$$\oint$$

Except there was one other item on the agenda. Chris-Chris had been handed off to his mother. Cake and ice cream had been procured. Dinner—a ready-made lasagna from the frozen foods aisle—was prepared and eaten. Dessert was in progress when Bernard opened his laptop and did the Nachtnebel Foundation fly-around once more, spending considerable time on the roof sequence and views of all possible approaches to that flat area where the ugly mechanical stuff was tucked away.

Aside from getting up there, something else niggled at him. Which service entrance to use? That depended on where they led. The treasure room lay almost dead center, just a hair to the west, while the gallery that led to it lay a tad to the east. Based on his memory of the rooms' dimensions, he figured there would be a staircase very close to the gallery. But how close? The roof route might present the same problem as the connecting door.

Shawn would have to provide that intel with the floorplan, so Bernard set it aside for now and reflew the fly-around. He quickly spotted a curious feature just below both service entrances. On the east and the west, near each end of the flat section, a barely-visible ladder ascended from a third-floor balcony to the roof.

He showed Melody the footage. "Piece of cake," he said.

She cut him another slice and put it on his plate. "That's your last tonight. I don't want you getting fat and falling off that ladder."

Sometimes their little misunderstandings had benefits. For a cake bought from a store in Aschimos, this one wasn't half bad.

"Shawn owes me a floorplan," he said. "But barring any surprises, I think we've got it."

Melody looked at him over the rim of her glasses. Not that she wore glasses, but if she did, that's what she would have been doing. "Bernie. Your plans are full of surprises."

Sadly, she was right, but he couldn't let that dampen his spirits. They needed a twenty-thousand-dollar win. "This time will be different," he said. But the words were scarcely out of his mouth before his brain chastised him: *You really shouldn't have said that.*

Melody raised an eyebrow. Then that yummy cake occupied her for a bit, until she looked up, puzzled.

"What?" Bernard asked.

"Why does Celeste want this song so bad?"

"Opera."

"Which is just a bunch of songs."

More or less. Either way, Bernard never meddled in the motivations of his employers. That could only lead to trouble.

But now that she'd started to wonder, Melody wasn't about to let it drop. "If she's hunting Nazis, why not expose his whole secret collection? And if not, well, like you told Dolley, nobody wants to be famous for stealing a stolen relic. What could she possibly do with it? Maybe..."

Uh-oh. When Melody assumed that look of concentration, there was no telling where it might lead. "I don't think we want to know, love," Bernard said. "So long as we get paid and our involvement doesn't make the news."

"I'll bet she could sell it, after all," Melody mused. "It would just involve a story. That's the only way. Make up a story so good, nobody will ever doubt it."

"Maybe," Bernard admitted. "You're the master in that area."

"True. Let's see. She's an artist. She's probably studied in Europe. While she was over there, she bought a trunk."

"Just the trunk?" Bernard asked with a twisted smile. "Not the whole elephant?"

"Quiet. I'm thinking. Yes, she bought an old trunk from a second-hand shop. To store art supplies. While cleaning it up—it looked like it had been in a bomb blast or something, see—she discovered a false bottom, and under that in a hidden compartment, she found the song. Oh, and there were some initials engraved on the outside of the trunk. A.H."

"A.H.?"

"Adolf Hitler. Or is that too much?"

"Definitely too much."

"Okay, no initials. Just the false bottom and the song. Then she could be famous for finding it."

"Except for one thing," Bernard said.

"Oh?"

He made a gun gesture with his fingers. "Gerhardt Nachtnebel, Jr. is reportedly a maniac who would kill her to get it back."

Melody leaned back and crossed her arms over her chest. "We only have hearsay for that. Shawn probably just heard an ugly rumor."

"Simeon Frankenberry said the same thing."

"Are you really going to take the word of someone who's named after a kid's cereal?"

"I'm just saying, there are two independent lines of supporting evidence." He finished his cake and pushed the plate away. "That was delicious."

"Flimsy evidence," Melody said. "And it was, wasn't it? Want to help me with the dishes?"

"No."

"Sure, you do." She batted her eyelashes.

"Oh, *that* kind of help."

They cleared the table together, then he mostly held onto her to keep her from falling over while she loaded the dishwasher. Not that she was likely to, but it was a pleasant way to help. Only, it did make the loading slower, because she kept turning around to kiss him.

His phone dinged about the time they were finished. With the dishes, that is. The ding announced an email from Shawn. An email with an attachment. A compressed, password protected attachment which, when opened and decompressed, contained two files, one a link to some freebie decryption software and the other a compressed, password protected, encrypted file. Bernard wondered if he should summon a cardiologist on Shawn's behalf, just in case.

He took Melody's hand and led her to the table to retrieve his laptop and then to his rolltop desk. He settled her in his lap so she could see the screen. In short order, he had the contents of the file displayed: a rough, hand-drawn floorplan of the vicinity of the fake restrooms with security details noted. Cameras, alarms, special locks, everything. There was also a note from Shawn:

Do not copy to other devices. Delete email when done. Delete all files, compressed and decompressed, encrypted and decrypted. Reformat hard drive. Remove hard drive and smash with hammer.

Smash cell phone with hammer. Scatter shards in three different areas in each of five different landfills. Not kidding.

"I'm starting to think," Bernard said, "we might not want to involve Shawn in further adventures for a while. It's bad for his health."

"Physical?" Melody asked. "Or mental?"

"Both."

They studied the floorplan together, although Bernard did more studying and Melody did more nibbling on his ear, which was beyond distracting, and she knew it. Even so, it only took Bernard fifteen minutes to realize what he should have realized in, oh, thirty seconds. "Look at this," he said. He pointed to a section of the floorplan. "One big room behind the two fake restroom doors, which spills into the private wing of the mansion. Let's call it the treasure room. Here's the little gallery we toured this morning. And the white door in that gallery—*voilà!*—connects them. All is explained."

"Except," Melody purred. She gave his neck a little bite. "How you get in."

Presumably, she was talking about the rooms, but one never knew with her. Bernard did his best to focus. "Ah, perfect. Shawn included the service access stairs from the roof. They run down to…" He blinked at the floorplan. "Huh."

"Huh?"

"Huh."

Melody turned his head and kissed his mouth. "Huh what?"

He turned back to the floorplan. "The stairwell descends alongside that gallery, with an access door into it. Should be, anyway, according to this. I didn't see that door. Did you?"

"Nope. I only have eyes for you."

"You're in a mood tonight, aren't you?"

She giggled. "Oh, you noticed."

It would be a shame to waste one of Melody's moods, so he closed his laptop and folded his arms about her. "Fine," he said. "You win. But promise we'll get some actual work done over breakfast."

Melody tweaked his nose. "Deal," she said.

Chapter 15: Tuesday, October 24, 2017

Chris-Chris didn't shriek at the crack of dawn, which fact Bernard failed to register until his cell phone did. He nearly threw the device into the closet, but he foolishly checked the number first and, recognizing it, was forced to accept the call.

"Rise and shine," Celeste said, but not in a sunshiny voice. Her tone invoked a severe thunderstorm gathering over Aschimos.

"I've risen," Bernard grumbled, "but I refuse to shine at this hour."

"Progress report."

That could have meant anything, including how he was progressing on waking up, but probably she wanted to know about *Rienzi* and the money she'd dumped into the expense budget. "Progress is being made," Bernard said.

"Details."

"Didn't have our coffee yet, did we? You sound like a..." He cut himself off before he said Gestapo officer. That would probably be in bad taste, given the circumstances.

"No games, Bernard. Details."

"In this sort of operation, the fewer details you know, the better."

"I'll take the risk. What's my four grand in operating expenses bought?"

Melody groaned and leveraged herself into sitting position. She leaned on Bernard's shoulder. "Tell them we don't want any," she said.

Celeste should have laughed at that. She didn't, which told Bernard more about her mood than her words had. "We've been testing options," he said. "It's a complex situation, but I think we've found a solution. I'm working on an implementation."

"Timeframe?"

"You should know better than to rush a work of art. Assuming you really are an artist." That was a risky interjection, but he was curious how she'd reply.

"If you don't deliver, my next work of art will be executed with extreme patience."

Ah, that was how. It wasn't so much the words. Anyone sufficiently annoyed might have said that. It was the north wind in her voice. It could have frozen Bernard's blood. But he had a policy: he refused to be intimidated. "Madam," he said in his most insulted tone, "when we promise to do a job, we do it. If we can't, you'll receive a full refund. Or we could issue it now and forget the whole thing."

"I don't want a refund. I want *Rienzi.*"

She cut the connection.

Bernard dropped his phone on the bed and flopped backwards, dragging Melody down with him. She snuggled up to him and whispered, "What was that about?"

"Celeste. She's getting nasty."

"Maybe she woke up on the wrong side of the bed."

"She probably sleeps in a coffin and only comes out at night."

Melody lifted her head and gaped at Bernard. "But Bernie, we met her in daylight. Wouldn't she have burned up if that was true?"

"Figuratively, love, figuratively. I wonder if she's really an artist at all."

"I say she's an assassin, but she must be an artist, too. She paints headless nudes. Who but an artist would do that?"

"Point. But you're right. She's not just an artist. I'd bet my Zephyr on it." He wrapped his arms around Melody and pulled her close. "How'd you like to do some more snooping, love?"

"I'd love to! I'll start at Chrissie's. Maybe someone knows her."

"And I'll check in with Allegra Fumagalli. Celeste claimed to have taken classes at Nachtnebel's. We need another class, anyway. Allegra ought to be thrilled to arrange that for her star pupil."

"Ask for a discount," Melody said. "A great artist like you deserves one."

Good point. Bernard stroked her hair. Maybe being mistaken for a rising talent had its advantages.

$$\oint$$

The prospect of snooping put Melody in a good mood. She fixed a breakfast of scrambled eggs, pre-cooked bacon zapped to perfection, coffee, and a can of fruit cocktail poured into a plastic serving bowl and garnished with coconut flakes. The coconut was a last-minute inspiration. She'd bought the bag six months earlier, intending to put it into a curry that for reasons she no longer remembered never got made. It was about time she used some of it, and she didn't have time to bake cookies or make German chocolate cake from scratch. Maybe once this Nazi business was behind them, she could do that. Far better to associate Germany with yummy cakes than disgusting Nazis, that was for sure.

After breakfast, she got herself dolled up in delicate makeup and a tight orange dress with little pumpkins printed all over it, a garment she'd picked up for a Halloween party that for reasons she no longer remembered they never went to. (She didn't think she was always this forgetful, but a lot of reasons for not doing things seemed to have poofed out of memory.) Fortunately, the dress would be in season one month a year every year, so it wouldn't go to waste. A pair of white slingbacks completed the outfit. Nail polish selection was a problem, although honestly, it always was. She could spend hours mulling over her hoard of little bottles arranged atop her dresser, even though usually she ended up picking a red. She thought about starting with the reds sometimes, but where was the fun in that? Besides, red wouldn't work with an orange dress. She settled on a yellow that blended nicely with her pumpkins.

She giggled at the inadvertent double entendre. She'd share that one with Felicity. They'd spend fifteen minutes laughing over it. Laughter being good for one's health, she might even save her friend's life.

In due course, she was ready to take on the world. She grabbed a little white clutch, made sure she had her license, keys, and other essentials, and set out for Chrissie's, blowing Bernard a kiss in passing. He was still at the table, food gone, messing with his cell phone.

The traffic was rotten, usual for a weekday, but she found a few gaps through which to thread her Corvette, so it didn't take as long as it might have. The drive was a bit loud, though, what with other drivers blasting their horns at her initiative. She found street parking only two blocks from Chrissie's—a minor miracle—and clip-clopped her way down the sidewalk, enjoying the cool autumn breeze and the cotton-ball clouds drifting far above the buildings and all the heads turning as she passed by.

Chrissie herself was seated in a chair, along with two other stylists—Claire and a new employee Melody didn't recognize—when Melody sashayed in. Whatever they'd been talking about was immediately forgotten as they all chirped greetings and Chrissie rose and hurried to her, took her hands, and as always inspected her from head to toe. "What you doing here, girl?" she said. "I can't improve a work of art like this."

They gave each other a loose hug.

"I'm not here for your services," Melody said. She pouted a little, both because it was rather sad that Chrissie wouldn't have a chance to work her magic, but also because Melody didn't want her to feel she wasn't appreciated.

Chrissie patted her on the shoulder. "Never you mind that. What's up?"

"Bernie and I went to that class last week at the Nachtnebel place. And guess what? It turns out I'm good, but Bernie is an absolute genius!" She bounced on her toes. "Isn't that amazing?"

The women all clapped and whooped.

"We're going to take another class soon," Melody went on. "But in the meantime, he's been doing a bit of studying on the side, and he ran across a local artist he'd never heard of before. She does amazing things with headless nudes."

That caused a moment of confusion.

"I mean, she paints them," Melody clarified.

"Oh," Claire said. "Thank goodness!"

They all sniggered.

"Anyway, Bernie is having trouble finding out anything about her. I thought maybe someone here would know something, given how cultured you and your customers are."

"I don't know about *us*," Chrissie said, waving her index finger around to encompass the staff, "but give us a try."

She was just being modest. Melody knew better. The stylists picked up all the gossip and considerable insider info from their wealthy clientele, who rarely kept their mouths shut. "The artist's name is Celeste," she said.

Chrissie frowned in concentration. Claire turned her eyes to the ceiling, as though the answer might descend from on high. The other stylist cringed. "Don't poke your nose into *her* business."

Melody arched her eyebrows.

"Really, stay away from her."

"Why?" Chrissie asked.

"She might be an artist, but I heard she killed someone once."

Melody knew it. Celeste was an assassin! Suddenly, those headless dancers made sense. She hadn't been unable to finish them. They'd been painted from life! Or, okay, death, which was even worse. Melody shivered.

Chrissie snorted. "Now where'd you hear a thing like that?"

"From Mrs. Cavenaugh."

"Honey, Mrs. Cavenaugh don't know her head from her big toe."

But Melody couldn't let it go. Bernie needed this information, for his safety if nothing else. She approached the stylist and offered her hand. "We haven't met, have we? I'm Melody Earls."

"I'm Ottawa." They shook hands. "Ottawa Floquet." She pronounced her surname like "croquet."

"Tell me the whole story, Ottawa. What did Mrs. Cavenaugh say?"

Sitting straighter and grinning like she really enjoyed having a captive audience—which probably she did, since how often does a stylist get to tell such a cool, dark story?—Ottawa launched into it before Chrissie could object.

"She said Celeste's real name is Celestina Bartosz. She had a grandfather—or was it a great-grandfather? No, I think it was a grandfather." Ottawa tried counting on her fingers, but that didn't seem to get her anywhere. "One or the other. Anyway, he was an officer in the Polish Home Army. They resisted the Nazis, see. So was her grandmother—or was it her great-grandmother?" She counted on her fingers again, then shrugged. "Somebody. She was captured by Nazi soldiers, and..." Ottawa shuddered before finishing, "Oh, it was horrible. I don't want to tell that part."

Melody patted Ottawa's hand. "It's okay, you can skip it."

"Anyway, Celestina is part Nazi, because one of those soldiers is her grandfather. Or maybe her great-grandfather. One or the other."

Chrissie shook her head. "I told you. Mrs. Cavenaugh don't know her head from her big toe."

Claire came to Ottawa's aid. "But it makes sense, right? That's what Nazis did. Horrible stuff like that."

"Just because someone's daddy's a Nazi don't make *them* one," Chrissie scolded. "It's a story told by a ditzy lady who loves attention. I thought you two had more brains than that."

"Just for giggles," Melody said, "what's this about Celeste killing someone?" Although honestly, it wouldn't be giggle-worthy if she really had.

"That Nachtnebel guy sent someone to kill her," Ottawa said, eyes wide, voice willowy, like she was telling a ghost story leading up to a shout of *Boo!* "But she killed him and buried the body in her cellar!"

"Uh-huh," Chrissie said. "And just how does Mrs. Cavenaugh know this? Did she help bury the stiff?"

Ottawa thrust her tongue into her cheek and pondered the matter.

"That's what I thought," Chrissie said. "Don't you listen to none of that, Melody. The lady probably jilted one of her lovers—you know how them artists are—and he started some nasty rumor about her, which got blown up like a blimp."

"Probably," Melody said, but she didn't believe that. Clearly World War II had come home to roost in southern Maryland. An odd choice of roosts, but then D.C. *was* just next door. This cast a whole new light on the *Rienzi* business. Celeste was probably out for revenge on her grandfather. Or great-grandfather. Whatever. And now she and Bernie were caught in the middle of it.

She was so worried on the drive back home that she forgot to speed or weave in and out of traffic or anything. It wasn't at all a fun drive.

𝄞

While Melody was unearthing the sordid history of a sinister artist, Bernard was wrangling a pair of seats for their next art class. It was a multistep process. First, he called the Nachtnebel Arts Foundation and asked for Allegra Fumagalli. She was no longer in residence. Could he have her cell number? Of course not. That would violate her privacy. Could a message be relayed? Of course not. That would involve work. Then could he talk to Mr. Nachtnebel? Mr. Nachtnebel is a very busy man. Yes, but this was Bernard Earls, Ms. Fumagalli's star pupil, who she personally invited to the private showing of Mr. Nachtnebel's extremely private collection yesterday, and certainly Mr. Nachtnebel could find thirty seconds to speak with him about contacting Ms. Fumagalli.

And so forth and so on. Eventually, the woman who took Bernard's call got so fed up with him that she promised to give Mr. Nachtnebel a message. Bernard thanked her and threatened to call back every half hour until he got a reply. Fifteen minutes later, the woman called him back and said his message had been relayed to Ms. Fumagalli. Bernard thanked her and threatened to call back every hour—he was feeling more generous now—until he got a reply.

Ten minutes later, Allegra's cheerful if wrinkled voice flowed from his cell phone. "Bernard! What a surprise! It's good to hear from you. What can I do for you?"

"After this past week," Bernard told her, "I'm full of artistic energy." (He didn't know if artists talked that way, but probably anything he said would impress her.) "Melody and I would like to take another class, but we can't afford it." (Starving artists and all that. With luck, artists really did starve. Not that he knew. Although, now that he thought about it, Celeste sure wasn't starving, which meant either she wasn't a real artist or she'd somehow beaten the system. Since Bernard himself was constantly trying to beat the system, he should investigate that possibility.) "I thought you might be able to offer a suggestion."

"Why, certainly. That's great news!"

Bernard wasn't sure whether she meant his wanting to take a class or his having no money. Or both.

"I'll arrange something for you," she continued. "Is another class at Gerhardt's convenient? Or would you prefer somewhere else, maybe closer to home, wherever that is? Swampside doesn't sound like your economic zone." She laughed.

In other circumstances, Bernard would have been insulted. Swampside certainly should be his economic zone, even though he was stuck in Aschimos. But he couldn't afford to take offense. "Gerhardt's would be great," he said. "I find the atmosphere inspirational." Which was true. It inspired him to find a way into that treasure room.

"I'll get the two of you free admission to one class. But just one, mind you. I only have so much pull with Gerhardt where money is concerned. Beneath his magnanimous exterior, he's quite the skinflint."

"I wouldn't dream of imposing on you further," Bernard told her, also true, since his dreams involved finishing this job and getting out as fast as possible. It was always best to tell the truth, if one could.

"Let me check the schedule," she said. "Hold on a moment." The sound of keys tapping followed, and a bit of hemming and hawing, and finally she returned. "There's a three-day oil seminar starting tomorrow. Knowing you and your talents, I think that would be a fine choice. I'll make sure your tickets are waiting at the registration desk. You only need bring yourselves. Supplies are supplied."

"Wonderful, Ms. Fumagalli, absolutely wonderful."

"Oh, please, don't be so formal. Call me Allegra."

"As you wish. By the way, I've been studying a local artist, or trying to. I can't find much about her. Do you happen to know a painter named Celeste?"

The silence was so deep, Bernard wondered if the cellular network had crashed, maybe struck by an unexpected stream of particles from space. But he had full bars, so that wasn't it.

"I know of her," Allegra said at last. "I suggest you find someone else to study."

"Oh? I've seen a few of her works. She seems quite creative." Headless nude dancers had to be creative. Probably.

"It's not so much her art as her personality. She's a thug."

Bernard all but laughed. Celeste sure didn't look like a thug, not in that smock hugging those oversized breasts. If anything, she looked like an exotic dancer about to go on stage. Then again, this morning's phone call had a distinctly thuggish tone to it. "What's she done?" he asked.

"I don't want to gossip. Suffice it to say, she and Mr. Nachtnebel are not on speaking terms. Best not to bring her up while you're in class."

"Understood. Well, thank you for the tickets. And for everything you've done for my development as an artist. And the warning."

"Don't mention it. Feel free to call me anytime. Just don't ask for more freebies."

Setting down the phone, Bernard pondered what she'd told him. It wasn't much, but it reenforced his sense that Celeste wasn't what she claimed. Oh, sure, she might be an artist, but she had some connection to Nachtnebel and some reason for wanting to steal from him beyond coveting a lost music manuscript. That manuscript was her key to something else. But what? Revenge? Power over her nemesis?

This business was turning ugly. And dangerous.

Celeste damn well better pay up once it was over.

§

By the time Melody got back, it was nearly lunchtime. After getting the scoop on Celestina Bartosz, a.k.a. Celeste, murderer and painter of disrobed headless figures, she chatted with the women for a good forty-five minutes about totally inconsequential stuff, by which time her friends had forgotten about homicidal artists. Then she strolled the shops in the area and picked up a solar powered snow globe that caught her eye.

Not really a snow globe. More of a star globe containing a model of the solar system surrounded by a sprinkling of stars that lit up whenever the globe caught some light. Best of all, it cost her nothing. Well, not quite nothing. Stealing from the rich was one thing. They could afford it. But stealing from small shops was tacky and mean. Alas, the star globe was so pretty she couldn't resist it. She slipped it into her purse and bought a bunch of Carmelicious Bars at the checkout to make up for it. Being a kleptomaniac with a conscience could be a real trial sometimes.

She stopped at the local Burger Bazzar on the way home and got lunch for Bernie and herself. Between the intelligence she'd gathered, the star globe, and the hot fries fresh from the fryer, she was feeling on top of the world as she all but skipped down the hall toward their apartment.

Then Chris-Chris shrieked, and little feet thundered back and forth through Mrs. Clarke's abode, and that good feeling went up in smoke. Poor Mrs. Clarke. She'd be dead by the end of the week. And Chris-Chris would be bound and gagged and charged with murder if Bernie had his way.

Melody tried to knock on Mrs. Clarke's door, but with her hands full of bags and cups of soda, she had to use her elbow. Even she couldn't hear it. Fortunately, Bernie burst from their apartment at just that moment, morphed from enraged to confused when he saw his wife, and got a grip.

"Allow me," he said. He pounded on the door.

Mrs. Clarke, normally the picture of respectability, was beyond disheveled when she emerged. Her gray hair was twisted and tangled, her eyes bloodshot, and a red stain spilled down the front of her dress. Probably not blood, since she was still breathing. Maybe ketchup? When she spoke, she sounded like a voice from the great beyond.

"Make it stop," she pleaded.

Roaring like a den full of lions, Chris-Chris charged into the foyer, saw Melody, and all but tackled her. The drinks went flying, dousing everyone. The burger bags hit the floor with a splat. Even Melody's purse was wrenched from her arm, but Bernard caught that as he simultaneously snagged Chris-Chris by the collar. He bent down and looked the little beast in the eye.

"Young man," he scolded. "Stop this right now."

Chris-Chris stuck out his tongue and hissed like a snake.

Bernard raised a hand as though to slap him, then folded his fingers into a fist, all but his index finger, which he shook in the kid's face. "Don't you take that attitude with me." Then he glanced up at Melody and muttered, "God, I sound like my father."

Chris-Chris tried to bite the finger. Bernard snatched it back with a millisecond to spare. "That's it," he said. "It's time you had a lesson. I'm taking you to jail."

"You're not the police!" Chris-Chris bellowed.

"No, but I know the police."

Melody nodded. That was true. They'd even given Bernie lodging once.

"And," Bernard added, "if I want you thrown in jail, they'll do it. Let's go."

Chris-Chris twisted out of Bernard's grasp and hugged his great-grandmother's wobbly knees. "Gramma, Gramma, don't let him!"

Mrs. Clarke pinched her lips. "Well," she said. "Mr. Earls has a point. You're being a little hoodlum."

"I don't got a hood. I got a hat."

"I mean, you're behaving very badly. And bad people do sometimes have to go to jail."

There followed a half hysterical, half tearful plea for mercy, which left none of them, not even Bernard, unmoved. Finally, Mrs. Clarke agreed to accept the boy's contrition and promises to be good. Once she had retreated into the apartment with her charge and silence reigned, Melody gathered up the remains of their lunch.

"Look at this," she said.

Bernard shook his head. "It's probably okay, except the drinks."

"It'll be cold by now, though. Those fries were perfect when I got them."

He kissed her cheek. "Even cold fries are perfect when served by you, love."

She melted into his arms. He always knew how to make everything better.

"Come on," he said. "I have things to tell you."

"And I have things to tell you. I'll bet mine are juicier."

"That goes without saying."

Once at the table with lunch reassembled—the burgers had become deconstructed in the fracas—and plastic glasses filled with crushed ice and cola served, they got down to business.

"According to Allegra Fumagalli," Bernard began, "Celeste is a thug and isn't on speaking terms with Nachtnebel. That suggests they've had an unpleasant run-in. I don't know what's going on, but we could be in dangerous waters here."

"That fits with what I learned," Melody said. She leaned over the table and whispered, even though it was just the two of them. Who knew, maybe Celeste or Nachtnebel or both had bugged the apartment. "Her real name is Celestina Bartosz. Her father was in the Polish resistance in World War II. Something called the Home Army. Nachtnebel tried to have her killed, but she took out his assassin and buried him in her cellar."

Bernard sat back, wide-eyed. "Who told you that?"

"Ottawa."

"Ottawa?"

"One of the stylists."

"How would a stylist at Chrissie's know about a body in an artist's cellar?"

"She heard it from Mrs. Cavenaugh."

"Who's Mrs. Cavenaugh?"

"A customer. Some rich lady, probably."

"Melody..." Bernard shook his head.

"There's more. Celeste's grandmother or great-grandmother was captured by the Nazis and, and, well, I don't even like to think about it, but they raped her. Celeste is part Nazi, genetically speaking."

Now Bernard's eyes were so wide, it was a wonder his eyeballs didn't roll from their sockets and bounce across the table.

"Think about it, Bernie. Nazis. Polish resistance fighters. Both DNA living in one body. Celeste must be a very conflicted woman, and I'll bet Nachtnebel's father is the one responsible."

Pressing his palms to the table, Bernard licked his lips. "Okay, first, 'Nazi' isn't a genetic condition. Second, that sounds like the plot of a grade-Z exploitation movie."

"Which is why it's probably true," Melody pointed out. "You know what they always say. Truth is stranger than fiction."

Bernard tapped his fingers on the table for a moment. Clearly he didn't find that convincing. "Third," he went on, "what does any of this have to do with a Wagner opera? Yeah, I think Celeste is out for revenge. Maybe she wants to humiliate Nachtnebel. They probably knew each other and had a falling out. But come on, Melody. Assassination attempts? Bodies in the cellar? That's nuts."

Melody sat back and crossed her arms over her chest. He sure could be stubborn sometimes, but so could she. She'd show him. "Look her up," she said.

"Look who up?"

"Celestina Bartosz."

"Fine." He went to his rolltop, retrieved his laptop, and began searching. He searched for nearly half an hour. His face grew grim. And maybe a bit white. In the end, he said only one word.

It wasn't a word Melody often heard from him.

Chapter 16: Still Tuesday, October 24, 2017

Bernard didn't say much beyond that one word until after dinner. He studied whatever he'd found online, tapped at the keys, studied more, ran his hand through his hair about a bazillion times, and muttered stuff Melody couldn't hear and probably didn't want to.

Given his state, she decided to treat him to one of his favorites, Hawaiian pizza with a side salad and cheese breadsticks made from scratch. Well, mostly from scratch. Refrigerated dough from a carboard tube was involved.

His mood lightened as they ate. He even managed a couple of smiles, some for the food, some for her. Once he'd finished and was patting his mouth with his napkin, she asked, "So?"

Maybe that was too soon. He slipped back into brooding silence. But only for half a minute. "You were right," he said. "Henryk and Emilia Bartosz were resistance fighters in the Home Army. They were both scouts. They provided intelligence for operations that sabotaged German transports making for the Eastern front. Henryk was caught and killed on the spot in December, 1943. Emilia was captured the following month. She was taken prisoner but escaped about a week later. She never talked about her captivity, but she bore a daughter nine months later, so…" Bernard shrugged.

That wasn't all he'd found. Melody could tell. She raised an eyebrow to prompt him to continue.

"Most of the rest is circumstantial. Over the next twenty-four years, a number of soldiers associated with the units who had captured and detained Emilia all died. A few were killed in fighting near the end of the war, but most were murdered in their sleep, shot at close range."

"Emilia killed them?"

Bernard nodded. "That's the theory. From the accounts, it sounds like the same M.O. in each case. The killings stopped right about the time Emilia herself died in a suspicious car crash. And then, two years later, they resumed with a difference. The remaining victims weren't just killed, they were marked. Each had the letter 'B' carved into their cheek."

Melody shivered.

"There's a small group of amateur historians who dig into this," Bernard said, "rather like those who insisted that Gilles de Rais was innocent."

"Who?"

"Marshall of France in the 1400's. Companion of Joan of Arc. He was executed on trumped-up charges as a serial killer of children."

"Why would anyone look into that?"

Bernard shrugged. "Obsession, I suppose."

"I wish you'd stick to the point, Bernie. What does an ancient French guy have to do with Nazis?"

"I'm just saying, there are amateur historians who—"

Melody gave him one of her looks.

"Never mind. What the Bartosz aficionados think is, someone was completing Emilia's revenge. No suspect was ever identified, but whoever it was had skills. There are certainly hints it might have been Emilia's only child, her daughter Aldona. For one thing, who else would have had the motive and knowledge to finish the job?"

"Oh, so her mother trained her."

"Maybe. A few years later, the killings stopped again. Aldona got married and had three children, one being Celestina. The assumption is, all the names had been crossed off the list." Bernard ran his hand through his hair again. "But all those murders occurred in Europe. What if someone slipped away?"

"Gerhard Nachtnebel, Sr.," Melody suggested.

"Exactly. He'd been a driver for some bigwig close to Hitler. Maybe Emilia couldn't get to him. He could have escaped Germany long before Aldona had a chance to find him. In which case, this might not just be about stealing a priceless artifact. Maybe Celeste means to finish the job and kill Nachtnebel."

Melody got all that, but then why steal an opera? Why not just kill him? She put the question to her husband.

Bernard pondered for a minute. "Maybe it's bait. Unfortunately, we're in the middle of it. We either we deliver *Rienzi* and duck out before she lures Nachtnebel in, or we flee to South America."

"Not South America," Melody objected. "That's the first place she'd look. All the Nazis went there, right?"

"Okay, then, Nepal."

"What's in Nepal?"

"Besides Mt. Everest? I have no idea."

Melody set her finger to her lips. Mt. Everest. That could work. They could hide among the hoards of climbers scrambling for the summit. She'd have to buy winter gear, though. It got a lot colder up there than it did here in Aschimos. Which was a problem, because nobody sold decent winter gear in Maryland. Nobody needed it. Oh well, there was always online shopping, although you might have to pay shipping if you went that route.

Bernard gave her a bemused look, as though he could almost but not quite follow her thoughts, which was likely the case. He always had been a bit slow when it came to shopping. "Anyway," he said, "we need to tread carefully. Let's see if Shawn's up for another consultation."

He got out his cell phone and called. Melody listened to his side of the conversation and tried to imagine the other. That was always good fun whenever Bernard and Shawn were talking.

"Hey, Shawn, are you and Felicity home tonight?"

"Oh, I see. When will you be home?"

"Ah. That late. No problem, you're young enough to pull an all-nighter."

"Of course you are."

"You sure are."

"Shawn, you're still in college."

"Oh, come on, you're a genius. You can code in your sleep."

"For God's sake! We just need a few minutes of your time!"

"Just to talk."

"Yes, the floor plan."

"Yes, I studied it."

"Yes, I know what—"

"I know what—"

"Shawn, I know what—"

"Damn it, Shawn, I just want to *talk*!"

"Yes, yes, tell Felicity there's money involved."

"Not that much."

"Not that much, either. Not half that much."

"I didn't mean that literally. We can discuss the amount once we're there."

"Eleven o'clock. Fine. We'll be there."

Bernard thunked his phone on the table and ran his hand through his hair one more time. Melody hoped he wasn't pulling too much of it out. He'd look terrible bald. "If he wasn't such a skilled accomplice," he grumbled, "I'd never talk to that kid again."

Melody reached out and squeezed his hand. "Ice cream?" she suggested.

He nodded, as she knew he would. Ice cream made everything better.

The thing about night in the Baltimore-Washington corridor was, it was never truly night, given the light pollution, doubly so when a blanket of clouds glowed yellow-white overhead, reflecting the wasted light from a quarter of a million streetlights and other forms of high-intensity illumination. Why human beings thought it was a great idea to spray all that light up into space where it did nobody any good was beyond Bernard's comprehension. Yes, everyone *thought* it made them safer, but people in Bernard's profession couldn't see in the dark any better than bankers and plumbers. That's why most property crimes occurred in broad daylight, and why nighttime graffiti artists and vandals took advantage of good lighting.

And then there were those LED headlights frying his eyeballs as he drove the now well-worn route to Felicity's apartment. Why were those things even legal? Okay, probably he wasn't the right one to complain about the legality of anything, but robbing from the rich was one thing. Blinding people and compromising everyone's safety was another. Even Bernard had safety in mind when he pondered such activities as climbing up balconies to sharply pitched roofs.

When Bernard and Melody arrived at Felicity's place, they found their young friends looking like reanimated corpses. Shawn's eyes were underscored by half-moons of darkened flesh, and Felicity lay flopped on the couch with the grace of a worn-out stuffed animal, yawning every twelve seconds. They were dressed sort of nice, she in a pink floral dress and he in gray dress slacks and a striped short-sleeve shirt, but they made both outfits look like rags draped haphazardly about their bodies.

Melody gaped at them.

Without much need, Bernard asked, "How was your cousin's rehearsal dinner, Felicity?"

She rolled her head in his direction and stuck out her tongue.

"Long," Shawn said.

"Loud," Felicity added.

"Burnt," Shawn finished.

Melody's eyes doubled in size. "Burnt!"

Felicity nodded, more or less. "Every single dish was burnt, so they had to remake them. Some had to be remade twice."

"Must not've been a five-star restaurant," Bernard quipped.

They all stared at him.

"It gets good reviews," Shawn told him. "But from the gossip among the wait staff, one of the cooks was..." He waived his hands as though trying to conjure a word.

"Aggrieved," Felicity supplied.

Sometimes she surprised Bernard by finding a good term like that. "Over what?"

"Who knows?" Felicity stuck out her tongue once more before continuing, "He just decided to ruin everything for us. Then there was yelling and screaming and pots flying around. Or it sounded like it."

"And then," Shawn finished, "the cops hauled him out in cuffs."

Bernard took Melody's arm, escorted her to a chair, and settled her in it. He sat in the adjacent chair. "So, all's well that ends well," he said with a churlish grin.

Felicity and Shawn glowered at him.

"Let's make this short so you two can get some sleep." Bernard had brought his laptop. He opened it and pulled up Shawn's drawing of the Nachtnebel mansion floorplan, then motioned his unwitting accomplice to have a look.

Shawn dragged another chair over and all but fell into it. "What?" he grumped.

Bernard explained while pointing out the key locations. "I'm trying to get into this storeroom here. These doors are deadlocked. I can't get in that way."

"What's deadlocked?" Shawn asked.

"Sounds like whoever locked it was killed," Felicity suggested. She yawned. "Like when pirates kill whoever helps them bury the treasure."

"It means," Bernard snapped, "I can't get in that way."

Shawn yawned, too. "You already said that."

Bernard glared at the screen. "Just listen. This balcony looks like an entrance from the outside, but it's not. The door isn't really a door. It doesn't open."

Instead of just listening, Felicity commented on that. "That's a stupid kind of door. What's the point?"

Bernard squeezed his eyes shut.

"What?" Felicity asked.

"Moving right along. I've been in this room here. It's a small art gallery that connects to the storeroom. You see this stairwell? It comes down from the roof and should be accessible from the gallery through this door. But when I was in the gallery, I didn't see a door."

He took a long breath while Shawn gave the screen a glazed stare.

"So?" Shawn finally asked.

"I can use the balconies to get to the roof. The Nachtnebel Foundation has drone footage of the mansion on their website. I noticed—"

"Oooo," Shawn said. Or maybe he was yawning once more. "Drone footage. That's a security risk."

You betcha, Bernard thought. "I noticed a ladder ascending the roof from just above one of the balconies. It leads to a service entrance at the top of this stairwell."

"Okay, so you'll break in up there, go down the stairs to the gallery and break into the storeroom."

"That's not the terminology I'd use, but in essence, yes."

Shawn leaned back, closed his eyes, and sighed. "What do we charge for that, Felicity?"

Felicity finished her latest yawn and, eyes likewise closed, replied, "Sounds illegal. Ten grand."

"Why do you always start so high?" Bernard griped.

"It's called negotiation."

Melody moved from her chair to the sofa, where she enfolded her friend's hands in hers. "We can't possibly pay that much. You know that."

"What're you stealing?" Felicity asked. In her exhaustion, she didn't seem to care that they were embroiled in an illegal venture. She might have been asking out of idle curiosity.

"I'm verifying the security of some artwork," Bernard said.

"Uh-huh. Ten thousand."

"One hundred," he countered.

"Five thousand."

"Two hundred."

"One thousand."

Bernard wished she'd shortcut the process, but that just wasn't her, and right now she was on automatic pilot. "Three hundred."

"Five hundred."

"Four."

"Deal." Felicity waved vaguely at Shawn. "Carry on, babe."

"Let me get some sleep," Shawn said. "I'll get you the security details tomorrow."

At least they were making progress. Shawn had no strength left for hyperventilating, so the prospects of getting shot, or worse, losing his job, held no terror for him. "You got it," Bernard agreed. He and Melody rose to leave.

Just before they closed the door behind them, Shawn's exhausted parting words reached their ears: "Last time, Bernard. For real."

Yeah. That's what he'd said the last few times.

§

All was silent when they crept into their apartment sometime after midnight. No elephants, no howler monkeys, no T-rexes. Naturally. Chris-Chris would have gone home long before. Given that he'd been threatened with jail time, Bernard hoped the kid would remain silent until Mrs. Clarke no longer had to babysit him.

They undressed, buried themselves under the covers, and wrapped themselves around each other. Melody fell asleep in record time. Bernard wanted to sleep, too, but something gnawed at him. Mentally, that is, although it did have a strange similarity to an annoying cat nibbling on his ear.

No, that *was* an annoying cat nibbling on his ear. Fifi had decided to join them. Bernard pushed her away. In a huff, she perched on his hip, digging her claws through the blanket for security. He was too tired to shoo her away, and besides, whatever had sunk its metaphorical teeth into his brain couldn't be chased off.

It wasn't the job. Not exactly. It was more the circumstances surrounding it. He got Nachtnebel hoarding stolen art treasures. That was the sort of thing Bernard himself might do, if he was rich enough to not sell them. He got showing them off to a select group of artists. A fun gloat. He'd do it himself, if he thought he could get away with it—which also came down to being fabulously rich. Those people could get away with anything. But the issue wasn't Nachtnebel, not at all.

It was Celeste.

Celestina.

Celestina Bartosz.

The woman was an artist *and* a killer. Possibly a killer. They didn't know that for sure. But assume she was an artist and a killer. She had good reason. For the killer part. Bernard had no idea why people might become artists, although granted, most people wouldn't understand his own career choice.

He was clearly beyond tired. Focus, Bernard, focus.

Celestina Bartosz lost her grandfather to the Nazis. Her grandmother Emilia had been raped and maybe tortured—raped for sure, and what was that but torture? Thus, both. Anyway. Celestina's very existence was an inescapable reminder of that horror. Emilia had tracked down and killed some of scum responsible for it, and Aldona, Celestina's mother, had presumably finished the job. Tried to finish it. Gerhard Nachtnebel, Sr. got away.

But so what? Why would Celestina target Gerhard Nachtnebel Jr.? He hadn't been born when her grandparents had suffered their fates. It wasn't his fault. He might not even have known about it. Whatever it was, it had to be some form of revenge.

Female revenge. Bernard wasn't an expert in that area, but he knew who was. He gave Melody a gentle shake to wake her.

No good. She was so sunk in slumber she didn't even mumble a complaint.

Never mind. She looked too lovely to disturb, even in the dark when he could hardly see her, although he didn't know how anyone that exhausted could look anything but exhausted. She was Melody, that was all. Best to let her be. His worries could wait until morning.

Until sunrise, anyway. Technically, it was already morning.

Chapter 17: Wednesday, October 25, 2017

For better or for worse, Bernard's worries largely evaporated in the morning glow and were banished entirely when they arrived at the Nachtnebel mansion. By happy circumstance, the oil painting class was in a smallish room on the third floor adjacent to the treasure room. He couldn't have been more pleased. For a couple of blissful minutes, anyway.

Then class started.

The instructor, a short fellow with a mop of stringy hair dyed blinding neon yellow with random neon green streaks, introduced himself as George Monroe. Bernard figured George was in his late twenties and probably clueless about everything except, one would hope, oil painting. Granted, that was a snap judgement, but anyone with hair like that deserved it.

The instructor wasn't the reason things went downhill, though. He proved innocuous, unlike his coiffure. After providing his name and zip about his background and experience, he told everyone they had two and a half hours to work. Then he beckoned toward a screen at the front of the room, a simple tri-fold draped in black fabric.

Bernard wondered why he would be signaling a screen to come forward. That made no sense. Someone must be behind it, or behind the black curtain covering the entire wall behind the screen. That would be the exterior wall, so it was one of the curtains he'd seen from outside. Probably it was there to block stray light from the balcony door. You didn't want backlighting in a photograph, so you didn't want it while you were painting, either, right? (Huh. He was getting good at this art stuff.) But was the balcony door real? Maybe,

maybe not. Regardless, that curtain had Bernard's full attention rather than the screen, because what of any interest could the screen possibly be hiding?

He found out when someone stepped forth from behind it.

She was a lovely young woman with long, black hair, her body wrapped in a white terrycloth robe that stopped at her knees. Barefoot, not looking at the assembled students, she strode to a red velvet couch at the front of the room, removed the robe to reveal nothing but skin beneath, and reclined on the sofa in a relaxed pose. She might have been gazing out a window, had there been a window.

The students began painting, all but Bernard, who somehow forgot everything he knew about art. (Not that he knew anything to forget.) It was Olivia O'Leary all over again, only in color. He turned his eyes upon Melody, an expression of dread frozen on his face.

Melody sighed.

"Don't look?" Bernard whispered.

"Shoulders up?" she suggested.

He supposed he could put the model's head on Melody's body, except that would be weird and just plain wrong.

His expression must have broadcast all that weirdness and wrongness, because Melody sighed again and said, "It's art. Just paint."

Which only made matters worse. Bernard had no idea how to paint. He had no idea how to draw, either, but at least he'd done that before. He snuck quick glances at the other students to see what they were doing, and at George, who had taken a seat beside a small desk at the side of the room, settled his elbow on a large sketch pad lying there, and was flicking through his cell phone. The only sounds were the swishes of pigments being mixed and applied to canvas.

Mix. Right. Bernard supposed that's how they got the colors they wanted from the six tubes supplied them. He gave it a shot.

Oddly, no matter what he mixed, he got a sickly shade of purple. He studied the model, who hadn't a spot of purple on her. Not one bruise, not one blemish, not anywhere on her.

"You don't have to look *that* closely," Melody scolded.

Bernard flushed. He hadn't been, not really. He was only searching for purple. He watched Melody mix paint and spread it on the canvas. She certainly got more colors than sickly purple. She also was pretty good at applying it. The model's form began to emerge on her canvas.

Hell with it. If all he had was purple, purple it would be. He'd paint a purple woman on a purple couch, blurring her sensitive parts. He couldn't paint in that much detail anyway, not to save his life, plus Melody couldn't be too upset if he left certain things to the imagination. And hey, the result would wow everyone with its avant-garde audacity, or some such nonsense.

For over two hours, he labored on his purple lady reclining on her purple couch, first building up her form, then adding shadows and highlights with splotches of slightly darker or lighter purple. He had to admit, it wasn't bad. Rather sci-fi/horror in conception, but not bad.

And then George put down his phone, rose from his chair, and announced, "Time. Clean up and prep for lunch break."

The model rose, donned her robe, and returned to the screen as though she'd just finished reading a book in private. She slipped from view, might have vanished from spacetime itself for all Bernard could tell.

Bernard knew as little about cleaning up as he did about painting, but he watched the others and learned, and soon his brushes and palette were depainted and ready for the afternoon session. Arm-in-arm, he and Melody filed out with the other students and made for the bistro.

This lunch was more pleasant than any from the prior week, since Bernard was just another student now. They hadn't critiqued each other's work, so nobody was in awe of him and nobody interrupted their meal. The weather had warmed to nearly eighty, fine weather for dining *al fresco*. They took their food out on the balcony. Bernard studied the approach to the roof as they ate. He located the ladder with no trouble, perched above the second balcony over. He'd done the traverse before. He could do it again. He'd just need to unlatch the ladder's extension and lower it. Piece of cake.

And then something *very* interesting happened. On that very balcony below the ladder, the model from their class stepped through the sliding glass door, still wrapped in her robe, and lit up a cigarette. She stuffed the lighter into her pocket, leaned on the balcony, and gazed out over the grounds.

Perfect. That balcony door was real. Forget traversing. He could slip directly from the classroom onto the roof.

The model flicked away her cigarette and straightened. As she turned toward Bernard and Melody, her robe fell open, exposing— well, too much. The tie hadn't been tied. She tugged the fabric back into place, secured it, and noticing them, gave them a wave before she went inside.

"Shameless," Melody said.

"Oh, I don't know," Bernard teased. "She's probably so used to people seeing her naked that she doesn't think anything of it."

"I sure couldn't get used to it."

"It's a tough job," he admitted, "but somebody's got to do it." He gathered her into his arms and kissed her. "And hey, you're used to me seeing you naked. In fact, I rather think you like showing off for me."

"That's different." She pushed him away but not without a teasing smile. "You buy me cedar chests and stuff. Come on, we'll be late for class."

The afternoon session was more of the same, except they were starting over with fresh canvases. The red couch had been replaced with a marble pillar, or more likely a plaster pillar molded in fair imitation of marble. And the model who emerged from behind the screen was ebony-skinned and robed in green. She put off her covering and leaned against the pillar, eyes directed into the distance as though waiting for a bus outside a museum. If she had been, every bus in the fleet would be at her beck and call.

The students set to work. Bernard mixed his paint, hoping for something at least approaching the deep brown of the model's skin. Instead, he got...

...purple.

Damn it.

He darkened the purple and got...

Dark purple. Obviously.

Okay, a splash of white for the pillar, dark purple for the woman. He'd make it work.

A couple hours later, George called time. The model covered up and ducked behind the screen, and the students performed their cleaning rituals. The time for critiques had arrived. George circulated among the easels, nodding, making small comments on each student's two paintings, generally liking what he was seeing. Or maybe he just didn't like being critical. He winced a time or two, but he never said an unkind word. He complimented Melody. And her paintings. And then he paused at Bernard's work.

Dead silence.

He retrieved Bernard's morning work from the floor, borrowed Melody's easel, and situated the two purple paintings side-by-side. His eyes flicked from one to the other until it made Bernard dizzy. Finally, George's eyebrows rose so far, Bernard was afraid they might crawl into his yellow hair and get lost. "Interesting," he said.

Bernard folded his hands before him and waited for more.

"Allegra said you had talent," he said. "Everyone, come here. Look at this."

Here we go again, Bernard thought.

The students gathered 'round and studied Bernard's work in fascinated silence. For ten whole minutes they studied it, none venturing an opinion.

"Thoughts?" George prompted.

One of the women raised a tentative hand.

George motioned her to speak.

"I like it," she said.

Everyone nodded.

"Anything specific?" George asked.

"The gestalt of it. It's so moody. So evocative."

"I didn't see that in either model," one of the men said.

Who would've? Bernard thought.

"But now that I see this," the man continued, "I can see that."

George gave Bernard a thumbs-up. "Can't wait to see what you do with tomorrow's subject," he said. "Class dismissed."

On the drive home, Melody was uncharacteristically silent until, as they pulled into their apartment complex's parking lot, she asked, "Why did you paint them purple?"

"I couldn't make any other color," Bernard replied. "Every time I mixed the paints, I got that hideous purple."

"Yes, it was hideous." Melody smiled a wicked little smile. "But they deserved it, dropping their clothes in front of everyone."

"Oh, come on, Melody. It's art, not pornography. You said so yourself."

"As your wife, I'm allowed to be conflicted."

"What about that naked flower people photo you liked?"

"That was clever. It doesn't take cleverness to lie on a couch with nothing on."

Bernard wasn't qualified to judge cleverness. Not in art, anyway. In burglary, yes. Accessing a secret treasure room via a roof access, that would be clever. But what constituted cleverness in art? Did art even require cleverness? He wasn't the one to discuss such matters, nor could he win a debate on them. He sure did land in a lot of those debates, though, especially when Melody was the other party. He pulled into a parking space and turned off the engine.

She set a finger to her lips. "Although, painting her purple *was* clever, even if it was an accident. I'll give you that. I imagine most people would have asked the teacher for help with the colors, but you dove right in and used what you had."

"So, I'm a genius?"

She undid her seatbelt, leaned over, and kissed his cheek. "Sure are. You married me, right?"

He got out, circled the car, and helped her to her feet. "Come on," he said. "I'm hungry. And maybe later, I can dive right in and use what I have."

Melody laughed, slapped his shoulder, and leaned on him all the way to their apartment.

&

Consumed with artistic fervor, Bernard hadn't checked his cell phone all day. In fact, he'd forgotten it was silenced, almost forgotten it was even there, which felt strangely liberating. But now that they were at the table, dining on spaghetti doused in fire roasted red pepper sauce from a jar, accompanied by a bagged salad and garlic bread heated from frozen, he placed the device on the table and noticed he had an email from Shawn.

He finished eating first. Classic Italian cuisine was best savored without the intrusion of business. Once done, he studied the email. "This is interesting," he told Melody.

She pushed her plate aside, rested her elbows on the table, and cradled her chin in her hands. "More interesting than me?" she purred.

"Nothing's more interesting than you, love." He said it automatically as he re-read the message.

"You're so sweet."

"So you always say."

"And what does Shawn say?"

"If he knows what's good for him, Shawn won't say anything like that to anyone but Felicity."

"He won't. He always blushes instead."

"Regarding the job, he says there's no video surveillance on the roof, but the maintenance access doors are alarmed. He can deactivate them. The stairwell does indeed open on that little gallery we were in on Monday. We already know that white door connects the gallery to the treasure room, so it's a straight shot through there. I don't need to risk going down the hall. Shawn used the video system to examine the gallery. He couldn't see the stairwell door. Seems it's disguised to look like part of the wall. But he found the security keypad that unlocks it."

"He can turn off the cameras and give you the codes, right?"

"Yep. All I need now is time."

"During lunch break?" Melody suggested.

"With any luck."

Melody clapped her hand over her mouth. "Oh, Bernie, don't invoke your luck!"

Oops. He'd probably just jinxed the operation. "I'll invoke yours, then."

Relieved, Melody fanned herself. "Don't scare me like that."

"Sorry. Anyway, we have two more days of class, which gives me two shots at it."

"No shooting. We're peaceful bandits."

"Just an expression, love, just an expression."

Melody slipped from her chair, circled the table, and came up behind Bernard. Folding her arms about him, she whispered, "Enough shop talk. Express something else."

That sounded good to him.

Chapter 18: Thursday, October 26, 2017

The cacophony of war jarred Bernard from sleep the next morning, or at least a caricature thereof.

"Bang! Bang! Bang!" it went. "Bang bang bang bang bang bang bang BOOOOOOOOOM!"

Melody shoved her head under her pillow and pulled the covers over the top for good measure.

"That kid's about to become a casualty," Bernard growled. He rolled out of bed and stomped down the hall. He made it halfway before realizing he wasn't wearing anything. He stomped back to the bedroom, retrieved yesterday's clothes from the floor, and stuffed himself into them. Then back down the hall, out the door, and across to Mrs. Clarke's, where he bellowed, "Chris-Chris! What did I tell you?"

The thunder of little feet approached, accompanied by more mock shooting and explosions and Mrs. Clarke's weary voice struggling to crawl out from beneath it all. "Don't open the door, Chris-Chris. Remember what I told you about that."

The kid wasn't remembering any of his lessons today.

The deadbolt clicked open. The door opened a crack. Mrs. Clarke's bloodshot eyes peered up at Bernard. "Oh, Mr. Earls," she moaned. "I'm so sorry."

Bernard took a breath to reduce his blood from boiling to a gentle simmer. "It's not your fault, Mrs. Clarke."

Chris-Chris pushed between Mrs. Clarke's knees and the door and grinned up at Bernard as though about to commit murder most foul and thoroughly enjoy it.

Bernard pointed a finger at the little monster. "It's your fault, young man. I'm starting to think you *want* to go to jail." It was alarming how often his father was speaking through him lately.

"Nope," Chris-Chris said. "You go to jail!"

"Now Chris-Chris," Mrs. Clarke scolded. "That's not very polite."

"He's not polite. He's a meanie."

"You don't know the half of it," Bernard said. Before he could expound further, another racket erupted at the far end of the hall. Stomping and semi-synchronized chanting and laughing spilled from the stairwell, accompanied by the rattle of plastic bags, and then Dimetrice and Osheena, Bernard's other noisy neighbors, also spilled out, almost literally, so giddy they could barely stay on their feet. Each was hauling a bag stuffed full of something, while the words they were rapping weren't fit for Chris-Chris to hear. Mrs. Clarke slapped her hands over the little tyke's ears, although he probably had no idea what was being said.

A moment into their stumble toward their apartment, they realized they weren't alone, and the rap faded away, replaced by non-stop guffawing. As they drew close, Osheena waggled her fingers and squeaked, "Hi guys!" while Dimetrice waggled his arm over his head and pointed and barked, "Bernard, my man! Mrs. C! How ya doin'?"

"I think the question," Bernard said, "is what are you doing?"

"Upgrading the sound system!" Dimetrice answered. "Look at this!"

He plunked his bag down and with some effort extracted a box nearly half his own height. A frighteningly loud speaker was pictured on the box. Or at least, Bernard suspected it was frighteningly loud. What else could overwhelm Dimetrice with such euphoria? Osheena plopped her bag on the floor and struggled with its contents until she had unveiled the speaker's mate.

"God help the eastern seaboard," Bernard grumbled. "How the—" He glanced at Chris-Chris. Mrs. Clarke had uncovered his ears once the dirty lyrics had stopped. "How could you afford something like this?"

"Oh." Dimetrice waggled his hand. Bernard had no idea what that was supposed to mean.

"My brother got a deal," Osheena said. "His girlfriend's cousin's roommate's buddy has an uncle who gets things wholesale."

Before Bernard could work out that relationship, Dimetrice leaned in and whispered, "He don't get 'em wholesale. He sells 'em wholesale. He knows where the truck's parked." He nudged Bernard, just in case the point hadn't been taken.

It had. Not that Demitrice would know, but Bernard had experience with truck spillages. His own big screen TV, for example. "With any luck," he said, "these units got smashed when they fell off that truck."

Dimetrice laughed. "Come on, babe," he told Osheena. They rebagged their ill-gotten gains and wrestled them into the apartment, after which their voices raised once more in rap, this time sufficiently muffled by the walls that the words were unintelligible. Thank God for that.

"I wanna big candy bag like them," Chris-Chris announced.

Mrs. Clarke patted him on the head. "Your bag is big enough."

"Big! Bag! Big! Bag! Gimm-eee! Big! Bag!" Chris-Chris chanted, in fair if far cleaner imitation of Dimetrice and Osheena.

Bernard pointed his finger right between the kids eyes. "If you don't settle down, not only will you go to jail, you won't be carrying a candy bag at all. You'll be sitting out Halloween." Which might be a good thing. The last thing Chris-Chris needed was a sugar rush.

Chris-Chris's eyes nearly popped from his head. "Nooooooooo!" he moaned. "I'm gonna be Hulk!"

How appropriate. "Not if you're in jail," Bernard warned.

The boy stomped his foot. "Not fair!" he cried. "Not fair, not fair, not fair!"

"If you want to be the Hulk," Bernard told him, "be quiet until Halloween. Then you can stomp and snarl and smash all you want."

Yet again, he really shouldn't have said that. Especially not the smashing part. But the threat convinced Chris-Chris to reflect upon his behavior, as much as a boy his age could.

"Okaaaaaaay," he said, sunk in the depths of disappointment. But then he brightened. "I wanna go trick-or-treating with Melody!"

Bernard took a step back. "What?"

"Oh, that's a wonderful idea!" Mrs. Clarke said. "I couldn't manage taking him around, and he had such a lovely time with the two of you before. The apartment complex is doing a trunk-or-treat on Sunday. Would you mind?"

"I'll, uh, have to check our plans," Bernard said. "We might be busy."

"Mel-o-dy! Mel-o-dy!" Chris-Chris chanted.

Before Bernard could object further, Mrs. Clarke said, "Thank you, Mr. Earls. Thank you so much. It will mean a lot to me, and…" She cast a less than enthusiastic glance down at her great-grandson. "…Chris-Chris."

What could he say? He was a saint. Or so she always insisted. "Don't mention it, Mrs. Clarke."

"Yaaaaaaaay!" Chris-Chris bellowed. Then he clapped his hands over his mouth and shrugged in apology.

𝄞

Melody hummed through breakfast preparation—pancakes and fake maple syrup and pre-cooked sausage links zapped in the microwave. She didn't seem to notice Bernard's apprehension as he sat at the table, eyes glazed, fingers idly poking at the keys on his laptop. Once everything was on the table and she had melted with pleasure following her first bite, she noticed he wasn't eating.

"Something wrong?" she purred.

"Um," he replied.

"You slept well enough, I'm sure." She giggled.

"Yeah, sure, until the explosions started."

But that was just Chris-Chris, and Melody had learned to tune him out. Almost. At least, first thing in the morning. Really, it was no different than any other morning noise, be it phones going off or whatever. She just covered up her head and let Bernard deal with it. Simple.

"Chris-Chris wants to go trunk-or-treating with you on Sunday," Bernard said.

"Oh, that will be fun!"

"You think so?"

"Sure, he can run around and blow off some steam."

"Melody, that kid doesn't blow off steam. He's a natural gas explosion."

Bernie could be so critical sometimes. Although, he did have a point. But still, it was Halloween, and kids were supposed to get a bit crazy on Halloween, right? Even adults did, sometimes. When she was growing up, there was a family down the street that turned their entire yard into a horror movie every Halloween, with headstones and skeletons crawling out of graves and spiders spinning ginormous webs and ghosts hovering in the trees and on and on. She hated going by that house in October. It scared her to death. But she had to admit, those people were creative. In any case, she didn't see the harm in taking Chris-Chris around to collect candy, aside from the fact that Mrs. Clarke probably wouldn't be able to cope once he got all that sugar into his bloodstream.

"Don't worry about it right now," she said. "That's three days still, and you have a priceless stolen artifact to steal."

That was the right thing to say. Bernard winked at her and turned his attention on his food. He shoveled half of it down before speaking again. "I was thinking about what you said about my luck," he told her. "Today will be a dry run, just to ensure everything works as planned. I'll abort if anything goes wrong, even the least little thing."

"Good idea," she said. "And I'll think up a plan B."

Bernard set down his fork and gazed at her.

"What?" she asked.

"You know how much I appreciate you and your talents," he said slowly, "but please don't. Improvisation will only get us into trouble."

"Did I say improvisation? I said plan B."

"Your plan B's are always improvisation."

Now that was picky. "And your plan A's always go wrong." Which wasn't entirely true, but it wasn't entirely false, either.

"Remember who we're dealing with, love. We're stuck between the trigger-happy son of a Nazi and the murderous daughter of a Polish resistance fighter, who by all accounts hate each other's guts. It's not the time for winging it."

It was better not to press the issue. Bernie could be so inflexible sometimes. But he would need her plan B—she knew he would—and by God she was going to have it ready when he did. Even if she had to wing it.

"Whatever," she said. "Finish your breakfast. We gotta get to class."

&

Most men—those not used to it, anyway—would find the prospect of staring at a naked female model exciting, but Bernard had his mind on his plan, and anyway he was still annoyed that he couldn't concoct any color but purple. That, and he knew Melody would take exception should he grow excited over any woman but her, which made excitation damn near impossible. In other words, he had too much on his mind to think about the model.

Which, it turned out, he didn't have to think about anyway, because the model this time wasn't a woman but a Great Dane that had been trained to sit perfectly still and stare out the window for ridiculous amounts of time. Bernard wondered if that sort of training would work on Chris-Chris. The dog's trainer was in the room, just in case. Maybe Bernard could ask him about toddler training. With luck, it wouldn't involve doggie biscuits.

Great. He was starting to think all crosswise, like Melody. Focus, Bernard, focus.

The session proceeded apace but with interruptions. Instructor George Monroe called for breaks every forty-five minutes, during which the trainer took the dog out for a stretch and, upon return, settled him in the exact same position. Painting a well-behaved dog was a welcome break from both painting nude women and threatening ill-behaved youngsters with prison. As Bernard mixed his paints, he felt suddenly light-hearted, as though he'd escaped the bonds of the material world and was soaring into the realms of the spirit. His euphoria banished all other thought, even of Nazis and Polish resistance fighters and stealing stolen operas. He mixed and painted with wild abandon, scarcely conscious of what he was creating. His eyes and hands played without the interference of analysis or criticism from his brain.

Beside him, Melody must have been in much the same mood, for she was humming her way through her painting, soft and quiet so as not to disturb others. The sound added to Bernard's mood, even though the tune was "Bored to Death" by blink-182, which seemed inapt, but whatever. It seldom paid to try to figure Melody out. Best just to run with it. Bernard hummed along with her. She shot him a smile, which he returned. And they painted on.

When the morning session ended, Bernard finally stepped back and looked—really looked—at what he'd painted. It wasn't so much a Great Dane as Cerebus, the multiheaded hound of Hades and guardian of the gates of the underworld. The creature seemed to be sunk in shadow, all of him rendered in shades of dark...

...purple.

Damn it.

The form of the dog was all twisted and contorted, too, more like a child's nightmare of a dog than any creature that ever walked the Earth. All of which meant he was bound to be acclaimed as a genius yet again. Resigned to his fate, Bernard began cleaning up.

Melody's dog, he noticed, was rather cute, not a masterpiece but a nice picture anyone would be happy to hang on their living room wall, as opposed to Bernard's, which ought to be consigned to the dungeon, if one had a dungeon.

George began making rounds, once more restricting his comments to subdued praise and occasional suggestions. And then he came to Cerebus and nearly jumped out of his skin.

"Whoa," he said.

Bernard waited for the inevitable.

"Whoa. That's dark."

"I do my darkest work when I'm happy," Bernard quipped.

"Hmm. Do you have a therapist?"

"No."

George set his finger to his lips. "Hmm."

Which probably meant, "You should," but Bernard decided not to hold it against him. He'd probably think the same thing if their places were exchanged.

"It's exquisite, anyway," George finally decided. "Although, how you pulled that from the soul of a Great Dane, I don't know. They don't call them the world's biggest lap dogs for nothing."

Shortly thereafter, the class filed out of the room for lunch. Bernard and Melody hung back a bit then loitered in the corridor while the other students vanished into the bistro. Once all was quiet, Bernard said, "I forgot something. You go on ahead." Melody nodded and proceeded to lunch.

A small ruse, in case anyone was listening, and protection for her, too. If asked later, she could honestly report what he'd said to her. He slipped back into the empty classroom, made for the back, and ducked behind the screen from which the models had emerged the previous day.

There was a slight gap in the curtain covering the back wall, and behind the curtain the balcony door. Yesterday, the model had passed onto the balcony without hinderance. Bernard could just unlock and open it, but he trusted neither Nachtnebel nor Fitzroy to be that sloppy. Pushing between the curtain and the wall, he found a keypad to the left of the door, an alarm control. It had been deactivated.

Huh. Someone *had* been that sloppy. Maybe George unlocked it during class so the models could step outside for breaks?

No sense questioning a gift. Probably it was Melody's luck at work. Bernard slipped onto the patio and scanned the area. Nobody on the other patios, nobody roaming the grounds. Perfect. Overhead, the ladder to the roof beckoned. He found the release, lowered the extension, and climbed up. The metal frame jiggled and clanked as he ascended. He squeezed the life out of the rungs until his fingers and palms hurt. Even if one's brain was used to heights, one's body didn't much like hanging from the side of a building. *Next time*, he told himself, *bring work gloves*. He reached the top without slipping, though, and swung himself over to the flat part of the roof.

The view was fantastic: the sprawling grounds, flocks of birds lifting from the crowns of trees and settling back again, a red tail hawk and a couple of turkey vultures soaring overhead on the thermals. If only he'd brought a canvas and some paints with him! But no, that wouldn't have worked. He would never have made it up the ladder with them, and when he got here, he'd end up painting some horror-story forest shrouded in dark purple. He didn't know why he was in a purple period, but there it was. He could never paint something as bright and alive as this.

But never mind that. He had work to do. He went to the west service entrance, texted Shawn, and received the reply. The access door's security had been deactivated. Barnard picked the lock in about ten seconds.

The stairwell was pitch black. He turned on his cell phone flashlight and by its aid descended to the third floor. Another text to Shawn. Another reply, this time not *hi* but the six-digit code for the interior doors, providing not only that intel but also signaling that the cameras inside the gallery had been dealt with. Bernard entered the code into the keypad. The door clicked open. Quiet and slow, he pulled it open a crack and peeked into the darkened gallery. Empty. No people, not even any art on display. Perfect. He closed the door behind him, crept to the treasure room door, and keyed in the code there.

The treasure room slumbered in darkness, too, silent as a country graveyard at three in the morning. He quietly closed the door behind him. It had been ridiculously easy. For him, anyway.

He'd kept Shawn plenty busy, and it wasn't over. Bernard hoped the kid wouldn't lose his nerve.

Turning on his cell phone light, Bernard prowled among the wares. Unlike ancient treasure rooms unearthed by Hollywood archeologists, there were no piles of gold, no chests of jewels, no haphazard mounds of ancient artifacts. The place was crowded but organized. Paintings hung on the walls and rested on easels. Statues stood guard on pedestals. Glass cases protected ornate tableware and jewelry and precious papers. A bit of a maze, with displays forming corridors that twisted through the room, but neat and tidy, and gaps between the displays allowed Bernard to move from one section to another without taking the grand tour.

A lot of good stuff, all begging to be stolen. Bernard' fingers began to itch. *Nope*, he scolded them. *We're just here for the music.* They almost listened. Almost. As he worked his way through the collection, an ornate armoire caught his eye. He loved furniture of bygone eras and couldn't resist a peek. Lifting the top, he found a collection of gold and silver jewelry of such elegance, he just had to pick out something for Melody. Earrings, maybe. Yes, those silver pendant earrings with mother of pearl inlays, studded with tiny rubies. She loved rubies. Of course she did. They were red. He pocketed them and moved on, focused solely on paper treasure.

Problem was, there were a *lot* of papers, not one of them written in English, a fair number of them music scores, many rendered in atrocious handwriting. Bernard examined them one by one, but he had very little time. Lunch period would soon be over. He had to find his target and get out.

He moved quickly, bypassing anything that wasn't music, hoping when *Rienzi* showed up, it would say so in legible script. The minutes ticked by. He was about to give up when there it was, right before him, a sheaf of papers with the magic word inscribed in beautiful, elaborate penmanship above the first staff.

He didn't have time to jimmie the case, but tomorrow would be different. He knew the route, knew *Rienzi*'s resting place. Tomorrow, he'd make short work of it. Piece of cake.

He really shouldn't have thought that. (Thinking such things had become a reprehensible habit.)

As soon as he did, the lights came on.

$$\text{\large\&}$$

"I should have had her killed when I had the chance," Gerhardt Nachtnebel, Jr. grumbled.

"Oh, sir, that would have been imprudent," someone else said, someone soprano, someone with enough experience in managing a filthy rich employer to understand the importance of tone. The words were a rebuke, but the delivery suggested deep concern for the master's well-being. "She's made contingencies. You'd be exposed and lose everything."

The moment the lights came up, Bernard slipped through a gap between a pair of glass cases and hid behind a seven-foot display cabinet filled with porcelain and silver dining implements. He turned off his cell phone light and stood as still as the statuary, barely breathing, listening for footsteps while taking in the conversation.

"I'd have gotten away with it," Nachtnebel said. "I always get away with it. Money has that effect." But he didn't sound too confident, and the servant didn't comment.

They'd entered from the gallery, same as Bernard, and had gone directly to the display case containing *Rienzi*. "It's still here, at least," Nachtnebel said.

"You don't really think anyone could get in here, do you, sir? Your security's impeccable. They say nobody can defeat Fitzroy's latest systems."

"If anyone could find a way, it would be Celestina. She's not just a ruthless bitch. She's clever. Oh, yes, my sweet little cousin—" He put an ironic emphasis on *sweet*. "—could worm her way in here no problem."

"But why warn you?"

Bernard's whole body knotted up. He bit back the urge to scream, "*What?*"

Nachtnebel didn't speculate. "I want cameras in here. How fast can Fitzroy do it?"

"For you, they'll come immediately."

"See that they do. Limit access to one worker. And make sure they sign a nondisclosure agreement. I don't want anyone babbling about what they see in here."

That should have ended it, but for some reason Nachtnebel and his assistant didn't move. Bernard still heard their breathing. Why were they stalling? Time was about up. He had to get out of here. But how? Maybe the fake restroom doors. If they were keyed from the inside, he was stuck, but it was worth a look. *Trust to Melody's luck*, he told himself.

"It's a beautiful thing," Nachtnebel said. His tension must have evaporated. He sounded almost in love.

"It is," the servant agreed.

Bernard inched toward the nearest fake restroom door, careful to make no sound, careful to keep large objects between him and the master of the house.

"It's not just music. Not even just Wagner. *Rienzi* is history in the deepest sense."

"How so?" the servant asked.

"Hitler saw the opera as a young man. This is the original score. He requested and received it as a gift on his fiftieth birthday.

He was so taken by the story's unification theme that it changed the world."

Bernard was at the door now and still out of sight of Nachtnebel. Melody's luck came through. The lock wasn't keyed. It was an escape deadlock, like those on hotel doors. He texted Shawn: *Emergency. Turn off third floor hall cameras.* He hated being that explicit, but he had no choice. He could only hope it wouldn't come back to bite him.

"Perhaps not for the better," the servant suggested.

"That depends on how you look at it. Hitler's particular vision of unification bred others, some of which are still with us today. Call him a lunatic if you will, a madman, evil, even..."

Done, Shawn texted back. Slowly, quietly, Bernard lifted the handle, covering the click of the deadbolt with the conversation.

"...but at the root," Nachtnebel went on, "he had the right idea. Sure, he was overzealous in pursuing it, as was Stalin or any of a host of other madmen since. But it was the right idea."

"I see," the servant said, although her tone suggested she didn't.

"That's why Celestina wants *Rienzi.* Oh, sure, she wants to humiliate me, but she wants the artifact as much as I do. And I swear, Carly, I swear on my life..."

Bernard didn't catch Nachtnebel's actual swearing. He cracked the door, ensured all was clear, and on impulse dug the earrings from his pocket and packed them into the deadbolt hole. They filled it nicely, right to the edge. He closed the door, then tested opening it again. Perfect. Blocked by the jewelry, the bolt failed to engage. He did feel a pang of regret, leaving Melody's gift behind, but so long as nobody discovered the tampering, he could retrieve it later.

When he arrived at the bistro, the students were just clearing out and returning to class. He found Melody tossing her trash into the wastebasket.

"So?" she asked.

He took her arm and led her out. "Had a close call," he whispered, "but I found it."

"So we're good?"

"Not quite. Didn't have time to pick it up. And we have another problem. Several, in fact."

"You shouldn't have said anything about your luck," Melody scolded.

"I know, I know. But your luck got me out. Let's get to class. I'll tell you everything tonight."

Once the students were situated, the afternoon's subject was ushered in. This time it was a snowy toy poodle, carried to a pink couch by a lovely young lady who Bernard assumed was her trainer. But she defied his expectations by settling herself on the couch with the dog in her lap and removing her t-shirt. She leaned back and gazed at the dog, and the painting began.

Melody set to work while Bernard obsessed over how not to make purple paint. This scene couldn't tolerate even a dab of purple. His first attempt at mixing went awry again. Purple, purple everywhere. There was nothing for it. No more mixing. He'd use colors straight from the tube.

The painting that emerged was garish but probably no worse than some of the stuff hanging in famous art galleries. On his canvas, the woman's bright red hair and yellow face lent a curious lightness to her green shoulders and blue breasts—was that a sign of a heart attack?—and the pure white fluffball of a dog with beady black eyes. Probably she was an alien and the dog a demon. The couch was black because he wasn't about to attempt to mix pink and get purple, plus he didn't like the idea of two red elements.

Upon review, Bernard's work got George more excited than he'd ever been. "Wow!" the instructor effused. He invited everyone to critique the painting, and after the whole class said, "Wow!" in unison, he dismissed them.

Once they were in the car on their way home, Melody said, "Wow, Bernie."

"Is that for me, or my painting?"

"Your painting. I've never seen a woman *those* colors before."

"With luck, nobody has," Bernard said. "In hindsight, it was pretty scary."

"Why did you do her that way?"

"I was sick of purple."

Melody laughed. "I guess that's what makes you a genius."

"What's that?"

"Your unique approach to art."

"Maybe, but I expect I'll give it up once this job is over. I can't stand being famous."

She leaned over and rested her head on his shoulder. "You're stuck with it. You'll always be famous with me."

Which was good enough for him.

𝄢

After dinner, they curled up together on the sofa with Fifi in Melody's lap and Bernard on more or less every other part of her while they watched *Spider-Man: Homecoming*, which had been released on DVD less than two weeks before. Melody had the good fortune to be gifted a copy by a friendly stranger in the mall. She said that was okay, because the stranger was an older fellow who had just come from a jewelry store where he'd spent ten thousand dollars on diamond baubles for his wife. Using his debit card. Ergo, he could afford another copy of *Spider-Man*. Bernard liked her logic.

After the movie, they remained on the couch, immersed in each other's warmth, until Melody asked, "What's our new problem?"

Bernard didn't want to go there. It was too pleasant holding her, listening to her breathe while Fifi purred like a well-tuned engine. But business was business. "I infiltrated the treasure room, no problem. I even found *Rienzi*. But I didn't have time to snatch it, and before I could get out, Nachtnebel showed up with one of his servants."

Melody gasped and looked up in alarm.

"They didn't see me," he said. "The good news is, on the way out, I rigged the fake restroom door for easy access. So long as nobody discovers that, I won't have to climb up the roof again."

Melody tightened her arms around him. "Oh, good. I kept thinking of your broken body splattered on the ground."

"You shouldn't think things like that."

"I know, but I can't help it. Remember that time you ended up dangling from that hotel balcony? And I already had the jewel."

Bernard remembered. He rather didn't want to. While he was failing to get to their target, a fabulous jewel, she'd wormed her way in and nabbed the wrong one because she liked its color better. Red, of course. Plus, since it was such a *nice* red, she wouldn't let Bernard sell it. At least he hadn't died while not getting paid.

"Anyway," he continued, "I overheard something encouraging and something disturbing. Which do you want first?"

"Encouraging," Melody said without hesitation.

"Nachtnebel didn't send someone to kill Celeste. He said he wished he had, but that was probably just grousing."

"Why would he be hunting grouse in his treasure room?"

"I mean, griping."

"Then why didn't you say so? Why was he griping?"

"That," Bernard told her, "is the disturbing part. Nachtnebel knows someone's trying to steal *Rienzi*."

Melody disentangled herself and set Fifi on the sofa next to her. Fifi meowed piteously and snuck back into her lap. "How could he know that?"

"Celeste told him."

"*What?*"

"That's just what I said. Or almost said."

Melody's frown of concentration was almost painful. "But why?"

Excellent question, for which Bernard had no clear answer. "Nachtnebel knows she's Celestina Bartosz. He called her cousin. You were right. His father must be Celestina's grandfather."

"This is terrible!" Melody said.

"Sure is. We might get caught in the crossfire."

"Plus, it's a horrible family dynamic."

Bernard opened his mouth, but no words came out. Having no use for a speechless mouth, he closed it again.

Melody shrugged. "Oh, well, that's their problem. We'll just do our job, right?"

"Except Nachtnebel decided to install cameras in the treasure room."

"Shawn can take care of those."

"Yeah, but we only have a hundred left in the expense fund, and I haven't even deducted meals yet. I'm not sure I want to ask Celeste for more, under the circumstances."

Melody leaned into him again. He wrapped his arms around her. "Don't worry," she said. "I'll talk her into it."

Bernard didn't know about that. Melody could charm all the socks off a millipede, if for some inexplicable reason it happened to be wearing socks, but this situation was far from typical. Then again, so was Melody. Then again...

She must have sensed his doubt. "I will," she insisted. "And you'd better let me do it, too. If you try, we'll end up buried in her cellar alongside that other guy. Although, I guess that other guy *isn't* buried there. I wonder if there even was an other guy?"

"Nacthnebel said he should have had killed her when he had the chance," Bernard mused. "He must've had an operative within striking distance of her. Sounds like there's a history between them. Dueling cousins."

"Like I said. Horrible family dynamic."

Bernard nodded. "Fits with what Allegra Fumagalli told me. I'll make arrangements with Shawn, then you can charm the money out of Celeste's bank account." He pulled out his cell phone and dialed his hapless assistant.

Shawn didn't say hello, but he did say something that rhymed: "No."

"No, what?" Bernard inquired as politely as he could, which wasn't very.

"No, I'm not helping you further."

In the background, Felicity asked, "Is that Bernard again?"

"Who else?" Shawn griped. "I told him no."

"I know you told him no. I heard very clearly."

"Can I just—" Bernard began.

"No," Shawn repeated.

"Don't say no until you know how much," Felicity instructed.

Shawn sighed a miserable sigh. "How much?" he asked. "And then, no."

Felicity corrected him again. "Never ask how much. Never say how much either, not until you know what for."

"I'm about to give someone what for," Shawn snapped.

"Can I just—" Bernard began again.

A minor scuffle interrupted him, then Felicity's voice returned, louder. "You're on speaker. What for?"

"CanIjustsayIhaveaproblemandneedhelp?" Bernard said in a rush.

"No," Shawn told him.

"He already said it," Felicity informed Shawn. "What's the problem?"

At least he'd gotten that far. "I need to run another experiment tomorrow."

"No," Shawn insisted.

"It's easy, just the hall cameras this time. Oh, and there's a new wrinkle."

"No."

"Yes, there is. Nachtnebel's installed new cameras in the target area."

Shawn didn't say no that time. He didn't say anything.

Bernard wondered if he'd disconnected, but the call was still active, so probably not. "Are you there, Shawn?"

"Why would he install cameras in a restroom? Isn't that illegal?"

Okay, probably Bernard should have admitted somewhere along the line that it wasn't really a restroom. But he didn't have hindsight ahead of time. Of course not. That's why they call it hindsight. "Don't worry about that. He just did, is all, and for tomorrow's test, you'll need to deactivate them."

"That's not too bad," Felicity said. "Sounds like a thousand to me."

She was letting him off cheap. Finally. "I only have one hundred left."

"No," Shawn said.

Felicity overrode him. "Get more cash."

Bernard looked to heaven for deliverance. "How much more?"

"Five hundred," Felicity suggested.

"Two," Bernard countered.

"Four."

"Three."

"No!" Shawn snapped.

"It'll help with wedding expenses, baby," Felicity cooed, then to Bernard she said, "Deal."

Bernard figured they ought to already have enough for two weddings, but then it had been a while since he was involved in such matters, and anyway, Melody's parents footed the bill, maybe with what remained of the Kensington crown jewels. Or the dregs of the McGirl bootlegging stash. Or both. "Same signals," he told Shawn. "About noon."

Neither Shawn nor Felicity answered, but Bernard could imagine the conversation they were having with their eyes.

"We good?" he asked.

"Yeah," Shawn said, injecting such misery that Bernard almost wanted to apologize.

Nah, not really.

Chapter 19: Friday, October 27, 2017

Bernard wondered if his hearing, or maybe his brain, had been permanently damaged. As he locked the apartment door on their way to class, he could have sworn a T-rex bellowed. But the sound was cut short and didn't repeat. He glanced at Melody, who was checking her purse for God knew what. She didn't react in the slightest. Must've been his imagination.

"You got what you need?" she asked.

He patted his jacket to indicate one of his hidden pockets, within which a pair of latex gloves and a large manila envelope were stashed. "Right here," he assured her. The gloves were more to protect *Rienzi* than to avoid fingerprints. He would slip the manuscript into the envelope for transport to its new owner. "What about you?" he asked.

Melody tapped her temple. "I got all I need right here," she replied.

Which was both comforting and a bit scary.

The D.C. area traffic was lighter than usual this morning, meaning instead of a hellacious crush of vehicles moving between zero and five miles per hour, the hellacious crush maintained a minimum speed of one—most of the time—and sometimes rocketed to ten. Melody paid more attention to her phone than the road, but even without looking up she had some helpful suggestions.

"There's a gap two cars up in the left lane."

"You can get into the right lane now. Oh, you missed it."

"Get ahead of this guy."

"You have five seconds to...never mind."

Bernard's failure to take her suggestions didn't seem to bother her. After twenty minutes of it, he had to ask. "Why do you do that?"

"Do what?"

"Tell me what to do."

"Do I?"

"You do."

Eyes still on her phone, she shrugged. "Habit, I guess."

"Telling me what to do is a habit, huh? Okay, I can see that."

"No, silly. Driving is."

Bernard could already feel the conversation flipping over and spinning out. "You aren't driving. I am."

She tapped something into the phone. "I'm driving virtually."

"Then you shouldn't be on your phone."

"I wouldn't be if I were really driving. See, I can virtually drive and really browse or text, or I can really drive and virtually browse or text. I can even virtually drive and virtually browse or text. I just can't do both for real at the same time. Well, I could, but it would be harder to sweet-talk the cop who pulls me over." She smiled at the phone. "Although, that might be a fun challenge."

"Don't even think it," Bernard snapped.

"Too late."

"Melody—"

"The problem with you is, you can't tell fantasy from reality."

He was pretty sure that was her problem, but whatever.

"I'm not telling you what to do," she went on. "I'm telling myself what I would do if I was driving."

Which made as much sense as anything else in their lives. Bernard decided he could live with it, although he couldn't let her off that easily. "Then maybe," he suggested, "you should apply that skill to our work."

"I do, all the time."

"Yeah? What do you imagine for today? Suppose I get caught in the treasure room, like I almost did yesterday. How do we get out of it?"

Melody flicked through a series of screens on her phone. "Oh, that's easy. Just say you thought it was the restroom."

"Perfect, except the restroom door is deadlocked. How did I get in?"

She turned a dull look on him. "Come on, Bernie. Someone rigged that door for easy access. You just pushed it open. How were you to know it was supposed to be locked?"

"Maybe the 'out of order' signs would have tipped me off."

"Maybe you were too desperate to notice the signs."

"But not too desperate to run out again when I discovered it wasn't a restroom?"

Melody sighed and tucked away her phone. "How can such a great artist have no creativity? You were so amazed by the treasure, you forgot you had to go. Just like, you know, when you're reading a book you can't put down?"

Bernard gave up. "If I'm that hopeless, maybe you should come with me."

She perked up "Really?"

No, not really. He didn't want Melody in the clutches of a maniac son of a Nazi who'd sent someone to not kill his archenemy cousin. Okay, the not killing part wasn't so bad, but what *had* he sent someone to do? Probably not to deliver a cake. Probably not to borrow a set of socket wrenches. Alas, Melody was so excited at the accidental invitation that he didn't have the heart to say no. He therefore said nothing, just drove, if creeping along in this crush could be called driving.

She kissed her index finger and touched it to his lips. "I'd love to!"

Bernard feared she really shouldn't have said that.

&

Shortly before arriving at Nachtnebel's, Melody placed one last call to Celeste, keeping it off speaker so Bernie wouldn't become distracted. Or blow it with ill-timed sarcasm. "We need one last little favor," she said.

"Should I be worried?" Celeste asked, although given her tone, it was less a question than a threat. Melody figured she just hadn't had her morning coffee yet.

"Noooooo," Melody cooed. "We need a bit more funding for our contractor ."

"It's not a favor if you have to pay him."

"He's giving us a deal. He's sweet like that."

"Uh-huh. How much?"

"Oh, not much." Melody counted on her fingers. Not that she needed to, but she figured the pause made her sound more thoughtful. "Two hundred."

"I'm paying you twenty thousand, assuming you don't botch the job. You can't cover two hundred yourselves?"

"It's not so much that. It's the art supplies."

Celeste didn't reply, but that in itself was a reply.

"And," Melody added, "meals."

"Meals!"

"Oh, yes. That bistro charges two arms and a leg and a half." Now, that might be something Celeste could paint. Dancers with no heads, no arms, and half a leg each. No, never mind. That was terrifying.

"I can't deny that," Celeste said. "How much do you want?"

"Let's call it four hundred," Melody suggested.

"Fine. But rather than another MoneyMonkey, I'll just add it into your payoff. Assuming you don't botch the job. If you do, you refund everything I've sent you."

Melody was so annoyed by that insinuation that she couldn't even giggle at MoneyMonkey. She was starting to understand Bernie's irritation. Maybe she should allow him one sarcastic jab after all. No, better not. "Don't worry," she said. "Bernie has mad skills."

Bernard shot her a look.

She disconnected before he could get sarcastic.

𝄞

Bernard worried all through the morning painting session, which involved a silver folding table adorned with roses red, yellow, and orange, apples red and green and yellow, and in their midst, a plastic terrarium containing a frighteningly large tarantula. He was so worried, he didn't even find the arrangement odd; so worried, he didn't worry about purple; so worried, he didn't notice that he hadn't mixed any purple at all, not until the end of the session.

George made his rounds, stopped at Bernard's painting as usual, and gave it unusually long consideration. "Monochrome," he said. "Interesting."

Only then did Bernard realize he'd rendered everything in shades of gray. "Is that good?" he asked.

George crossed his arms over his chest, stepped back, cocked his head. "It's not a matter of good or bad. It's a matter of intent."

"What did I intend?" As soon as he asked it, Bernard realized what a stupid question that was.

Or maybe not. "I'd say," George decided, "you're highlighting how evil casts a shadow over good."

That could work. Maybe. "Interesting interpretation," Bernard said, hoping that was a reasonable thing for an artist to say.

Must've been. George moved on. Melody whispered in Bernard's ear. "See? You *can* be creative."

"Nice to know," he whispered back. But he wasn't creative enough to find a way to discourage her from accompanying him into the treasure room, so he didn't try. He just told himself it would be all right. If they got into a jam, she'd get them out of it. He hoped.

The class adjourned for lunch. Bernard and Melody took their time leaving, guaranteeing they would be the last out, and hung around the bistro door until everyone else had filed in. After checking the time—Brian the guard wouldn't pass by for a good twenty minutes—Bernard sent Shawn the *Hi* signal to glitch the hall and treasure room cameras.

A pause ensued, then Shawn's reply came back: *Hi.*

They strolled to the fake restroom door and took a quick look around. They were alone. Bernard nudged the door. It opened easily. Keeping his body between the door and Melody, he retrieved and pocketed the earrings from the deadbolt hole. Not only were they to be a surprise, he couldn't afford her squealing with delight just now, which she would if she saw them. She had a hard time containing her emotions where sparklies were concerned.

They slipped inside. Bernard closed the door. The deadbolt clicked into place. Taking Melody's hand, he used his cell phone flashlight to lead her through the maze to their target. She leaned over the case, mesmerized by the notes flowing along the staves. "It's beautiful!" she murmured.

"Twenty thousand dollars beautiful," Bernard told her.

"Is money all you ever think about, Bernie?"

"Nope. Sometimes I think about you. But not while I'm working. That's dangerous."

She sighed happily and stood back so as not to distract him. Bernard picked the case's lock with ease, slid open the back panel, and pulled on his latex gloves. With excessive care, he lifted the stack of paper and settled it on the glass top of the display case. He then pulled the manilla envelope from the large pocket inside his jacket and eased the manuscript in. He folded the flap over but didn't seal it. Then he gradually slid the envelope back into his pocket, careful not to bend it, and finally closed and locked the case.

"And that's that," he told Melody. She kissed him on the cheek. Back at the fake restroom door, he checked the time, peeked out to make sure that Brian Garfunkel hadn't inexplicably altered his routine, and escorted Melody out. The door clicked shut behind them, deadbolt engaged. Nobody would ever know they'd been there. They returned to the bistro, where Bernard texted Shawn to restore everything to working order.

And that was that. They just had to suffer one more painting session. Easy peasy.

Yep. He'd thought it again.

$$\text{\textbf{\&}}$$

That final session was curiously simple. Maybe George Monroe was testing them or trying to impart some artistic wisdom via osmosis. Bernard had no idea. But then, he'd been clueless the entire time, at least where drawing and painting were concerned. In any case, the subject was a vase on a folding table. The folding table was black. The vase was clear glass, wide at the bottom, narrow in the middle, not quite so wide at the lip, no ostentation, just smooth glass. No flowers in the vase. Not even a weed. Not even water, in fact.

The other students dove into the subject with the same focus they had afforded tarantulas and naked women. Bernard just puzzled over it. He puzzled so long he almost forgot to paint. Ultimately, he just splashed some black onto the canvas for the tabletop and some light gray over it for the vase. Neither had true form. They were just splashes of black and gray.

He pondered adding a dab of purple, just to see what George would say, but decided against it. He was sick of purple, and besides, no point making stuff up, right?

In the end, it wouldn't have mattered. George never got to Bernard's painting. He was halfway through his inspections when a young woman in the official Nachtnebel Foundation uniform scurried in, caught him by the arm, and whispered in his ear. Then they gaped at each other, eyes nearly popping from their sockets. For five whole seconds they did nothing but gape, then she rushed out.

George gave his class a befuddled examination before clearing his throat as if preparing to speak for the first time in his life. "I'm sorry," he said, "but everyone must stay here for...for...for a bit." He fumbled his way to a chair, dragged it to the folding table, and nearly fell into it. The vase tottered.

"What's wrong?" one of the female students asked.

"There's been an...a...an...incident."

Uh-oh, Bernard thought. Melody hooked her arm through his and leaned into him, implying the same sentiment.

"Everyone please stay here until it's..." George ran a hand through his hair. "...resolved."

"Like a fire?" someone asked.

"Bomb threat?" someone else suggested.

"Active shooter?" another proposed.

"Sprinkler system rupture?"

That last one inspired silence all around.

"No," George said. "We're safe. It's just...we...we have to...have to...wait here. Why don't you..." His gaze wandered the room, the floor, the windows, the ceiling, as though seeking some repair job to which a bunch of artists could apply themselves. But there wasn't any, so he shrugged.

For a few minutes, the students stood in confused silence, then they began to congregate in small groups, talking to each other, then they gathered up their week's work and stacked it along the wall, ready to take home if and when they were allowed to leave. Curiously, nobody questioned why they were being held without charge, but Bernard knew. Nachtnebel had discovered *Rienzi* missing, and he'd locked down the mansion.

Fifteen minutes passed in befuddlement before a pair of guards, Brian Garfunkel and a shorter, thinner, more female associate, burst into the room. "All right!" Brian barked. "Men line up on that side of the room, women on that side."

"Now just a minute," George protested. He held up a finger. He met Brian's eyes. He put down his finger and, head hung, went to the male side of the room. Muttering their confusion, the other students complied. All except Melody. Already in his assigned spot, Bernard motioned her off and mouthed, *Go*. Best not to draw attention to themselves. Okay, yeah, they'd been the center of attention for the past two weeks, but best not pile it on, not now. Alas, Melody seldom worried about that, seeing as how she could hardly avoid a certain amount of attention. Her strategy frequently involved becoming the focus.

Like now. She marched right up to Brian, planted her fists on her hips, and stared him down. Literally. He returned her stare for all of five seconds before looking away in embarrassment.

"What's this about, Brian?" she demanded.

Bernard wondered if it being on a first name basis with a guard was a positive or negative thing. For him, definitely a negative. For Melody...

"Look," Brian said, more apologetically than he no doubt wanted. "We're just following orders."

"Oh yeah? That's what all those Nazi soldiers said. Just following orders. And look where it got *them*."

Bernard winced. Maybe they shouldn't bring up Nazis.

"Mr. Nachtnebel is *not* a Nazi," the female guard snapped. She met Melody's stare without fear, not having encountered her before. That was about to change.

Melody made a show of squinting at the woman's name tag. "Colleen Corduroy," she read. "Is your family in textiles?"

"What?"

"Textiles. Linen. Satin. Corduroy."

Collen cocked her head. "No, why?"

"Maybe an ancestor?" Melody suggested.

"Not that I know of. What does that have to do with Nazis?"

"Nothing. I was just curious. My family was royalty on one side and bootleggers on the other."

"That's..." Colleen glanced at Brian, who shrugged and continued to look anywhere but at Melody. "That's beside the point. Line up over there." She pointed to the women arrayed along the wall.

"Not until I know why," Melody said. "This is the United States of America, and we have rights."

A murmuring broke out among the students. Not too loud, but loud enough to indicate they hadn't thought of that before, but now that Melody had mentioned it, yes, it was a fair point.

Colleen bit her lip, clearly not liking the insinuation that she was colluding with Nazis, or thugs anyway, when she herself was a U.S. citizen. "Look," she said. "Something was–"

"Quiet!" Brian snapped.

"Oh, I see," Melody said. "You think we're stupid."

Now grumbling broke out among the artists. Bernard put his hand over his face and shook his head. Aside from angering Brian and Colleen, provoking a riot was about the worst thing Melody could do. But he was powerless to intervene. Once she got going, only an act of God could stop her.

Brian puffed himself up and tried to look brave, which his quivering fingers said he wasn't. He was losing control of the situation. "No," he said. "We just think you should do as your told."

That got a bigger grumble from the crowd. Even George didn't like it.

Melody waggled a finger in the guards' faces. "Shame on you. It's obvious, isn't it? Something's been stolen, and you think you're going to search us."

That's exactly what they think, Bernard thought, *and they're right. How do I get rid of this thing?*

"Exactly," Brian admitted, and Colleen nodded, and they both tried to stand straight and strong and tall, although Colleen wasn't that tall.

"You need a warrant," Melody informed them.

Which technically was wrong. Technically, they couldn't get a warrant, not being officers of the law. At most, they could detain everyone until the police arrived. But given the way Brian and Colleen looked at each other, Bernard knew they had no clue about legalities. All they knew was what they'd been ordered to do.

He scanned the room for some way out of this jam, and he quickly found one. On the desk by the wall where George usually sat while the class painted lay a large sketch pad and some pencils. Bernard slipped over and picked up the sketch pad while the guards and students and George were all focused on Melody.

"We do not," Colleen said. "Somebody here is a thief, and Mr. Nachtnebel has a right to retrieve what they took."

"Not by illegal search and seizure!" Melody snapped, waggling her finger in their faces again.

God, she was beautiful when she was angry. Or, okay, any other time. Bernard took the envelope from his pocket and tucked it into the sketchbook. With all eyes on the confrontation, nobody noticed. Then he flipped the book open, snagged a pencil from the desk, and began to sketch. Brian. Colleen. Melody. Dark clouds and lightning overhead. Very melodramatic.

"We aren't the crooks," Brian insisted.

"You will be if you do this," Melody replied.

"You're probably the crook!" Colleen poked Melody in the shoulder. (*Oh, that was a bad move!* Bernard thought.) "Maybe we should search you first!"

Melody poked Colleen back. "Listen, sister," she warned, "touch me again and I'm suing this place for everything it's got. This will be my mansion. And as a Kensington, a direct descendant of royalty, I know how to run it properly!"

Colleen nearly made a grab for Melody's wrists, but then she caught a movement out of the corner of her eye and whirled. Pointing a finger at Bernard, she demanded, "What the hell are you doing?"

Bernard added a few pencil strokes to his masterpiece. "Drawing," he said. He hummed a few notes of *Bored to Death*.

"Put that down!"

"It's an art class," Bernard objected. "We're supposed to be drawing and painting and whatnot." He hummed a few more bars as he worked.

Abandoning Melody, Colleen and Brian marched over to Bernard. Keeping a grip on it so *Rienzi* didn't fall out, he turned the book so they could see it: a somewhat childish rendering of two monsters attacking a beautiful woman in a terrible storm.

"Huh," Brian said. "That's pretty good."

Colleen punched his arm. "That's us, you moron!"

"Yeah, but it's pretty good."

The male students gathered 'round and murmured compliments, then the female students crossed the room and admired Bernard's work. A few of them also whispered more personal admiration in his ear, but he ignored them.

Finally, Colleen had had enough. "Put that down," she snapped. "All of you get back where you belong."

Grumbling, the students complied. Bernard closed the sketchbook and returned it to the desk by the wall, where it was soon out of sight, out of mind. He gave Melody a surreptitious wink. She gave him a sultry smile in return.

Another pair of guards arrived a few minutes later, with Gerhardt Nachtnebel, Jr. himself smiling behind them as though all was right with the world. "My friends," he said, "I'm sorry about this, but something terrible has happened. Someone has stolen one of the most precious pieces in my collection. I'm sure all of you are entirely blameless and don't deserve this intrusion, but I'd like to ask your cooperation in apprehending the thief. I've already conducted searches of everyone on my staff, including the security guards themselves. They were all most cooperative, which I deeply appreciate. Unfortunately, the artifact has not turned up, so I'm forced to the sad conclusion that one of the students has done this terrible deed. It's a shame I must ask this, because I'm sure everyone in this room is innocent, but if I could have your cooperation in conducting a search, I would deeply appreciate it."

He sure knows how to lay it on, Bernard thought, half in admiration.

Nachtnebel's appeal worked. Placated, the artists allowed themselves to be taken one by one into a storage closet at the back of the room and patted down, the men by the male guards and the women by the female guards. Once cleared, they were given permission to leave. Bernard and Melody, too.

On their way out, Bernard passed by the desk to retrieve the sketchbook.

It wasn't there.

Chapter 20: Late Friday, October 27, 2017, blurring into Saturday

When Bernard got in one of these moods, Melody never quite knew what to do. He was furious. And depressed. He wanted to blow up the whole world. He wanted to kick himself clear to Wyoming. He wanted to slink into a dark cave and never come out. He *really* didn't want to face the wrath of Celeste, a.k.a. Celestina Bartosz, and who could blame him for that? But most of all, he wanted to find whoever had taken that sketchbook and suspend them by a fraying rope over a pot of boiling oil.

And that was, you know, not very nice at all.

Being such a convoluted mass of emotion, in the main Bernard flopped on the sofa and sulked. Melody tried stroking his hair, holding him, whispering it would be okay. But she might as well not have been there. She gave up and retreated to the kitchen. She was hungry even if he wasn't, and maybe—just maybe—something yummy would pull him out of his funk. Good food always worked for her, anyway.

Melody kept a well-organized kitchen, and though they didn't have money for extravagances most of the time, she did stash away a few surprises, mostly canned goods picked up on sale and forgotten until that magic moment when she rediscovered them and turned them into a divine repast. Like this little can of chopped chipotles. She mixed them into some hamburger, squashed the burger into patties, and broiled them. Then she toasted a couple sesame buns, poured a bit of salsa onto each half, and added the burgers and some pepper jack. A side of nacho corn chips and cheap lemon-lime soda completed the meal.

After setting everything on the coffee table, Melody sat next to Bernard and turned on *Guardians of the Galaxy*. She found the film strange, but he always got a few laughs out of it. It took a while this time. Though her plan didn't seem to work at first, over the next half hour he slithered back into the light, nibbled at the burger, complimented her on it, even chuckled at the film.

Two hours and some odd minutes later, movie over and dishes loaded into the dishwasher, Melody rejoined him on the couch and leaned into him. "So," she said. "Where do you think it went?"

He shrugged. "Somebody took it."

"Maybe it spontaneously combusted."

"Really, Melody?"

She tweaked his nose.

"Oh. That was a joke."

She nuzzled his neck. "Who do you think took it?"

Bernard closed his eyes and leaned back. He put an arm about her shoulders and drew her close. She figured that meant he hadn't a clue. She didn't either. She hadn't kept an eye on the sketchbook, although she'd intuited what he'd done while she was distracting Brian and Colleen.

"Problem is," he said at last, "whoever took it might have picked it up by accident. They might not have known *Rienzi* was in there. Could've been anybody."

Melody nestled her head against his. "Oh, that's true. They probably wanted to steal your sketches."

"Why would anyone want to steal my sketches?"

"Because you're a famous artist. Or could be, someday. Everyone at that school knows it."

Bernard grunted. "Yeah, right."

"Don't be so down on yourself, Bernie. You excited two teachers and two whole classes."

"Female students particularly." He peeked at her to gauge her reaction.

"Yeah, well, you *are* irresistible." Which was both a blessing and a curse, but Bernie had eyes only for her, so she supposed she could put up with the curse. Still, if a student had taken his sketchbook…

Bernard had the same thought. "Whoever took it will discover *Rienzi*, probably sooner rather than later. If they turn it in, I'll be fingered for the theft. I'll have Celeste *and* Nachtnebel gunning for me. Literally."

"Look on the bright side. They stole your sketchbook to get your work. They're a thief, too, just like us. Maybe they'll see *Rienzi* as a bonus."

"Maybe."

"What can we do?"

"Wait and see what happens."

He sounded thoroughly miserable. "Tell you what," Melody said. "I'll bake us some brownies. That will give me time to think up a story to deflect attention from you. And once we know who took it, you can just steal it back."

That got her a smile and a kiss on the cheek. "You're too good to me," Bernard said.

"Not a bit of it." She hopped to her feet. "You deserve me."

𝄞

They slept late. Real late. Eleven o'clockish late. The zoo across the hall remained silent. Showered and dressed and famished, they decided to go out for lunch and pretend for a couple of hours that none of the preceding two weeks had happened. "How about Watson's?" Bernard suggested, naming the cozy little pub in Silver Spring where their adventure with Dolley Madison Plaskett's family had been resolved. Melody was on board.

Even at midday, the lighting was subdued, but it lent a sheen to the polished wood and the reds and golds of the décor. The sound was subdued, too. The whole place had a sleepy air to it, a sense of comfort so rich it could lull you off to dreamland before your server arrived to take your drinks order. Bernard had hesitated to bring Melody here the first time. He was sure her blazing personality would set the place on fire. But Watson's had survived, and since then they had enjoyed an occasional foray to its refined confines.

Melody ordered a turkey club, Bernard a cheesesteak sub, both with loaded cheese fries. The "loaded" part was bacon, which came with a premium cost even though it was just average bacon, but creature comforts sometimes added value, and this was such a time. Anything to get their minds off what might happen next.

Mid-meal, Bernard's cell phone went off. He checked it. Celeste. He let it go to voice mail. "How's the planning for Shawn and Felicity's wedding?" he asked.

"Mostly set," she told him. "Felicity didn't like my purple people eaters idea. I mean, she liked it, but she didn't *like* it, you know? So we went with something more traditional."

"I thought that was a joke."

"It was."

"So why did you tell her?"

"Just in case."

Bernard finished off his sandwich and wiped his fingers on his napkin. "In case what?"

"In case she liked it."

"Which she didn't."

"Oh," Melody said, "she did, like I said. But she didn't *like* it like it."

"And the guest list?" Bernard said to get past who liked what without liking it.

"That's become a nightmare," Melody said. "They both wanted a small wedding, but every time they thought about it, they realized there were five or ten more people they just had to invite. I think they're up to about five thousand by now."

Good thing Bernard wasn't eating. He would have choked to death. "Five thousand!"

A few diners at nearby tables gave him a dirty look.

He lowered his voice. "How can the two of them even know five thousand people?"

"They don't know most of them, but they know people who know them, or know people who know people who know them, you know?"

"All I know is, they'll never be able to afford that kind of wedding."

Melody finished her turkey sandwich and licked her fingers. She looked like she was in heaven. It must've been smoked turkey. "They know. They're trying to whittle it down."

Bernard's phone went off again. "Thank God for that," he said as he checked the caller. George Monroe, it said. How had George gotten his number? He answered anyway, since it could only be about his future as a great artist. "Hi George, what's up?"

"Bernard," George said. "We need to talk."

"About what?"

"Art," George said, then didn't explain.

Well, yeah, art. Bernard let the silence hang for a moment. "How did you get my number?"

"From Allegra Fumagalli."

Of course. "I see. Go on."

"It's best we meet somewhere," George said.

The mental light bulb flashed on. "About my sketches," Bernard suggested. "Of the guards."

Melody looked up, astonished.

"Um, so, well...yes."

George was the culprit. Okay, it could have been worse. With luck, he hadn't yet gone to the police. Or Nachtnebel. Probably he wanted something, probably money, probably far more money than Bernard stood to make from Celeste.

"Where do you suggest?" Bernard asked.

"Harper's Ferry. The Jefferson Rock."

Bernard blinked at Melody. Melody cocked her head. Having heard only half the conversation, she couldn't know what he was thinking. Bernard himself didn't know what he was thinking, except maybe, *What the hell?* "Okay," he said. "When?"

"As soon as possible. Alone."

That would be an hour and a half drive, maybe two hours if traffic misbehaved, which it usually did. The clock was closing on one thirty now. "Four thirty," he told George. "Melody will join us, but nobody else. Nobody."

"Nobody," George agreed. "Just the three of us."

After pocketing his phone, Bernard bent over the table and whispered the details to Melody.

"What do you think?" she asked.

"I think he better not be setting a trap for us."

"How do we know?"

"We don't. Let's get there as fast as possible and scout the area. With luck, he won't have the same idea."

Melody took a sip of her drink, giving Bernard a thoughtful look over the rim of the glass. She set down the glass and patted her mouth with her napkin. "Okay," she said. "I'll think up more stories. Just in case."

"Atta McGirl," he said and winked.

𝄞

Harper's Ferry had a long and checkered history. Situated at the confluence of the Potomac and Shenandoah Rivers, the ferry for which it was named was established in 1733 by one Peter Stephens. Stephens sold the land in 1747 to Robert Harper, who had come to build a Quaker meeting house and was dazzled by the promise of the waterpower latent in the two great rivers. The town boomed, both figuratively and literally. Industry sprawled along the river. Interchangeable manufacture was birthed here. The first successful American railroad connected the town with the world. John Brown staged his famed insurrection, which failed spectacularly. North and south coveted the town's strategic position so much that no less than five Civil War battles engulfed it, and it changed hands eight times. The war all but obliterated the place. Today's Harper's Ferry is located a bit upstream and uphill, with the historic site owned and operated by the National Park Service.

And Jefferson Rock? Yes, Thomas Jefferson indeed stood on that great rock jutting from the cliff's edge on October 25, 1763, overlooking the rivers, awed by nature's beauty, as have thousands over the ensuing two and a half centuries. Alas, the rock became unstable. At first it was shored up, but eventually the Park Service declared it off-limits.

Bernard and Melody now stood there, too, not on the rock but beside it, 254 years and four days after Mr. Jefferson, as near the edge as allowed, and it was indeed beautiful. The late, great president would have seen it as they saw it, fall colors lining both banks of the rivers, a cool breeze picking at the leaves that remained on the trees, a carpet of reds and golds and browns at their feet, while 165 feet below, the Shenendoah rushed through a jumble of boulders protruding from the water.

"Just think." Melody breathed in the forest scent. "Only a tenth of a mile from the road."

"A tenth of a mile straight up," Bernard added.

She gave him one of her looks. "It wasn't *that* bad."

"No," he admitted. "Only that first part."

There had indeed been a steep climb up a stone staircase. And then, after a brief respite, another stone staircase. And then a longer, less gentle respite and a few more steps.

"It's the Appalachian Trail," Melody scolded. "What did you expect, a wheelchair ramp?"

"I've learned to expect the unexpected." Which was true. He was married to Melody, after all. Life was a constant adventure.

Tourists filtered through, not as many as during the summer peak, but enough that the Earls duo weren't alone. It was coming up on three forty-five and George wasn't in evidence. Bernard took in the people flowing by while pretending to soak up the scenery. Mothers and fathers with their children, teenagers, an occasional older couple who'd survived the climb. Nobody suspicious that he could tell. He and Melody settled themselves on a small boulder just past the famed rock. Above them, the trail bent and continued south along the crest of the cliff. They watched the river, the tree-shrouded slopes across the river, the people, the specks of cloud floating by, the people. And especially, the people.

"We should find a nice restaurant for dinner," Melody said.

"We already spent money on a nice lunch," Bernard objected.

"Maybe George will buy."

"Why would George buy?"

"To make up for this." She looked up and smiled. "Hi, George!"

Bernard hadn't missed his appearance. Nobody had. He stood before them in a beige trench coat, dark glasses, and a trilby hat. "When did you take up espionage?" Bernard asked.

George glanced around. Everyone was snickering and trying not to stare at him.

"Take that thing off," Bernard suggested. "You couldn't be more obvious if you tried."

George removed the hat and sunglasses but kept the coat on. "It's a bit cool," he explained.

"You're not exactly blending in. I guess that means you haven't been briefed by the cops on how to do this. Good. Here, sit down." Bernard scooted over to give George room to sit. And to bring himself into physical contact with Melody, which was a bonus. She wriggled over a bit, but she couldn't go far without falling off their rock.

George sat and fiddled with the hat in his hand.

"Did you bring the sketchbook?" Bernard inquired.

He shook his head.

That much was smart, anyway. "But it's safe, I suppose."

George nodded.

"How much to return it?"

George shrugged.

"Do you plan on talking?" Bernard inquired as respectfully as possible, which wasn't much. His patience, already thin, was developing a hole.

"I saw you put something into it," George explained. "I was curious. I thought maybe it was another sketch. I like your work."

"So you stole it. I'm flattered."

"I just wanted a look. I was going to give it back." George stopped fiddling with the hat and looked across the valley. "But then I found *Rienzi*."

"Is that any reason for not returning my property?"

"You can have the sketchbook. *Rienzi* isn't yours."

"It is now," Bernard said.

"Nope. It's mine now."

Fair point. "How much, then?"

George rose and sauntered to the edge of the cliff, which wasn't half as bold as it seemed. Bernard wouldn't push him off, probably not even had the sketchbook been in his hand. And especially since it wasn't. "I'm not sure how to handle this," he said.

What was to handle? Name a price, haggle, arrange payment and return of the opera. The only sticking point was price. Bernard had nothing until he got paid, and even then he had very little compared to the artifact's true value.

Melody rose and joined George at the edge. She took his hat from him and settled it on her head, took his sunglasses and tucked them into his pants pocket, took his hands in hers and stroked them. "What are your options?" she asked.

People passing looked at her, but this time they weren't snickering. They were awestruck. Bernard didn't know how she could look more beautiful than ever in that trilby, but that was Melody. She could make ashes and sackcloth look good.

"I thought about returning it to Mr. Nachtnebel," he said. "But there would be questions. And honestly? I hate that guy's guts."

Score one for George. He went up a notch in Bernard's estimation.

"I thought about keeping it, but what could I do with it? You can't sell something like this, not without raising more questions. And Mr. Nachtnebel would hear of it and come after me."

George scores again, Bernard thought. *How about that.*

"Which makes me wonder why you want it. What could you possibly do with it?" George looked at Melody, wide-eyed. At first it was just inquiry. Inquiry morphed into wonderment, which morphed into—maybe—a different sort of inquiry.

Melody stopped him there. She released his hands and shrugged. "What do you think?"

"I think you're working for someone."

Damn, this guy was good. What was he doing in art school?

Melody gave him a demur smile and returned his hat.

"Which means," George went on, "you're getting paid. So, I guess I want a cut."

"Oh, George," Melody purred. "How much do you think we're getting paid?"

He shrugged. "A lot, I suppose."

"Not really."

Bernard about choked. Yeah, okay, "not really" was nonspecific, but twenty thousand was nothing to sneeze at.

"Not compared to *Rienzi*'s value, I guess," George admitted. "But a lot."

Melody rolled her eyes and shook her head. "This isn't about money at all."

He bit his lip. "I knew it. Celeste."

Okay, now George was getting *too* good. Bernard rose, intent upon redirecting the conversation, but Melody waved him down. He sat under protest.

"Who?" Melody asked.

"Celeste," George repeated. "Mr. Nachtnebel's cousin. She hates him."

"So do you," Melody reminded him. "So what?"

"She'd do this to spite him."

"And just how do you know that?"

George shrugged and gazed out over the Shenandoah gorge. "It's not exactly a secret. Or, okay, it is, but most of Mr. Nachtnebel's inner circle know anyway. Word is, Celeste's been pressuring him to open his private collection to the world. But he can't, not without facing a lot of questions and probably losing control of the art. He allegedly tried negotiating with her, even offered to pay her off, but she refused. She wants him ruined, plain and simple."

"Hmm," Melody said. "It's a shame people can't get along, but that's a family matter. We're just providing a service."

"How much *is* she paying you?"

Bernard about choked again when Melody said, "Not much." Okay, George had nailed it. He'd guessed they were working for Celeste. But Melody shouldn't have confirmed the fact. That couldn't end well.

Bernard rose again. She waved him down again. This time, he refused to sit. He joined Melody and George at the cliff's edge and raised a finger to make a point.

Melody gently enclosed his hand in hers and pushed it down. "I have an idea," she said.

George raised his eyebrows. Bernard bit his lip. "Melody," he began.

"Sush," she told him. To George, she said, "Why don't you return *Rienzi* to us and keep the sketchbook?"

George mulled that over, his gaze locked with Melody's. "I don't get it."

"Oh, George, come on. You're an artist. An art teacher. You saw Bernie's work. You think it's great."

"Yes, but–"

"Allegra says Bernie's a genius who will die in poverty and be remembered for all time." She beamed at Bernard, pride all but oozing from her pores.

Bernard shuffled his feet. "Now look–"

Melody didn't let him continue. "George, listen. You have in your hands–well, not literally in your hands, but somewhere hidden away in your house or apartment or teepee or whatever–an original Bernie that the world has never seen. Someday, it'll be worth a fortune!" She bounced on her toes. "Isn't that worth a silly old music manuscript that you can't ever let anyone know you have?" In case he wasn't convinced, she leaned in and kissed him on the cheek.

George blushed and turned away. "Um," he said. "Well. Um."

Melody winked at Bernard.

Bernard looked skyward in an appeal to the Almighty. George couldn't possibly be that stupid, not after his brilliant display of detective work.

Except he was. "Okay," he said, a smile finally breaking on his lips. "I guess that works."

Had he not been on the edge of a cliff, Bernard might have fainted. Given the imprudence of such a reaction, he shoved his hands in his pockets and made do with a question. "When can we have it back?"

George ignored him and told Melody, "But I want one other thing, too."

"What's that?" she asked.

"I want Bernard to paint my portrait."

Bernard ground his teeth and vowed to give George purple hair. "When can we have it back?" he repeated.

"Is that a yes?"

"Yes, damn it. When—"

"As soon as we get to the parking lot," George said. "It's in my car trunk."

Chapter 21: Sunday, October 29, 2017

They'd done it. They'd stolen a priceless relic from under the nose of a maniac son of a Nazi, nobody got shot in the head, and nobody but George, Celeste, and Dolley Madison Plaskett would ever know. Which was at least one person too many, but George had zero intention of letting Gerhardt Nachtnebel, Jr. know of his involvement, so that was okay. All that remained was delivery and payment. And, well, George's portrait, but that could wait.

Okay, no, there was one other thing, as they were reminded Sunday morning.

Saturday evening, they had celebrated with a luxurious meal at a Harper's Ferry restaurant with the curious appellation Skunkweed Ridge Manor House. Bernard later researched but found no Skunkweed Ridge anywhere in West Virginia. Or in the whole of the U.S., for that matter. Skunkweed, he discovered, was another name for the odiferous skunk cabbage, which reveled in the eastern wetlands and certainly not on ridges, where wetlands were few and far between, but come on. Why name a restaurant *anywhere* for it?

Anyway.

After dinner, they'd come home, further celebrated with cheap wine—pretending it was a thousand-dollar-a-glass vintage— and completed the evening in proper marital fashion before falling into a deep sleep that was only interrupted at eight-thirty Sunday morning when a rhinoceros bellowed in the hall and tried to beat down their door with its horns.

As Bernard sat in bed shaking with fear that the world was ending before he even got paid, and as Melody groaned and stuffed her head under the pillow one more time, a shrill voice beckoned. "Chris-Chris! Get back here! Don't bother Mr. and Mrs. Earls!"

"Trick! Or! Treat!" the rhino chanted, bashing the door with each word. "Trick! Or! Treat! Trick! Or! Treat!"

"Not until after lunch!" Mrs. Clarke scolded. "Get back in here, or there will be no trick-or-treat!"

"Awwwww!" the rhino complained, and silence descended.

Bernard flopped back onto his pillow. Melody crept out from under hers. "The recidivism rate in his age group," Bernard observed, "is horrible."

"You were a boy once," Melody said.

"But never an escapee from the zoo. Or from the Cretaceous."

"Jurassic."

"Cretaceous, love. T-rex was a Cretaceous animal."

Melody rolled over and settled her head on his shoulder. "Then why was it called Jurassic Park?"

"Try saying 'Cretaceous Park.' It doesn't exactly roll off the tongue."

They were awake, but neither wanted to get out of bed, so they spent another twenty minutes in stimulating intellectual discussion of dinosaur movie titles, reaching no firm conclusions save regarding each other's obstinacy. Still, it wasn't a serious disagreement, so it didn't ruffle them much. Impending doom aside, they were in too good a mood to allow serious ruffling. A twenty-thousand-dollar good mood. A beautiful cedar chest good mood, in Melody's case.

Bernard decided to let the good mood last a while longer and didn't immediately call Celeste. Melody made a celebratory breakfast of eggs and sausages and toast and hot chocolate. They pondered a vacation in West Virginia, then decided to swap it for

Florida. Soon. Before tourist season and unbeachlike temperatures kicked in. They talked new clothes and new furniture and stuff to stuff into the new cedar chest. In short, they talked about all kinds of things they seldom had the money to talk about. And it was good.

And then Bernard's cell phone went off, and it was Celeste.

He didn't wait for pleasantries. "I have it."

"I know," she said.

"You know?"

"I know."

"How do you know?"

"Gerhardt called last night."

That made sense. Nachtnebel had known Celeste was after *Rienzi*. Because she'd told him. Whatever that was about.

"You did well," she added. "He's clueless. So, I gather, is his security company. He's threatened them with a huge lawsuit."

"Poor Fitzroy," Bernard said, his voice dripping irony. The company could afford it. And deserved it, for making it so hard for honest thieves to make a living.

"Oh, he won't do it," Celeste said. "He can't without revealing the nature of his treasures to the world. Or his family background. He'll just have to suck it up."

Better and better. "When should we stop by?" Bernard asked.

"Three o'clock. Don't be late. I have a full schedule."

Bernard agreed, but he couldn't let her go just yet. "Normally I wouldn't ask this sort of question," he said, "but I'm very curious."

"About what?"

"Why tell Nachtnebel your intentions?"

Celeste was silent for a moment. Bernard almost thought she wasn't going to answer. If she hadn't, he wouldn't have pressed the matter, but he could still hear Nachtnebel trash talking her. It gave him chills, and not the good kind.

"Let's not discuss that on the phone," she said. "I'll explain when I see you."

Bernard set down his phone next to his plate and frowned at it as though it had told him a bad joke. Something wasn't right. Not the phone, the situation with Celeste. Or maybe he was just paranoid.

"What's wrong?" Melody asked.

He told her what Celeste had said.

She put down her fork and gazed out the window. "Oh," she said dismissively, "she's probably just being careful. Unless she's being sneaky. Women can be sneaky, you know."

"So can men," Bernard informed her.

"Not in the same way."

That sounded like a good discussion to avoid. He stuck to specifics. "How's she being sneaky?"

Melody shrugged, picked up her fork and knife, cut off a bit of sausage. "That's the trouble. You never really know with a woman. Not until you know, that is. You know?"

"No."

"You should. You've lived with me long enough."

"I know," Bernard said. "But that doesn't mean I know."

Melody winked, said, "I know," and popped the bit of sausage in her mouth.

At least one of them knew. Still, he was uneasy. While he couldn't put his finger on anything specific, he sensed Celeste wasn't done with them yet.

𝄞

Just before three, they arrived at the wrought iron gate guarding Celeste's three-story brick Georgian home. The old trees shading the neighborhood had lost nearly a third of their leaves in the past week. The remainder hung like a colorful afghan draped about the neighborhood. Bernard lowered his window and pushed the button on the speaker box by the gate.

As before, static erupted from the box.

Here we go again, Bernard thought. "Hello," he called.

Static.

"Hello!"

Static.

"It's Bernard and Melody."

Static, static, static, with a bit of voice behind it.

"Maybe you should get this thing fixed in the coming years," he told the voice.

Static underlaid with laughter. Maybe. The gate opened.

He pulled up to the garage, and by the time they got to the door, it was open. Celeste stood in the doorway, tall, tanned, as lovely as before but not in a smock. Today, she wore a dress that could barely contain her curves. "Going clubbing after?" Bernard asked.

Melody swatted him.

Celeste laughed. "You two are such fun to work with. Come on in."

She led them through the statuary standing guard about the foyer into the foliage-draped sitting room, where an unpleasant surprise met them.

True to its name, the sitting room was furnished for sitting, with couches and love seats and wingback chairs, all in pastel colors, arranged in three groups that each allowed for intimate conversation but were accessible to each other for wider interaction. A gas fireplace at one end separated two of the groups, with miniature replicas of famous statues adorning the mantel: Venus de Milo, The Little Mermaid, Michangelo's David.

None of that was unpleasant. The unpleasant bit was the other guest seated in one of the wingbacks, his elbows on the chair's arms, his fingers steepled before him, his eyes watching Bernard and Melody over the tops of his gold wire rim glasses. He said nothing, just watched, but Bernard could tell. Gerhardt Nachtnebel, Jr. thought he recognized them.

Melody, to her credit, didn't react to Nachtnebel, but she did give Celeste a nasty glare before taking Bernard's arm and pulling him close. Bernard put his arm about Melody and waited.

Celeste didn't introduce them, didn't say anything at all. She merely extended her hand to Bernard, palm up. Bernard drew the envelope from his inner pocket and handed it to her. She opened it and extracted the pages of *Rienzi*, then she leafed through them, taking her time over each sheet. Her eyes glistened. She was either about to cry with joy or maybe drool with something approaching lust. When done, she tucked the sheaf back into the envelope and handed it to Melody.

"Hold this for a moment," she said. "It's a bit chilly in here, don't you think?"

"I don't think so," Melody said. She tucked the envelope under her arm.

"Not at all," Bernard agreed. He found it distinctly warm, no doubt the effect of rising adrenaline. What was she playing at?

Celeste sauntered to the fireplace, flashing Nachtnebel a mean sort of smile in passing. She turned the control knob and pressed the igniter button until flames began to lick the fake logs. "Wherever are my manners?" she said, voice dripping sarcasm. "My friends, have a seat."

Bernard escorted Melody to a love seat facing Nachtnebel. He eyed them the whole way, but not the way men usually eyed them. Most men eyed Melody almost exclusively, only ever looking at Bernard to gauge his level of irritation as they ogled his wife. This wasn't that. This was curiosity if anything. Nachtnebel wanted to know who they were and how they'd stolen his treasure. He probably also wanted to see them six feet under, but if so, he was doing a fine job of hiding the fact.

Celeste didn't sit. She came to Melody's side and held out her hand once more. Melody returned the envelope to her. Celeste pulled out the music and leafed through it. "This is what comes of being so full of yourself," she said.

"Me?" Nachtnebel laughed bitterly. "You're so full of yourself, you're delusional."

"You think you can escape justice."

Nachtnebel turned his gaze on Bernard and Melody. "Cousin Celestina has me confused with my father. My father did some terrible things. Many people did back in his day. But I've only ever been an honest businessman. I wasn't born with a silver spoon in my mouth. I applied myself and prospered."

Celeste, still studying the music, shuffling pages, wandered to the fireplace and leaned against the wall beside it. "Your father was a thief, a murderer, and a rapist. Your wealth is built upon treasures he acquired through his crimes."

"Not at all. My wealth is built upon my own hard work. Those treasures never had anything to do with it, aside from inspiring me. I could never sell them. I could almost never show them. They've been largely locked away, lost as far as most of the world knows. I'm not my father. I'm an honest businessman."

Celeste smirked. "You sent your thug to threaten me."

"To negotiate," Nachtnebel corrected.

"But he did threaten me."

"You tried to expose me!"

"You deserve it!"

Nachtnebel rose and balled his shaking hands into fists. "No more than you do!"

It might not have been smart, but Bernard didn't want to be caught even on the periphery of an altercation that would lead to police intervention. Or the death of all witnesses, which was likely if Nachtnebel really did want Celeste dead, or *vice versa.* "Children," he snapped. "Can we all remain calm?"

Celeste and Nachtnebel glared at each other, then both turned their eyes on Bernard. Still smoldering, Nachtnebel drew a long breath and resumed his seat. "She *does* deserve it," he grumbled.

"Deserves death?" Bernard asked.

"I didn't say that."

"There's already a rumor running around," Bernard said. "A rumor that your thug..." He pointed at Celeste. "Her term. Your thug tried to kill her and is now buried in her cellar."

The cousins stared at Bernard as though he'd suggested they juggle flaming kabobs while whistling *The Star Spangled Banner.*

"Who told you that?" Celeste asked.

Bernard didn't care to mention it was a hairdresser at Chrissie's. "That's the word on the street."

"Don't be an idiot," Nachtnebel grumped. "I just wanted Celestina to lay off. Yeah, okay, I told Bruno to rough her up a little if she didn't listen to reason, and she smacked the dumb oaf's skull with an easel when he tried, but that's all."

"Bruno?" Melody asked. She put a hand to her mouth to stop herself from laughing.

"An easel?" Bernard asked. He didn't bother stopping himself. He laughed in their faces. Across the room from their faces, anyway. "A novel weapon."

"The point," Nachtnebel said through gritted teeth, "is that nobody died."

"Glad to hear it. Now let it go." *At least,* Bernard added silently, *for our sakes.*

"Who the hell are you, anyway?" Nachtnebel snapped.

Bernard shrugged. "Nobody important. Nobody near as rich as either of you, at least. Which may be why I'm better behaved."

"I know you from somewhere."

Bernard shrugged again.

Nachtnebel waved a finger at him. "You were at an event not long ago."

What could he say? Nothing, which was also the most prudent response, so that's how he responded.

"They're just my operatives," Celeste said. "Don't bother with them. This was all my doing." She rattled *Rienzi.*

Nachtnebel sneered at her. "Damn right it was. What happens now?"

"Now you face a choice. I warned you this was coming. I'll give it back, on one condition."

"No."

"You don't want it back?"

"I want it back, but not on your terms. That belongs to me." He thrust out his hand to receive the opera, as though she might actually return it.

Celeste rattled the pages at him. "After you open your secret collection to the world."

"I'd be thrown in prison."

Celeste snorted. "Don't be melodramatic. You're no Nazi."

"I'll be ruined, though."

"Naturally. Your father may have escaped justice..." A dark look stole over her face. "...but you won't."

Nachtnebel ground his teeth. "This isn't justice, and my collection remains private. You may as well return *Rienzi* to me. You can't do a thing with it, and you know I'll come after it. This doesn't end until I get it back."

"Last chance," Celeste said. She held the precious pages out as though offering a gift, but it wasn't a gift at all. It was a taunt. "Come clean, and it's yours."

Nachtnebel might have spat on her if Bernard and Melody hadn't been present.

"Pity," Celeste said.

And she flung *Rienzi* into the fire.

𝄞

The rest remained a blur in Bernard's mind. Nachtnebel yelped and would have dove into the flames himself to retrieve his precious manuscript, but Celeste snatched up the poker from the tool stand and brandished it like a sword to keep him back. The pages blackened and curled and disintegrated to ash, rendering one of Richard Wagner's most precious lost manuscripts truly lost to history. Bloodshed would have followed had Nachtnebel not been so distraught—and so unarmed—but in the end he had no recourse. He stormed out, never to be seen again in Ford's Ford.

After that, Celeste was in such a good mood, she offered Bernard and Melody champagne. She offered them dinner, too, but they begged off, having a prior engagement to escort the Incredible Hulk on his Halloween rounds. Then Bernard asked a most important question: "I assume we get paid now?"

She handed over a manilla envelope. "This includes final expenses and a bonus for a job well done."

Bernard opened the envelope and did a quick count: two hundred twenty hundred-dollar bills. Twenty-two thousand in cash. He tucked it into an inside pocket and thanked her with all the grace he could muster, which was considerable.

"One last thing," he said, then hastily added, "Which you don't have to answer."

She was in too good a mood to refuse him. "Ask away," she said.

"What the hell was this about?"

Celeste sipped her drink and leaned back in her chair. She gazed into the flickering flames. "My grandmother was with the Polish resistance in World War II. She was captured, imprisoned, and raped by Nazi soldiers. After she escaped, she hunted down and killed the perpetrators. She died before the job was done, probably killed by one of her persecutors, so my mother dealt with those who remained. Or so she thought. But one escaped."

"Nachtnebel's father," Bernard said.

Celeste nodded.

"You made it your job to get him."

"Not at first. At first, I wasn't interested. I didn't even know, really. I just wanted to pursue art. Then I took some classes at the Nachtnebel Foundation. When I saw Gerhard for the first time, I got curious. The photos of him when he was younger bear some resemblance to my mother at a similar age. I contrived to get a DNA sample from him one day. A small accident with a palette knife. I had tests run, and yes, we're closely related. Rumors have swirled around Gerhard for some time, rumors of stolen art smuggled out of Germany by his father. Gerhard, Sr. was dead, of course, but I knew what I had to do. I had to give my grandmother closure."

Melody pouted. "You never cared about *Rienzi* at all, did you?"

"I cared about justice. I couldn't kill anyone. I'm not like that. But I could make him suffer."

"You hit Bruno with an easel," Bernard pointed out. "That's just a step removed from killing."

"Self-defense. Not the same thing."

Bernard didn't argue the point, but he had heard the arctic wind in her voice before. She could kill someone if she had cause.

"I probably shouldn't have told him I was after *Rienzi*."

"You sure shouldn't have," Bernard said. "You jeopardized the operation."

Celeste shrugged. "Believe it or not, I had faith in you. Dolley vouched for you. She's a shrewd judge of character. And anyway, I couldn't help it. I knew Gerhard wouldn't capitulate. I wanted him to fight back and fail. I wanted him to come to me, to be here at the end." She grinned an evil grin, as evil as those who had started all this. "That opera meant more to him than anything in the world. For the rest of his life, he's going to remember standing by helpless while it burned to ash."

"That was mean," Melody told her. "And you destroyed a treasure. You should be ashamed of yourself. For both things."

"Probably," Celeste admitted. "But I don't care. And you got paid, so why should you?"

Chapter 22: Still Sunday, October 29, 2017

Had Melody been her parents' age, or maybe her grandparents' age, she might have found modern Halloween traditions a bit sad. She'd heard stories of swarms of children moving up and down streets like locusts, ringing doorbells, shouting "Trick or treat!" and gathering enough candy to gag a giraffe. Everyone—most everyone, anyway—participated and had fun. And then one dark day in Chicago in late September, 1982, everything changed, and Halloween was never quite the same.

That's what they told her. But she wasn't born until later. Traditional trick-or-treating was a ghost story for her.

Ghost story. Melody giggled. There weren't so many ghosts now. Some, yes, but most of the kids had dressed up as animals and superheroes—a lot of Spider-Mans, or Spider-Men, or whatever—and *Star Wars* characters. And instead of going door-to-door, they were going car-trunk-to-car-trunk. Trunk-or-treating. In a designated area of the apartment complex parking lot. Yuck.

Still, the kids were having fun, although some of the parents looked frazzled. So did Bernard. Chris-Chris, in his Hulk costume, insisted on dragging his chaperones from one end of the area to the other and back, then to the food truck the complex had brought in, then back to the trunks for a second round, then back to the food truck. For the first half hour, he hadn't spoken anything but Hulk, which consisted mostly of roaring like a T-rex. Or at least, Melody couldn't tell the difference. Adults laughed every time he bellowed until, maybe fifteen minutes later when they didn't laugh quite so much, and then fifteen minutes after that when they started giving the kid dirty looks.

Bernard suggested he roar more quietly.

Chris-Chris responded with his loudest roar yet.

Melody suggested a hot dog.

"Yay!" the Hulk cheered, and after that his ferocity decreased somewhat, although not because he'd eaten well. After insisting upon a generous coating of mustard, ketchup, and relish, Chris-Chris downed just two bites. The rest was victimized by the Hulk, who threw in on the ground and smashed it into a smear of pink, yellow, red, and green.

After a later stop at the food truck for some ice cream—half of which Hulk consumed and half of which he smashed—Chris-Chris tried to pull Bernard and Melody into a third round of candy-grubbing.

"Twice around is enough," Bernard declared.

"Grrrr," Chris-Chris objected.

"You need to leave some for the other kids."

"Grrrr!"

"Now look—"

"Chris-Chris," Melody purred. She squatted before him and said soothingly, "Wouldn't you like to eat some of your candy now?"

"Grrr?"

"We can take you to grandma's, and you can have a few pieces of candy before dinner." Which wasn't ever what Melody's parents had told her, and probably not what Mrs. Clarke would have told her great-grandson, but if it would soothe a savage green monster, why not?

Chris-Chris nodded and said with enthusiasm, "Grrr!" He pulled a fistful of candy from his bag, threw it on the ground, and stomped it into oblivion, snarling the whole time.

"That's enough of that," Melody purred. She patted his head, took his hand in hers, and nodded to Bernard. "Come on, Bernie, let's get the little lizard home."

Chris-Chris stomped his foot. "Not lizard!"

"You're green, aren't you?" Melody figured all that gamma radiation had probably reversed Bruce Banner's evolution somehow, which is why he turned lizard-green.

"The kid's right," Bernard said. "Lizards are members of the suborder Lacertilia in the order Squamata. I doubt the Hulk was ever classified, taxonomically speaking. However—"

"I don't think Chris-Chris cares about that," Melody interrupted. Why would he? *She* certainly didn't care.

"It's science," Bernard huffed. "He ought to care."

"Grrrrr!" Chris-Chris commented.

Melody led the menfolk away from the treat-laden trunks into the building and up to Mrs. Clarke's apartment. When she opened the door, Mrs. Clarke smiled at Chris-Chris and asked, "Did you have fun?"

"Grr!" he said.

"I'm glad. Thank you, Mr. and Mrs. Earls. I don't know what I'd do without you."

"Oh, it was nothing," Melody said. "We had a great time, didn't we Bernie?" She winked at him, then raised an eyebrow to signal the correct answer.

"Yep," he said, although with less enthusiasm than she'd hoped.

Mrs. Clarke didn't notice, or maybe didn't care. She'd had her respite, and that was sufficient for now.

"Your two weeks tour of duty is about over, right?" Bernard asked.

Melody elbowed him.

Mrs. Clarke sighed. "I didn't think I'd make it this long. Fortunately, I've gotten the hang of it." She gave Bernard an apologetic smile, then looked away.

Melody felt Bernard's whole body go rigid. She felt a touch of dread herself.

"Unfortunately," Mrs. Clarke added, "my daughter's new daycare arrangements already fell through. It will be a while longer."

Melody smiled on the outside. On the inside, not so much. She turned to Bernard. Bernard turned to her. They shared a deep, unified, silent scream.

Mrs. Clarke brightened. "Maybe we could do Thanksgiving dinner together?"

"Yaaaaaaaay!" Chris-Chris shrieked. He charged into the apartment, gobbling like a psychotic turkey. The unceasing noise filled the hall.

Across the way, a door opened partway, and their lanky neighbor Dimetrice poked his head out. "What the hell's all that noise?" he asked.

Must be bad, Melody thought, *if he's complaining*.

"Baby!" Osheena called from somewhere behind him. "I got the new speakers figgered out! Wanna do a sound check?"

"Crank it up!" he told her.

Thunder shook the building.

Mrs. Clarke shook her head and closed her door.

The thunder stopped.

"Up a notch," Dimetrice told Osheena.

Fists clenched, Bernard turned on him. "Damn it, Dimetrice..."

Melody took his arm and nodded toward the exit. "Take me out to dinner again?" she asked.

Thunder shook the building.

Bernard hustled her to the parking lot.

𝄞

Old habits die hard. Here they were, sitting on a 20K payday, and the only spot that came to mind was Burger Bazzar. But they got everything large, even the chocolate shakes. They deserved a treat.

They didn't talk much, probably because they were recovering from shell shock, but by the time Melody swirled up the last bit of ketchup with the last fry and drained the last of her shake, melting with pleasure at the tangy salty sweetness of it all, Bernard had recovered. "This job changed everything," he said.

"Sure did," Melody agreed.

"We're in a new league now."

"And I can get that cedar chest."

"That, too." He reached across the table and tweaked her nose.

Melody giggled and returned the gesture. "Plus, you're now a famous starving artist."

"Not starving anymore. Anyway, I don't think I'll return to the art world. That was weird."

"How so?"

Bernard took her hands and squeezed them. "I'm no artist, love. I couldn't draw a straight line or mix paint to save my life. They only thought I was great because I was so bad."

"Don't be so down on yourself, Bernie. I think you're great, and not because you're bad." She giggled again. "Sure, you're a thief, but us McGirls always were a bit bad, ourselves."

"And the Kensingtons?"

"They weren't so innocent, either. Royalty never is."

He had to give her that. "Anyway, the job was the real work of art. Speaking of that..." From one of his secret pockets, he extracted a jewelry box and passed it to her. "From me to you," he said.

Surprise and joy mingling in her eyes, Melody took the box. "For me?" She opened it and gasped, then lifted from it the silver pendant earrings. The mother of pearl inlays glowed and the rubies glinted in the restaurant's lighting. Tears flooded her eyes. "Oh, Bernie, they're beautiful!"

"I saw them in Nachtnebel's treasure room and thought of you."

They were screw-back earrings, something she'd never worn before, but she figured them out and clipped them onto her ears. "Take a picture!"

He snapped her photo with his phone, then showed it to her.

"They're perfect, Bernie, absolutely perfect!"

"Of course they are. They're on you."

She reached across the table, took his face in her hands, and pulled him into a kiss.

Once her emotion subsided sufficiently, he suggested she put them away. They were too, too much for Burger Bazzar. She did so, settling them back in the box and tucking the box into her purse.

Bernard hadn't felt this good in a long time. "I think we should get started on that Florida vacation," he suggested. "We don't need to work for a bit, and we can be selective about our next job."

Melody smiled a crooked smile.

"What?" he asked.

"We may never have to work again."

He laughed. "We didn't get paid quite that much, love."

"No?" She was still smiling.

Uh-oh, Bernard thought, the good feeling slipping away. "What did you do?"

Melody made a show of rummaging through her purse before producing a business envelope, unmarked and unsealed. She extracted a folded paper from the envelope, unfolded it, and set it on the table in front of Bernard.

Bernard leaned forward to examine it. It was a single page of music, a score written in Richard Wagner's elegant hand. "What's this?" he asked, although he knew as soon as the words were out.

"What do you think?" She winked at him and leaned forward to gaze upon the page with him.

It was *Rienzi*. Part of *Rienzi*, anyway. Just one page. Just the first page of the original manuscript for *Rienzi*. "But how..."

Melody kissed her finger and pressed it to his lips. "From me to you," she said. "I pinched it when Celeste handed me the envelope. Now it's the only surviving page. It's priceless!"

"But..." A swarm of conflicting, impossible thoughts buzzed through Bernard's brain. "We can't sell it, love. There would be so many questions. How could we ever explain..."

"Oh, I'll think up a story. Might take a while, sure. It's got to be *really* creative. But I'll work it out."

If anyone could, it would be Melody. Bernard sat back as it sunk in. They'd be rich. Maybe not right away, maybe not this year or next year, but once Melody had her story, once enough time passed, once an auction house turned that single page to gold...

Melody cocked her head, no doubt seeing the stars in his eyes. "Promise me something," she said.

"Anything," he replied. Foolish, making a rash promise, promising literally anything to anyone, even to Melody. Maybe especially to Melody. Her imagination was capable of conjuring literally anything.

"Promise it won't change you. Promise you'll still be my great starving artist."

"I promise," he said and meant it. After all, he would always be hungry for her.

Thank you for reading! Please leave a short, honest review wherever you purchased this book. I greatly appreciate it, and it will help others discover my books.

About the Author

Dale E. Lehman is an award-winning writer, veteran software developer, amateur astronomer, and bonsai artist in training. He principally writes mysteries, science fiction, and humor. In addition to his novels, his writing has appeared in *Sky & Telescope* and on Medium.com. He owns and operates the imprint Red Tales. He and his late wife Kathleen have five children, six grandchildren, and two feisty cats. At any given time, Dale is at work on several novels and short stories.

Visit https://www.DaleELehman.com to find out more about Dale's books.